"*Fossils* ... drew me in from the [...] a character whose voice is urge[...] bubbles and snaps with an ener[...] as changeable as its teen protagonist. Convinced she and her brother Joshy have been born into the wrong existence, Sherrie-Lee reaches out for companionship and care from the unlikeliest of sources, and in so doing, challenges our assumptions about the goodness of people. Sherrie-Lee is a girl trying desperately to escape her situation, who finds solace in the sharing of stories. But in seeking a new identity, she finds herself caught in a trap of her own making, with a lie that puts her in grave danger. This is a novel that tugged at my heart, with its blend of humour and wisdom and rage ... a stunning, important novel about poverty and hopelessness, compassion and resilience."
Emily Devane

"*Fossils*, Alison Armstrong's debut novel, is a moving and vivid piece of storytelling. With great skill, Armstrong captures the inner life of Sherrie-Lee, a young girl without a safety net who has been left to fall between the cracks. Sherrie-Lee's exposure to darkness and the dangerous place she finds herself in is described in haunting, lyrical writing that is at all times compelling and frequently surprising." **Will Mackie**, New Writing North

FOSSILS

A novel

Alison Armstrong

Saraband

Published by Saraband
3 Clairmont Gardens,
Glasgow G7 3LW

ISBN: 9781913393366

Printed and bound in Great Britain by Clays Ltd, Elcograf SpA.

10 9 8 7 6 5 4 3 2 1

For my mum

'The fairy tale ... was once the first tutor of mankind [and]
secretly lives on in the story ... Whenever good counsel was
at a premium, the fairy tale had it ... The fairy tale tells us
of the earliest arrangements that mankind made to shake
off the nightmare which the myth had placed upon its chest.'

Walter Benjamin, 'Illuminations'

'And you can see only those who stand in the light,
While those in the darkness nobody can see.'

Bertolt Brecht, The Threepenny Opera

1

The light came down or across, dazzling in all directions at once, so that in the blink of an eye or in a glance, first this way and then that, it was impossible to see clearly, to maintain an impression of how it all was and then hold it to any kind of realisation. On top of that there was a wobble in the eye, a focus floating away in the aqueous mechanics of vision.

At each aisle she moved into, she noticed him. The security man, appearing at one end or the other. He was onto her. You could just about bet on that. She hovered in the photography aisle, looking at the photo frames with happy smiling people already encased in them, trying not to look for him. Trying to be calm and hold it together so he would see that there was nothing going on here. Just a girl thinking about buying a photo frame. There were a lot to choose from. Wooden ones, metal ones, others that were just all glass or plastic. The perfect teeth repeated in each frame depressed her. It was as though identical smiles had been stamped onto each person. This is how to smile, they seemed to echo. This is how to be normal. How to be happy in the world. She dared a backward glance across the length of the aisle to where she thought the security man might be. Streaks of light rose up and fused together in the tremor of her vision. Not there. She directed her gaze back towards the frames and studied them. The sizes were all given in inches, she noticed. She forced herself to count three details about them before looking for him again. All the sizes of each style were placed together, big to small, running from left to right. There was not one single person who was not smiling in those frames. That was three details ticked off. Her mind turned back to the security man, holding off the moment when she would look again for him. She didn't want to look anxious and give the game away. You had to keep an eye on them. When you lost track of them, that was when they grabbed you. Collaring you out of the blue. She looked along the length of the aisle. Yep. There he was again. She couldn't tell if he was looking at her, she didn't dare to look at him for long enough. *I'll be for it now,* she said, inside her head, with her reluctant-reprimanding voice. *Been coming a long time, Missy.* Missy is what her nan used to call her. She had taken to using it whenever she needed to give herself a talking to. There were not many people in the shop, that had been the problem. And a kid in the shop on a school day, that had been another. She had stood out too much. Rookie mistake. When she glanced sideways to check on him, the shop lights bounced off all the mirrored and shiny surfaces, which made it difficult to focus, in a quick glance. To see what he was doing. To see what he had seen or not seen. She felt dizzy. Had he seen her pocket the eyeshadow trio? She didn't even wear makeup. Is that what she'd say if he collared her? Maybe she should take it out of her pocket, hide it behind the frames, but she knew he'd be watching. *You've gone and done it now, Missy.* Though technically that wasn't stealing, that was replacing something. Putting something back. He wouldn't see it like that though, she could tell. That type could be very unreasonable. She could imagine his whole life, right down to the pouring himself into the black and white of his job, of his uniform. His little bit of authority gone straight to his head. If he'd had more authority, he might have had some empathy. But having just a bit meant that it expanded inside his head, and didn't allow any other stuff in. *Let it be a lesson to you. Never take nothing you don't need.*

Spotting a shop assistant in her white uniform, she walked over to her. The woman turned to smile at her as she approached. Hello. Can you tell me where the deodorant is?

It's over there by the door, she said, pointing in that direction. Perfect. Sherrie-Lee knew very well where it was. She was just hoping that the assistant would point over there, so the security man could see.

Thank you. She smiled a big, grateful, wonky-toothed smile. She could turn on the charm when she needed to.

She walked across, pausing at the lines of roll-ons and sprays, so he'd slow down, thinking he had more time. She was sure he was following, and then – one, two, three – she was out the back doors, quickening her step.

Four doors down was the stone entrance to the bank. She turned to go in so she could look back discreetly. The security guy was nowhere in sight.

Inside the bank, the air was cool and still, despite the high, vaulted glass roof. She looked up and saw that beyond the glass was another roof, protecting it, shading it from the outside. She let her eyeballs roll back in her head, her eyelids close. It's what she did when she tried to make herself feel relaxed. Make an outward show of it. Trick it into being real. There was a queue of about six or seven people. She joined it, with no more intention than giving herself time to rest, time to think of what to do next. She felt the plastic casing of the eyeshadow trio in her pocket and thought about getting rid of it somewhere, just in case. When she was second in line, she'd pretend she'd got tired of waiting and leave. Any shenanigans with trying to follow her or catch up with her would be over by then. She didn't have an account here. Had no account anywhere, in fact, unless her mother had one for her and hadn't told her. She doubted that. These days, her mother could barely hold it together to finish a shopping list. But maybe that was unfair. Sometimes she surprised her. Once she brought

3

her a brand-new pair of Adidas trainers, completely out of the clear blue, after two years of being chased up and poked at by school for not having a PE kit. They had been slightly the wrong size, but a perfect fit with a wad of toilet paper shoved in the front and the laces tied extra tight, and it made them last much longer.

Why was she constantly stealing stuff? Stuff she didn't need. Lately, she felt she was getting too old for all these adrenaline-goings-on. It was the habit of it, and the need to keep it practised. A kind of skill for life, like they talked about at school. You never knew when you were going to need it. There was something else, too, a kind of stepping out of yourself, leaving yourself aside. She imagined herself on a psychiatrist's couch, like she'd seen on TV. Telling her secrets to the darkened figure of the psychiatrist, who was sitting, cross-legged, pencil and notepad in hand, silhouetted by a meagre light coming in through the slats of a Venetian blind. A large, leafy plant sharing the frame of the window. No one was even half-aware of what she, Sherrie-Lee Connors, was capable of.

The bank was one of those old stone buildings, but they had done everything they could to hide that. Everything was overly bright and modern looking. All glass and streamlined to make it look open plan and inviting. Lines of red and grey, the colours of the bank logo, were emblazoned on the walls at odd angles. A could-be-anywhere sort of place. A non-place. Anonymous and indifferent. As if anyone really gave any more than zero shits about the bland décor. You could bet that what people really wanted would be another teller, another person behind those counters, so that they could do something else with their lunch hour instead of queueing here at the bank.

She looked back towards the door every few minutes. Not too often, so as not to look nervous, but just enough to check on the security guard situation. That's when she saw them come in. There were two of them.

Two men in dark long-sleeved tops and masks, each of them carrying a large, dark blue hold-all. *Oh boy!* she said to herself. *It was turning into one helluva morning.* One of the guys, the one in a black balaclava, held back and stood behind her. The other one, wearing the rubberised head of Prince Charles, had grabbed the arm of the man on the welcome desk and pushed him forward to the front of the queue. The woman, second in the line, started to turn towards them to complain about the pushing in or something, but stopped herself when she looked at him and took in the headgear. By now the whole bank had gone silent. The people in front of her seemed to creep into themselves. Nobody wanted to stand out.

The one that stood at the back was moving his weight from one foot to the other. Nervous, she thought. She could relate to that. It was how she had felt ten minutes ago. But she had kept her cool. She had learned the simple fact of life early on, that when it all hits the fan and everyone is giving up, that's really when you needed to keep your cool. When it was on its way out the door, that's when you needed to hang on to it. Make it bide its time. He needed to hang on in there. In a wild moment of sympathy, she felt like telling him so. Giving him advice so he didn't bottle it. But then she thought against it. It wasn't really done; she knew that, even though this was her first bank robbery. You could just tell that it wasn't high on the list of bank-robbing etiquette. He was wearing trainers, the guy behind her. Black Nike trainers. That was a mistake, she thought. They were too distinctive, with a fluorescent orange tick running down the side. If she were robbing a bank, she wouldn't wear anything with a logo. These places have cameras everywhere. He'd have to throw them away. There was grass sticking to the sole of his right trainer, like he had stood on something, and his laces were tied in a double knot. Why was she focussing on this stuff? she thought. All the trivial shit. *Have you not grasped the situation, Missy? Are you not scared?* She tried

5

to force herself to take it more seriously. A couple of over-nervous dudes were robbing the bank she was in. It could all go horribly wrong, at any minute, and all she could focus on were all the absurd, random things. All the little irrelevant things were too interesting, as though they pulled everything towards themselves and held all the significance. All the meaning. She was aware, too, that probably all was not normal in her own head. She probably had some kind of syndrome.

Prince Charles, who was still holding the man from the welcome desk by the upper arm, also had some kind of shotgun. Sherrie-Lee imagined that that was what it must be, though she had never seen one in real life before. He pushed the reception desk bloke along with his forearm, nudging him. He pointed with the gun to get the teller to pull up the other blinds.

Nobody gets hurt if everyone does exactly what they're told, he said. *You*, he gestured again with his gun, this time towards the reception guy. Take this bag and the other one and get them to fill it with cash. He nodded towards the woman behind the counter with a slight cocking of his head. One of Prince Charles' ears flapped with the movement.

His partner passed his bag forward and the reception man took the two bags and punched in the code to let himself through to the other side.

If you hit the alarm people get hurt, he shouted through the glass, so everyone heard.

The bag, she noticed, also had a logo on it. *Complete Fitness Gym!* Maybe it was a red herring, she thought. More and more she was deciding that they were amateurs. Opportunists. Did that make them more or less dangerous? More, she decided. Definitely more. They were more likely to get spooked, shoot someone by accident or make some mistake and then go into panic overdrive. And the people too, the hostages. She wondered at the word, thinking that that was probably what they were now. At what point do people stop being bystanders and start being hostages? Maybe there was some kind of scale to measure it. Boxes to tick. Standards to reach. The woman in front of her, she was just the type to grab pepper spray from her bag and start spraying at the one with the gun. Or the old guy at the front looked like he could be tempted towards some kind of heroics, grabbing him by those ears, getting Prince Charles in a head lock, making a move on the gun. All hell would be let loose then. They'd all be for it. Prince Charles was definitely the ringleader, Sherrie-Lee could tell. The way he directed every-one. Pushed himself to the front. There'd be no mercy from him.

Out of nowhere, Sherrie-Lee became aware of the smell of lavender. Not strong, like when you brush by a lavender bush, but a slight waft of it lingering in the air. It was probably coming from the woman in front of her. She lifted her nose slightly towards the woman, but it didn't get any stronger. And, when she moved closer to her, slowly and slightly so nobody would notice, there was no extra strong smell of it arising. She moved back again towards the robber behind her, maybe the smell was coming from him. She imagined news reports, describing the robber smelling of lavender. Perhaps he would get the nick-name Lavender Jack or something. But again, the intensity of the smell did not seem to increase the closer she moved towards him. Some things in life were meant to stay a mystery.

Behind the counters, a bag had been given to each of the tell-ers. The red-haired one looked nervously towards Prince Charles, who was doing all the talking. He brandished the gun and she went through into the unseen part of the bank with the bag. You have three minutes to fill it, he told her. The other teller, a man with short black hair and the red tie of the bank, began filling the bag from the drawers behind the counter.

Two minutes, Prince Charles called. The man with the tie looked at him and moved to another drawer, which he quickly opened and began emptying of money. One minute left. Prince

Charles leaned towards the glass as he spoke. His voice was clear, sounding out all the consonants, posh-sounding to Sherrie-Lee. Not from round here. An absurd thought came to her, that it really was Prince Charles. It would be a perfect disguise. Masquerading as his own identity. Nobody would ever get it. She felt a giggle surge from somewhere near her stomach. She managed to thwart it into a cough. She didn't want to be laughing and drawing attention to herself.

Come on, Prince Charles said angrily. His left hand banged and then tapped against the counter. There was a delay, a shuffle from the back. Everybody seemed to hold their breath at once in anticipation. It slowed the circulation of air in the room.

A shot was fired. It broke through the glass above the counter. The glass was punctured. It was followed by an elongated echo as everything seemed to slow. Most people crouched down, protecting themselves. The woman in front of her just gawped at the punctured glass.

Fuck, she heard the man behind her say. Sherrie-Lee sensed him move back, and she moved back with him. Stepping away from the line. Nobody seemed to notice them. It was as though they were all frozen in the after-shot. As though time had stood still for a few moments and only Sherrie-Lee and the second robber could move. At the entrance, they turned and walked out of the bank quietly. There were a few people walking by in the street. It seemed like an ordinary day. The only thing was that people were looking over at the two of them on account of the man's balaclava. She saw him reach up to take it off.

Don't take it off, she said. There are cameras here. She gestured towards one stuck high above the cut-price card shop, with a slight flick of her head.

What the fuck? he said, looking down at the small girl walking with a quick stride beside him as if it were the first time he had noticed her.

8

Well, that's nice. Where is your car? She looked up at him.

What car? He kept his eyes focussed ahead of him, trying to outpace her.

Don't you have a getaway car?

No.

Wow!

Look, who are you? You need to be on your way! I'm in a spot of bother, in case you haven't noticed.

I can help you.

He looked down at her. She had to incorporate a few running steps into her walk to keep up with his quickened pace. He half-laughed and shook his head as he looked ahead muttering to himself. Jesus, this is all I fucking need.

Walking quickly, they made short work of the length of the street. Soon they were passing the Kwik-Fit at the top of town and the big, closed-down pub on the corner. They crossed the road, picking up their pace before the lights changed. If we cut through here, she said, we can get on to the canal and out of town. There aren't any cameras there.

How do you know?

I make it my business to know. She tapped her nose theatrically. We are the most surveilled country in the world. I read it on the internet. Not sure how they measure that, though. A lot of the cameras don't work. Only we don't know which ones. Cheapskate security. Keeps you on your guard without going to all the expense.

She had taken the lead by this stage, and he seemed to follow blindly. He kept looking behind him. There seemed to be nobody following. It was bizarre how normal everything looked, even though his heart was still moving like a gymnast inside his chest and small tremors ran down his arms and legs. Just beyond the infirmary they went down some steps onto the canal path. She went under a bridge and he followed.

There was a stone caught in the hole in the bottom of her trainer and it sounded against the cobbles. It was a big, ball-like stone, more like a pebble, wedged into the sole where the rubber had worn away. Normally she felt embarrassed when something got caught in it and she heard it tapping against the floor, as though it made all that was defective about her stand out to other people. A soundtrack to the defective. She had meant to poke it out and get rid of it. But hearing it here, echoing under the bridge, it seemed transformed. Acute echoes, rising, each one curtailed by the next. They stood in the curved cooled underbelly of the bridge. The light caught on the surface ripples where the shadow of the bridge ended and was reflected onto the stone underside where it jumped and flitted, mirroring the movement of the water.

You can take it off here. She looked at him, an expectant expression on her face.

He hesitated, looking in both directions along the canal. If you see my face, you'll be a witness. You should buzz off now. Don't wanna be getting mixed up in this.

How ungrateful. She folded her arms and leaned against the barrel of the bridge. Three ducks appeared, swimming idly near to where they stood. Sherrie-Lee watched them, waiting.

He crouched down near to Sherrie-Lee, his elbows resting on his thighs. He chewed at his thumbnail.

Well, Sherrie-Lee said.

I am grateful. It's just not safe. You should go home. He looked about him again, anxious to get rid of this weird kid.

I don't have a home, she said, looking down in a contrived pose of forlornness.

He seemed to pause and look thoughtful for a minute. He was tiring quickly as the adrenaline dissipated. She was a skinny runt of a thing, with badly cut hair, fluffed up a bit at the back from lack of brushing. How old are you anyway?

Twelve.

Shouldn't you be in school?

School's over for the summer, she said. I'm already mixed up in it, by the way. I helped you, remember. I'm what's called an accessory to the crime.

He looked at her. She was making it up as she went along. How do I know you can be trusted? he said, falling into the game.

You don't.

What's your name, anyway?

Zadie. What's yours?

He hesitated, then said, Bob.

I had a cousin who was called Bob.

Was? Where is he now? He asked the question automatically; he didn't really want to know. He'd become used to the idea of it as a fake name and he couldn't imagine anyone having it for their real name.

I don't know. We haven't seen him for a long time.

Things kept rolling as though he had no control over them. Like he was trapped in some film. He was in it but had no say in what was happening. It started to feel as though he was already stuck with this kid. She wasn't going anywhere. He stood up and stepped towards the edge of the canal. In the shadow of the bridge, he could see about a foot into the depths, and could make out the outline of a clear plastic builder's bag half-submerged in weeds. Looking down, the balaclava obscured part of his vision and rubbed against his lower eyelids. He was overheating and felt claustrophobic inside it. He pulled and rolled the balaclava upwards and wiped at the sweat on his reddened skin. His brown hair was flat and damp and pressed against his head. He stuffed the balaclava into the pocket of his jeans.

You walk out first. In case a camera picks you up on the next stretch. They'll be looking for a man and a girl. I'll catch you up.

Not if I can help it, he muttered just under his breath, and he moved off.

11

She watched him as he strode away. She thought that she would count slowly to fifty and then follow him. That would leave enough of a gap between them. The canal looked narrow as it stretched ahead. It reflected the blue of the sky and the shapes of all the clouds. The surface was small and yet what it reflected was huge. A whole lot bigger than itself. The whole sky was reflected in its surface. Only at the edges, where the shadow of the side protected its surface from the light, did it show its true colour.

2

They walked by the old mill that bordered the edge of town, with its broken windows reflecting fragments of sky in sharp angular shapes. Its walls were stained a dark green in places, where the guttering was missing. Buddleia clung to the sides, roots penetrating the spaces between bricks. Into the scrubland, they passed a car with wheels and doors removed. Bindweed climbed and twisted into it. Further on, travellers' caravans, the old type and modern ones, were parked up on the verges, on their way to or from Appleby Fair. The old caravans were rounded and painted with flowers and patterns. Their piebald horses grazed in the field next to them. A man carried a large see-through plastic container of water to the back of one of the caravans. Each of them observed all this as they passed. They had gone into their own silences and Sherrie-Lee had stopped trying to make conversation.

Sherrie-Lee thought about the name Bob. You could just about bet that this was as likely his real name as Zadie was hers. What did it matter, anyway – nobody's name ever really fitted anyone. Her sister was called Grace, for fuck's sake, and she was about as graceful as a bag of potatoes, with a mouth on her that was even less deserving of the name. And if that wasn't enough, Grace's boyfriend, Luke, had a smelly bulldog whose name was Pearl. It sometimes made her smile thinking of Luke with his dog called Pearl and his girlfriend called Grace. She hated too her own name, Sherrie-Lee. She had a particular hatred for double-barrelled names. She had noticed that people with double-barrelled surnames were always quite posh. One name wasn't enough for them. They were too important for that. People wanting to push their poshness in your face so you'd know they were better than you. But the opposite was true with double first names. They were always poor people's names. Silly and sad, they seemed to Sherrie-Lee. The way people said them out loud, the last syllable raised or drawn out, and you would know how someone felt about you just by hearing them speak your name.

The sky was blue. An all-one-colour-blue all the way to the edges. A sky blue. No messing about. No dithering about what colour it was. A summer sky for a summer day, like you get on a postcard. If she'd gone to school she wouldn't be getting all this fresh air and feeling the sun on her face. That was much better than learning about Henry VIII and all his wives. She was quite good at school stuff when she put her mind to it, but it tried her patience, most of the things they had to learn. The irrelevance of it all. History was just the history of rich people: there was never any history about ordinary people, as though they weren't important enough, or as though nothing ever happened to them. Only when history touched World War One and World War Two did it look at ordinary people, because then they were needed as soldiers, as cannon fodder. History was the subject she found most annoying. The one that could be the most interesting but wasn't. Refusing all the things that could be interesting, for some reason of its own.

The sunlight caught the bottom edge of a tin can stuck into the ground and reflected back into her eyes. She had a visual flash of being in the bank. A rush of postponed fear surged inside her and was gone, though it left her with thoughts of what might have happened. What might have happened to the others they left behind. Leaving with one of the bank robbers. Almost like going to the heart of it was a way of conquering that fear. Even though it seemed from the beginning that it was Prince Charles who was the one you needed to keep an eye on. The one to watch. Not just because he was the one with the gun. There was something shifty about him. All these thoughts were squashed through Sherrie-Lee's mind, like playdough through a press. Changing shape. Existing briefly, then disappearing.

Her legs had started to ache. She kept it to herself. Instead, the word 'traipsing' came into her head. That was what she was doing. It was a funny word if you thought about it. Various sentences attached themselves to her thoughts. *She traipsed across the fields behind Bob. Bob led the way as they traipsed over the field. Traipsing across the fields, one behind the other.* It was like in those comprehension tests they did at school, which she never fully understood, where you had to choose the correct sentence to fit in the gap, but all the sentences meant the same thing and whichever one you chose ended up being the wrong one. It didn't bother her getting these wrong because she was good at almost everything else. It was the kids that got everything wrong that she felt sorry for. The pointlessness of the exercises just seemed like a trap to catch them out. Green marking scrawled on their work; green dots and crosses filling their answer sheets and exercise books. It was pitiful even for Sherrie-Lee to see.

On a long street, Bob turned off the pavement and sat down on the step, watching as Sherrie-Lee caught up with him. The twenty or so paces that had grown between them made her seem even smaller. She squinted at him in the glare of the sunlight and plonked herself on the step beside him. Are we there, then? she asked.

Where?

Is this where you live? Looks nice. She looked up at him, and then looked down at her trainers, straightening her feet so that they were parallel to each other on the step.

Look, you can come in for a tea and a bite to eat, he relented. He wanted to get inside his flat, get out of the sunlight. Since you've tagged along all this way. Then you'll have to leave. Okay?

Even as the words were exiting his mouth, he was thinking against it. He now regretted saying it, feeling that just the fact of letting her through the door would mean that the whole thing was going to drag on, that she would be shadowing him for longer. Though it was true enough what she had said an hour or so ago. The cameras would have picked up her face, would identify her and trace her. She needed to hide out for a day or two. They had not spoken since, though he kept coming back to her reasoning as his mind skated in and out of what had happened: the bright light of the bank through the prickled heat of the balaclava, the adrenaline, the gunshot, the look on the teller's face.

They had walked for miles, through a convoluted route, turning a two-mile trek into five or six. He was only vaguely aware of his surroundings in all that time. He thought she would tire of it and get lost, but she kept on following like a needy puppy. Now she knew where he lived too. He had kept telling her to go home, but the poor kid didn't seem to have anywhere to go home to. Seemed mad in this day and age, but then he thought of all the people he'd met inside who had lived like that as kids. One man he knew left home at ten years old and lived under an upturned boat in the same village as his parents, way out in the sticks. People used to put food out for him, the way you would for a stray dog. But that was a good few years ago. The guy had been older than he was now when they first met. He had even envied him at the time. Envied his freedom from other people. He didn't have the love of a mother to disappoint. It was easier for men who had nobody on the outside. They just had themselves to think about, they didn't have to feel bad for the people they'd let down. They could live entirely on their own terms.

Putting his key into the lock, he felt like an animal about to enter the refuge of its cave. And at the same time, he was conscious of himself, in a nagging way, of everything catching up with him, like he was entering some narrowing tunnel and was not sure when or if he would come out of the other side.

Not much of a place, is it? she said as she moved from the living room to the doorway of the small kitchen.

You didn't have to come in.

He walked to the window and drew the curtains and then spent a few minutes looking out of the window from behind the edge of the curtain. There were a few parked cars outside, but they were all empty and he felt they were familiar to the street. None of the others knew where he lived, or anything about him, but still he felt like someone could turn up. It wouldn't be hard to find him if they really wanted to. Though it wouldn't be yet. They would wait it out in case he was tailed, by someone other than this weird kid. It calmed him when he reasoned like this. Calmed the surface of things. And for a minute after his thoughts had stopped articulating themselves came a calm that spread out like the stillness of water. Then the doubts would blow in again, agitating the surface. There was always some unforeseen thing. One doubt laid itself on top of another. Still at first, then tapping against each other. Faster and faster. Like divining rods going at it. Demented. Reaching over the source of water.

He felt drained. Another reason why it would've been better to be alone. He could've just crashed out on the sofa. Not thought about anybody else. Pass out. Not think. That's what he really needed to do.

She sat down on the armchair, looking about the room. Bob glanced out again behind the edge of the curtains. They were thick and heavy and the room was cast into semi-darkness. There was only a dim orangey light coming through them, and two bright lines at either side where the light still got in. And from the other side of the room came a little light from the small kitchen window, otherwise it was all shadows.

Bob turned on the TV and went through a set of wooden, saloon-style doors into a kitchenette. Checking the kettle had water in it, he switched it on, and when he turned round Sherrie-Lee was behind him.

Cool doors, she said, swinging through and turning to admire them. They're like cowboy doors. You know – in the films. Got anything to eat, then? She looked past him, towards the fridge.

Not much. Do you like crackers? He opened the cupboard above the kettle. There was the sticker his girlfriend, Gina, had stuck on the inside of the door. A smiling apple, skipping. The sticker read, *Have you had your five-a-day?*

She looked into the fridge. Not much of a cook, are you?

Nope.

There's not even any cheese. What are we supposed to have with the crackers?

A bit fussy for someone who has nowhere else to go, aren't you? He took out the crackers from the cupboard and put them on a plate. Then he pulled out a tin of sardines and a bottle of hot sauce.

Here. Have these with them. I don't like cheese. He handed her the sardines and hot sauce and she carried them the short distance to the table. He passed her a plate and her tea and sat opposite her.

Do you have sugar? she asked after taking a sip of tea, grimacing at the taste.

He shook his head automatically, not really paying any attention.

Everybody likes cheese. Anyway, there's lots of different types you know, you just have to find one you like. A cheese for every taste. Blue cheese, green cheese, red cheese.

Nope. I just don't like cheese. Full stop. He rubbed his face with his hands and looked towards the curtained window, exhaling slowly.

There's even a cheese made of maggot poo.

No way.

Yep. I read it in a book. Maggots eat cheese and they make more cheese out of the maggots' poo.

He pulled a face, but felt that, if it was true, it was as good a justification for not liking cheese as any. Sometimes he got tired of having to explain it to everyone, as though not liking it was something he chose just to provoke people. Beneath all the chattering and the complaints, Zadie seemed quiet and on edge, the way she looked around the room, taking in every detail. She sometimes bit her lip like she was deep in some anxious thinking, and she looked at him as though she was unsure about something or was in the process of making an important decision. Perhaps she was one of those people that talked a lot to hide nervousness or shyness or quietness, or whatever it was she wanted to keep hidden. The light thrown from the kitchen window reached up to where she was sitting at the kitchen side of the table. She had thin light brown hair that held limply against her head, and freckled, pale skin. Even her skin was thin. You could see the small blue lines of her veins beneath her eyes and at her temples. It showed all different colours underneath, purple blotches, a salmony colour too, on her cheeks. Almost like you could see the flesh underneath. Sometimes her eyes looked a kind of brown, then in a different light they looked green. Her nails were bitten down to the quick, and the nail beds bulged with a red soreness from too much biting at them. The cuffs of her thin grey jacket were scuffed and layered with dirt.

You shouldn't really walk off with strangers, you know. Didn't anyone ever tell you?

She darted him a look, lowering the hand that had been about to put a cracker to her mouth.

You're alright here. I'm not one of those creeps.

She looked directly at him as though weighing him up and then glanced towards the TV and resumed eating the cracker.

She seemed hungry, the way she spooned on the sardines and ate the crackers. She had already had four before he had eaten his first one. She didn't touch the hot sauce.

Do you think the other guy got away? She wiped her mouth on the back of her hand, smearing a cracker crumb to her left cheek.

Which guy? he said without thinking. They hadn't talked about what happened at the bank the whole time they had been walking around. Not about the details of what happened.

Hmm, let me see. The real Prince Charles maybe, or the other one in the bank? Duh, the other bank robber. Stupid.

I don't like to be called stupid.

She looked down, embarrassed. In the afternoon light, Bob could see how her forehead and neck reddened, but her cheeks remained the same blotchy mismatch of colours. She said sorry after a minute or so.

He probably left too.

Do you think he shot anyone? Her eyes widened and there was red sauce on her chin where the sardines had dripped.

No. The bullet hit the glass, and then probably went into the wall at the back.

But there was another shot. As we were leaving.

I didn't hear no more shots. He frowned at the possibility, feeling the edges of it curl up from the hollow of his stomach.

There was. How come you didn't hear?

He shrugged, impaling a piece of sardine on the end of a knife. He tried thinking back, but he didn't remember hearing another shot. He thought the hollowness had been from hunger. He had been too nervous to eat breakfast. But he wasn't hungry anymore.

He a friend of yours?

No. I don't know him. Called himself Dom for this job. It was organised by someone else. I met him yesterday to go over the plan. Everyone had a false name. No one knows anything about anybody. That way, someone gets caught, they don't know nothing about anybody. He thought also that was why he could just leave like that, he didn't even know the guy. Didn't owe him anything.

So, Bob's not your real name?

Bob looked at her and looked away. Gary knew him though, he thought suddenly. He'd put him onto the job in the first place. Though Gary had said that he himself was not known to the group. But someone must know someone somewhere along the line. Connecting the dots of strangers. That second shot, if it happened, why hadn't he heard it? He thought, on the surface of his reasoning, that there had been no other shot. Panic and confusion could get things mixed up, could make people sense things that didn't happen, and not sense things that did. He wondered which it had been and thought about mentioning it, sounding it out. He tried imagining the possibilities of that second shot. Into the air? The ceiling? One of the bystanders? He imagined it until it all blanked out, numbing his head, his thoughts aimed like pebbles into the water, forming a series of ripples before disappearing, one after another.

The news came on the TV and they moved to the sofa to watch the local headlines. A hospital was closing and people were standing outside it with home-made signs. It flicked to another story; some school was doing a sponsored silence, but there was nothing about them yet.

Maybe it's too early. Maybe they don't report stuff like that, she said. The news is like that you know, just stuff they decide they want you to know. She was looking for other stuff whenever she saw the news. Wildfires had been burning in Australia for seven months, though it was hardly ever on the news now. If you wanted to find out about it, you had to look it up on the internet, find it for yourself. Although, sometimes she was glad it wasn't on anymore. Sometimes she didn't want to think about it. She still had nightmares about all the charred bodies of kangaroos and koala bears she had seen on TV.

Do you have any playing cards? She thought that would provide a good distraction, while away the rest of the afternoon. She knew a few games. She could even do a couple of tricks.

No.

3

The blanket he'd given her smelled of old dust and raw onions and rabbit droppings, but that was alright. She could stay here a while. She'd had enough of living at home. She'd show them. She might even move in here. Joshy too. She was sure that he would fit in just fine. Maybe in a few weeks, – she didn't want to be pushing her luck right now. Bob might need a bit of persuading in the meantime, but she was good at that sort of thing. No one would bug her here and it was comfortable. More than comfortable. The carpet reminded her of the carpet in her nan's house. The big brown and orange swirls, the way the pattern half-resembled an opening flower and half just fell into itself. Her nan had lived next door and they had spent most of the time there, her and Joshy. She would watch TV there on the sofa, or read, while Nan and Joshy would kind of talk to each other. Nan must have been losing her mind even then because she would ask Joshy things like where her mam and dad were, even though they'd been dead for over forty years, and where her husband was, dead for twenty. Joshy would say, *Gone park*. Or *Gone pictures*. Sometimes various answers all in the same hour. They satisfied her just the same. But, when she asked Sherrie-Lee the same questions and she'd replied something like gone to the park, she'd keep questioning her further. *Why would they go to the park? Why would they leave us here? They'd have been back from the park by now?* As though she didn't believe Sherrie-Lee, as though it was only Joshy's answers that could soothe her. As though they both had some special connection in the brain that nobody else could understand. As though the defective things in both their brains were transmitting some special understanding that couldn't be detected from the outside. Couldn't be understood or shared by anybody else. She'd sometimes call them the names of her own children. She would call Sherrie-Lee their mother's name Beryl, or Susan, their aunt, and Joshy would get the name of their uncle, Patrick. She would make them boiled eggs for tea and sit with Joshy for hours, watching television with him, or singing him all those old poor songs like *The Little Boy that Santa Claus Forgot*, and *Dear Old Daddy's Whiskers*. Sherrie-Lee thought about how she was always singing to them or teaching them songs. Joshy would never've talked so well as he did if it wasn't for all Nan's songs. She recited a few lines of a song to herself as she lay there on the sofa in the fading light. It came back to her easily, though it seemed sad the way it sounded, spoken rather than sung. The words came out flat and dry, sucked clean of all melody. Even as her nan was forgetting everything else, she could still sing a whole song right through to the end. Word perfect, too. But then she'd say something like – speaking over Joshy as though he wasn't there – *What's wrong with that kid? Why can't he speak proper?* As though she didn't know him at all. And Joshy would repeat *Wrong with kid* over and over. And it would become a thread for the whole afternoon or evening as it became fixed in both their minds. Nan repeating the question and Joshy repeating the words. It would've been more sad if it hadn't also been a bit funny, and they hadn't all been so used to each other. Sometimes her nan laughed at it too, when she asked it and heard Joshy repeating *Wrong with kid*. She would laugh and shake her head. Her laugh was loud and musical and when she stopped laughing, she would say softly to herself, *I don't know*. Sherrie-Lee missed that cosiness. It was never the same with just her and Joshy, almost like you needed someone else, a grown-up pulling it all together. She would visit her nan when she couldn't remember a name or a thing and cuddle up to her and start singing one of her songs and then her nan would join in and take over and sing it right to the end in her beautiful voice. A voice that her husband had said was like the voice of someone called Vera Lynn. She used to say that, before she lost her memories. She'd smile in a proud, happy way when she told them, but after a while she forgot even that. She had kept some of her habits though. Even after the time she was forgetting almost everything and started going outside and getting lost. Habits like the way she answered the phone. She never got over the newness of it, even though it was old-fashioned to have a phone line in the house when everyone had moved over to mobile phones. It seemed to startle everyone when it rang. The loudness of it. It didn't ring often, but when it did, the same routine was played over. They would look at each other in surprise. A kind of *who could that be?* took over, sometimes said out loud, sometimes just thought. Then, Nan would run over to the phone as though this had to be done to make up for the stunned moment of inaction, to make sure that the caller was caught in time, before hanging up. Then she would pick up the receiver and her normally loud voice would give way to a feeble, put-on voice, the voice of a weak, old lady. And then, depending on who it was that had called, the feeble voice would disappear in an instant, or be drawn out to continue whatever effect her nan was trying to create.

The only picture on the wall of Bob's living room was a small, faded photo of the sea and the edge of a cliff in a red plastic frame. It was so boring that it must have been some special place to whoever had bothered to put the photo in the frame. It wasn't even a good picture. The light in the picture wasn't that good and it looked dull and dim. The place needed cheering up a bit. It was all old-looking and she wondered if it was a temporary place, just for the bank job, or whether he lived here. She had learned that he didn't like too many questions. She would have to slip questions

24

in gradually. There were still a lot of things she needed to find out. His real name. What he was about. What his plans were. She would tell him stuff about herself too. That's what you needed to do when you got kidnapped. You had to get them onside, make them see you as a whole person so they felt empathy for you. She knew all about it. She'd seen *Silence of the Lambs* and that other film. If this was his permanent home, she could help him fix it up a bit. This involved just buying a new set of cushions, which is what her mam did when they moved to a new place. They'd done a lot of moving to different places before getting the place next to her nan. She thought it funny, that. All the different places they'd lived in, sometimes just for a couple of weeks, and then they'd ended up right next door to Nan's. Funny how it took all that time and the house had been there all along. Right under their noses. Her mother used to have a thing for motivational cushions. The more motivational the better. That's what her mam had thought. Sherrie-Lee had liked it when she bought them. Had liked seeing her involved in something. She helped her carry them back all the way from town. *Be Bold, Be Brave, Be You,* they said. *Believe it, Achieve it.* Or *Without the Rain There'd Be No Rainbows.* Daft stuff like that. Not that you'd ever find Sherrie-Lee buying crap like that. After a while, they always depressed her, as they got dirty and squashed out of shape. Their mottos seemed sarcastic and taunting. They made her feel extra sad - the way they mocked. The cheapness of them. They seemed to suck every last bit of hope out of you, every time one caught your eye. It had been a while since her mother had bought any motivational cushions or anything for their house. She looked around the room. Even if they didn't fix this place up it was fine the way it was. It was just a place. And more than that, it felt like a calm and easy place to be. It didn't ask anything of her. A bit like her shed at home, only here it was dry and warm. It wasn't really her shed, she just used it when she wanted to be on her own. It used to belong to the people who lived there before her. It still had stuff they'd left behind in it. A spade. A box of dried-up cans of paint. Some old bits of wood. She kept some of her own special things in there. Stuff she didn't want her sister poking into.

She felt wide awake. Lights stretched out in straight lines on the ceiling from passing cars, reaching out, then receding at odd angles, forming strange geometric shapes. She had been listening to the screeching of swifts outside but now they had quietened down for the night. Outside was a street lamp and the yellowed glow of it shone through the edges of the curtains. It was the end of June and it was gone ten and it had only just begun to get properly dark, though she could still see stretches of thin cloud, like cigarette smoke, high in the sky. Coming from the flat upstairs, she could hear the droning of a TV set. Every so often, music boomed out of it and then died down. It was comforting, the sound of somebody else's life nearby.

When she peered out and up at the sky, she saw that already a few stars were out. The nearest ones. The sky hadn't yet reached its deepest dark, when it threw up the light from more distant stars. The nearest star to the Earth was Proxima Centauri, which Sherrie-Lee had memorised and thought it sounded a bit like some Italian singer's name, or the name of an exotic dancer. It was a dull kind of star, though, and you couldn't always see it. Spotting them was difficult enough anyway and sometimes she pretended to herself that she had seen constellations or planets, otherwise star spotting got too frustrating. You had to make space for it in your imagination. Be open to a little fuddling. It was hard to find a way in with the stars otherwise. There was no order to them that she could find. They were just randomly out there. Sometimes knowing the constellations helped. Beyond that, there was nothing to help her with knowing them, with memorising their names and positions. If you wanted to travel to that closest star, it would take one hundred years to get there. She liked that they were all so far away, that they were so far away that what you see of them isn't really how they are. They aren't really little twinkling dots of light. Being all that distance away our view of them gets distorted, they could be anything, and if you thought about it, looking down from all that distance away, so could we. She knew all this because there was a great section on space in the library and it was one of the sections she was making her way through. There were 318 books about space. If you took one out every week it would take six years and two months to read them all. She had read twenty-three of them in two years, so even if she stepped up her game and read one a week, she would be eighteen by the time she had got through them all. She'd already made the decision that some of the more difficult ones she would leave to that last year. In one, she had read that because the possible number of other universes was infinite, it was likely that, some-where out there in the infinite vastness, there would be a planet that is just like ours, that had developed in the same way, under the same conditions. The librarian, who she found out was called Claire, had agreed with her that it did seem like a crazy idea. That's the thing with infinity, she had said, it makes anything and everything possible. That was also the great thing about all those books. All those ideas in there. It was mind-blowing. The library was her absolute favourite place to be. It was always warm and cosy and nobody harassed her there. Even when she was there during school hours. Nobody said shouldn't you be in school? Or gave her special sideways looks. It was as though they knew the same thing that Sherrie-Lee knew, that you could learn a whole lot more in the library than you could ever learn in school. It gave her space too to think through all her problems. The ones that she couldn't solve. It even helped her with those, too. It helped her draw her mind elsewhere, so she didn't have to think all the time about the same stuff. All those universes and possibilities out there. It helped her escape in lots of ways. And taught her stuff about the world that even most grown-ups didn't know. Even her teachers. And the best of it was she'd not even yet read one per cent of the books in there. So, there were all those other books just there waiting for her. It was Claire who always saved new books that came in about animals and space for her, because she knew that's what she loved to read. And stuff about saving the planet too, because that was one of the other things she was into. Saving all the habitats so the animals would have somewhere to live too, somewhere to find food and shelter. She liked the way Claire didn't look like anyone else she'd ever known. She had blue hair, for a start. Not punky and spiky, though. It was always combed neatly, in the style of a short bob. She didn't overdo it on the makeup either. Just mascara and eyeliner and purple lipstick, which made her teeth look really white. She always wore long-sleeved flowery blouses. Beneath the cuffs you could just make out the beginnings of her tattoos, which started just above her wrists. The kind that were not just lines, but shaded in so you could see the textures and shadows like real drawings. The kind of tattoos drawn by real artists.

4

Bob knocked on the door of the living room before he came through in the morning.

On his way to the kitchen, he said, I'll boil a couple of eggs and then you can have something to eat before you go.

Suit yourself, she replied. So he was still on about that, she thought. He wasn't much of a kidnapper, that was for sure.

- Put the news on, he said.

She picked up the remote and flicked at it until she found a news channel, even though she was actually, if anyone cared to notice, already watching something. There was an image of a big factory building on fire. And a news presenter in front of it saying how the firefighters had been working through the night to try and save it. They didn't yet know how it had started but eyewitnesses had reported hearing an explosion in the early hours.

Bob stepped back into the living room to see what was happening. There's always something, he said. Tell me if anything comes on.

The screen flipped to a picture of an old cinema, and somebody being interviewed said that it was important for our national heritage to save the old cinemas like this one, and that's what their community group was going to do. They had started a fund to buy it and restore it. Make it into a community cinema. Putting the community first. There were a couple of kids behind them, across the road, waving and trying to get on camera. They walked first in one direction and then turned to walk back so they could keep in the frame. It took them a while before they built up courage to wave at the camera.

29

She tapped into the egg, breaking the shell at the top with the back of a teaspoon. It was all dried up inside. I like my eggs dippy, she said, looking down into it with exaggerated disappointment.

I'll inform the chef.

I didn't mean to be ungrateful. Thanks for making it.

I can never get them like that, he said like he was genuinely sorry. It's hard to tell. They look the same no matter how long you boil them for.

They watched the last bit of the news, but there was still nothing on about them.

Listen, he said as she changed the channel back. My landlord is not so crazy about me having people stay.

He came to stand in front of her when he got no reply, and said it again. She was trying to get back into watching the TV. All the while, she could tell he was anxious about something, because he kept half-approaching her. Maybe that's why he didn't have any breakfast. She could see him, in the floating periphery of her vision, like he was rehearsing something. Preparing himself. He'd already ruined one show for her by making her switch to the news, and now he was ruining *ScrewIt* on top of that. It was a game show she'd gotten into this year. The contestants came on and tried to score as few points as possible by thinking of answers to questions that hardly anybody else had thought of. The answer must have been thought of by somebody though. It must be a genuine answer to a question. You couldn't just say some random thing to the question. Like if they asked the name of a popular zoo animal, you couldn't just say potato or even scarlet harlequin frog. It had to be an actual animal that someone else had said. And even though the scarlet harlequin frog was an actual animal, nobody would ever say it because it was so unusual. Nobody would even know it had ever existed, and now it didn't anymore because it was extinct. You scored a point if you chose a more popular answer than your opponent.

30

Every time a contestant scored a point an oversized plastic screw would screw into a block with their face pasted onto it, gradually pushing the block out of its frame. When they got to ten points the block would be pushed out of the bottom of the frame and that contestant would be out. The wrong answer sound would come on really loudly and all the lights in the studio would flash on and off and the loser would have to walk off the stage. The presenter called it 'the walk of shame' and some of the audience booed and hissed. It seemed mean but wasn't as bad as all the other shows that tried to humiliate people. It was just stupid. As dumb as any other game show, but she was really into it. Looking for it, whenever she turned on the television. It was on practically all the time, in the morning and then again in the afternoon. She even watched the repeats.

You really need to be on your way, Bob said, crouching slightly so he was nearer to her level. She had to act quick, jump in and change the reasoning.

You rob a bank and you're worried about what your landlord will say? She dug at him, trying to reverse his worries. Trying to make light of them so he'd stop bugging her and let her watch TV unhindered. It was deeper than that, though. She knew that. He didn't really want her around. Charming! After all she had done for him. He'd been raising doubts since the beginning. Trying to thwart her, so she'd felt like a tennis player volleying them back into insignificance. He didn't see the necessity of having her there yet. She told him how her mam wouldn't notice or care that she wasn't there. She often didn't even stay there, anyway. It was true too. Her mother had enough on her plate. Her little brother was probably autistic or something and her mother was often out of it, on prescription drugs for her addictions and all the back pain she was in from an accident years before. School was practically over for the summer. She didn't really have friends. None that would miss her anyway.

31

Maybe you should have me stick around, you know. You should be keeping an eye on me for a few days, a week at least. What with me being a witness and everything. Just until everything dies down. They have my face on the CCTV, they would easily trace me to my house. But here, how would they find me? Of course, I'd never say anything. But you never know how they question people. It's all psychological. Something might slip. We need to think of all the options very carefully. Make sure we work out everything. We don't want to be making any mistakes, do we? She kept watching Bob's reaction while she spoke. She knew she'd slipped up saying 'my house' after she'd told him she didn't have a home. But that was insignificant in the grand scheme of things and he didn't seem to notice. She could tell that he was seeing the sense in what she said. He was easy to read, Bob was. And she had to give herself credit, it was masterful how she was making such a watertight case.

He walked over to the window and lifted the edge of the curtain away from the window frame with his index finger, looking out at the street, first in one direction, then in the other, taking his time. He straightened himself, breathing deep and measured, like he was timing something. He needed working on a bit more. Maybe if she told him one of her stories, that might help.

She turned the telly off and sighed. She had begun practising telling stories and was making it her thing. She already had a repertoire of about twenty that she practised. She thought carefully about which one she might tell Bob. Dismissing one in favour of another because of what she thought he might like the best, before deciding on one of her favourites. A bubble of nervousness rose up her spine, bumping against all the notches. She felt anxious telling a story to someone for the first time. And she was careful who she practised them on - some of them were so fanciful that most of the people she knew wouldn't permit them, would look blankly and refuse to listen. People would regard them as outlandish. But sometimes, when she told one to herself, only the outlandish would do. Only the far-fetched, the improbable, so as to take herself as far away as possible from the here and now, to fly with it. It was the only way to exist. To save yourself. She thought about Bob, what she could get away with. What would pull him in. The story she chose was from a book she had at home. An old book that you could tell was something special from its blue cloth cover, which was faded and discoloured in parts and frayed at the corners. It said *101 True Animal Tales and Adventures* in lettering that had once been gold but that in places had faded to a dark silvery grey. Inside, the pages were foxed from all the damp houses it had lived in. Small brown spotted stains marked all the pages like big, spare freckles. She had become really good at telling stories and maybe if he saw how entertaining she was he wouldn't be so keen for her to leave.

I know a great story. It's a true story actually, which makes it even better. It's about a countess living a long time ago in France. She looked at Bob while she told him about the story, but as she was about to start she looked towards the wall, as though readying herself. This countess, she began, unlike a lot of the other countesses, was very beautiful. And, more importantly, she was rich and had lots of admirers. More than that, she had these two suitors. And it was well known that she liked exotic animals. One of her suitors had given her a parrot. All the way from the Amazon, it had come. Big and beautiful with brightly coloured feathers. They became famous, the countess and the parrot, and the other suitor became jealous. All the suitors were rich and they had all these contacts all over France, other rich people and their eccentric pets.

Why did everyone have weird pets? When he asked that she knew she was drawing him in, though he still stayed by the window, sitting on the arm of the sofa, bathed in the dulled orange light from the drawn curtain.

It was fashionable in those days. Explorers and trading ships had been bringing them back for a while. Anybody who was anybody, if you know what I mean, wanted to have a fancy pet. And the French were mad for them. The second suitor asked around and eventually found someone who wanted to sell their pet chimpanzee. The chimp had even worked in the kitchens, helping the cooks with their jobs. It would surely be better than any parrot. He was convinced. So when he purchased the chimp he went off with it, through the streets of Paris to the countess's grand house, which overlooked the Luxembourg Gardens. These were very famous gardens at that time, and somewhere where the countess could walk the chimp and the parrot. Parading round to show them off. It was all the rage then. Walking round, showing off. It's where the idea of a catwalk began. But they didn't walk moggies. It was big cats. Leopards and stuff.

The countess was overjoyed. She had never seen such a pet. Sherrie-Lee continued, and from time to time as she spoke she would steal a furtive glance at Bob to check his reaction. The chimp was big and handsome, but also gentle and affectionate. She enjoyed showing him off at parties, and the suitor that gave the chimp was becoming a favourite. She invited him to all her parties. The suitor that had given the parrot was becoming increasingly annoyed with the state of affairs, and spent a great deal of time plotting against his rival.

So people filled their lives with nonsense even then, Bob said.

She ignored his comment and continued, One day, the countess had to go out to a party and she couldn't take her beloved pets. So she left them together in her bedroom where they'd be company for each other while she was out.

Later, when she came back from the party, she rushed up to her room. The chimp was sitting on the window seat looking out at the street below. She hugged him and then looked for the parrot. She couldn't find him anywhere. Have you seen

Bertrand? she kept asking the chimp. That was the name she had given the parrot. Eventually the parrot was found cowering and shivering under her bed. He had been plucked of all his feathers and was trembling and naked beneath the bed.

It turned out that one of the jobs the chimp did when he worked in the kitchen was to pluck chickens and geese. When the suitor who gave the parrot found out about it, he was outraged and thought that the other suitor had planned it all on purpose. In humiliating his bird he'd humiliated him. There was only one thing to do in those days, so he challenged him to a duel. But in the duel he was shot. Just *here* – she pointed to her own chest, just below the heart – and eventually he died in agony from his wounds. Leaving the other suitor, who was an excellent shot, a veteran from Napoleon's wars, free to marry the countess.

The daft bugger, Bob said. Imagine that. You wouldn't catch me getting shot over that nonsense. Didn't he know he'd been a soldier? He stood up and moved to the other side of the window, shifting the curtain with an outstretched finger and leaning in to get a better look.

It's what they did then, the rich people. It was all about their honour and saving face. They were so busy being rich and doing nothing that they had to make up crazy things to do all the time. It's a true story. She eyed him from the sofa. She knew he would be the kind of person who would listen to a story. She had got quite good at telling the types. Some people couldn't even be bothered to listen, couldn't concentrate enough to get interested in them. Though he hadn't laughed at the funny bit when the parrot had lost all his feathers, she noticed. Of course, you had to catch people in the right mood too. And once you got their attention, tell them a story that was worth listening to. All these things she was conscious of learning. It felt good, like she was really getting the hang of it. A skill for her future life.

I don't think it's true, it doesn't sound right to me. Either a story ought to be true or it should carry a message. This doesn't have a message.

Maybe it does, she said, making it up as she went along. She didn't really think it had a message either. Stories didn't need to have messages, that was kids' stuff. She was smart enough to keep that to herself, though. Adults didn't like to be patronised.

What message?

Not to give exotic pets as presents, animals shouldn't be owned. Haven't you seen that sign in the backs of cars? *A dog is for life, not just for Christmas*. Especially not wild animals. She looked at him to gauge his reaction. Look what happened to the parrot man.

No, that doesn't sound right. He rubbed at his chin, thinking it over. The one who gave the chimp, he did alright from it.

Maybe messages shouldn't be so straightforward. Anyway, it's a true story. It said so in the book I got it from.

He narrowed his eyes. There was a bit of fluff on his lip and he blew on it. Two quick sustained blows until he had succeeded in getting rid of it. The chimp couldn't help what he did, he was just doing what he'd been taught to. Anyway, what happened to the chimp? he said finally.

I don't know, I think they probably kept it. The parrot too. Maybe they just kept them apart.

I bet the chimp found the parrot annoying. They don't really talk. You know that? They just mimic human sounds. The chimp probably found that annoying, the parrot impressing everyone and everyone thinking it could talk, and the chimp not being able to, even though it could understand a whole lot more.

She had never thought about that before. That birds couldn't really talk. But it seemed unfair to say, really, when you considered it. Some humans did the same thing, she felt sure. Joshy seemed to take up with talking just from imitating. That's how people learned to talk. And birds were a lot smarter than people thought. They didn't have big brains, but what brains they did have, packed a lot of punch. There was a lot of brain activity going on all the time inside their little bird brains.

She was glad that he seemed to like the story. He had taken it seriously, anyway. At home, only Joshy liked stories, although he never said so. He couldn't talk that well, although he was nearly eight, but she could tell he liked to listen to them because he would settle next to her when she read aloud and practised her stories. Sometimes leaning against her so she could feel his breathing against hers in the pauses in her reading. The rhythm of it. The shallow movements of his body as he breathed in and then out. And then afterwards, after the story was finished, still joined together for a little while, she would try to control her own breathing so it would fall in time with her brother's.

Just beneath the lobe of Bob's right ear he had a tattoo of two dice. Each one, if it was a real 3D die, would have been about one centimetre high, which, if you thought about it, was a pretty average size for dice. Only these dice were quite darkly tattooed. The tattoo artist had gone in for a bit of shading, but this, in Sherrie-Lee's opinion, had been a mistake. They were too dark and it was difficult to make out the numbers. You could see two sides of each die, but the top side was too flattened and dark to see the number properly. The sides that you could see each displayed a three and a four next to each other. That was another mistake: on a real die the three and the four are opposite each other. She knew that because she liked to see the pattern in things. It made things easier to understand. And one thing that she noticed with dice was that the opposite sides always added up to seven. The one and the six were always opposite. The five and the two, and the three and the four. She was going to say something about it, but didn't want to hurt his feelings.

Good job you had that dice tattoo covered up.

Bob looked at her.

You know, in the bank. I mean, you don't see many around. I mean it stands out, that tattoo.

Suppose so. I've had it a long time. I forget it is there most of the time. Self-consciously, he touched his tattoo with his middle finger, as though responding to its presence.

I'm gonna have one. When I'm old enough.

Yeah?

Either I'm gonna have the back of my head shaved and have two eyes tattooed there. You know, like the saying. She's got eyes at the back of her head. I like that. That's what my nan used to say about me. *She's got eyes at the back of her head that one. She doesn't miss a trick.* That was another one she used to say. *You've been here before, you have, Missy.* She used to say that too, I didn't like that one too much though.

That's just because you're smart. People say that about smart kids.

And the other one I might have if I don't have my head shaved is an eye just here, looking out. She turned round, lifting her hair and pointed to the back of her neck.

That's just weird, that is. You don't wanna be getting no tattoos. I wish I hadn't got this. He pointed to the dice.

You can always grow your hair longer.

Nah. That'd be worse.

Why a three and a four? Why not show the top more and have double six?

Three and a four. That's average. You don't often get double six in this life. Not unless you're born with loaded dice.

You got a one in thirty-six chance of a double six. So you'd get one pretty often.

You tried it out, then?

It's just the maths of it. If you tried it out, it probably wouldn't be like that. Because chance is chance, and it never works out like

38

the maths says it should. So, there is a one in six probability of one die showing six, and when you add another die, you times that six by another six. If you had three dice, the probability of rolling three sixes, well you'd just have to multiply the thirty-six by another six. So that would be one chance in 216.

We could get you on *Countdown*.

Sherrie-Lee shrugged. I just like numbers.

When I got this tattoo, I said to the bloke, do them showing a three and a four. You know, I meant showing a three and a four on the top, like an average roll. He just misunderstood.

Did you get mad?

Nah. No point.

5

At the back of the house was a long, narrow garden. The grass was thick and green, and some people might describe it as overgrown, but it was not overgrown, in Sherrie-Lee's opinion. It was just grown. Left to grow properly, when you thought about it. Better for nature like that. Along one side there was a hedge that had been allowed to run wild. It had brambles poking out all over it. Hard red blackberries were hanging from the brambles, small and not yet ripe. There was a fence at the other side that squared off across the back of the garden. Towards the bottom of the garden was a wooden shed. She'd seen it all from the kitchen window, but she'd never been out into the garden before. She thought it must belong to the flat upstairs.

The day was bright, and, after the interior darkness with the curtains always drawn, it burned the back of her eyeballs so that she had to keep closing her eyes to rest them. She let herself through to the garden by way of a large gate at the side, which, after she worked out the latch mechanism, pushed easily inward against the already flattened swathe of grass behind it. A male blackbird was busy beneath the hedge, picking up bits of ground and tossing them aside. It was jumping about in the shadows. It wasn't frightened of her at all. Every few seconds it stopped what it was doing and seemed to listen or look around, its head slightly cocked to one side, then it went back to its business with the soil. All of a sudden it called out wildly and took off. Sherrie-Lee looked around to see what had startled it, but she could see nothing that might have bothered it. She edged further down the garden and looked up at the top windows to see if anyone was looking out. It was a sunny day and she thought it would be nice to sit out here and read, but there were no books in Bob's house.

She went over to the shed to see if it was locked. Maybe there was a chair in there, or something she could use to sit on. It looked newer than her shed, with no missing planks of wood and no rotten bits at the bottom. The door had no handle, though, just a piece of faded twine that had once been red, but was now a kind of orange-pinkish colour, sticking out through the hole where the handle would've been. She pulled at it. The door opened slightly, but the string seemed stuck on something on the inside. There was a shifting movement. She stepped back. The movement stopped. Her heart thudded against her ribcage. It was too big to be a rat. More of a dragging sound, like one that a bigger, injured animal might make. She listened. Everything had gone silent. She listened and sensed that something was listening out for her, also. She called a weak hello through the gap. Still nothing. She pulled at the door again, until the string was taut and wouldn't give any more slack. She put her face up to the gap and peered inside. She could see a blue sleeping bag on the floor, a white trainer on top of it, and a denim knee sticking out on top of that. A short stacking tower of things she was not expecting to see.

Who's there? she asked in a big voice.

She peered in again. The trainer and the knee had moved.

Finally, a hand reached across and lifted the twine. The door swung open.

The trainer and the knee belonged to a man, who had short brown hair and brown eyes.

Hello, he said.

It seemed to Sherrie-Lee like an insubstantial thing to say when you had just been discovered hiding out in a shed. Though he looked harmless enough. He had a calm face, even though it was covered in stubble and his hair was sticking up. She was a good judge of character. She was always the one to spot the villain in films.

Who are you? she asked him.

My name's Mark. Is it your shed?

It's my dad's, she said, looking back at the flat windows.

You won't tell no one will you? I'll be gone in a day or two.

There was something about him that Sherrie-Lee found disarming. The simplicity of him. Just there on his own in the shed. There in a place where he shouldn't be. Helpless. Like he had turned his skin inside out – everything visible and vulnerable. She felt for him.

No. I won't tell no one. What you doing here?

My missus threw me out. We had a fight and I had nowhere else to kip down. She'll be alright in a day or two.

That's too bad. What did you fight about?

The question seemed to surprise him. He looked thoughtful and seemed to be considering the question for a few moments. Sherrie-Lee noticed that the bottom of his left earlobe was missing.

You know what, I don't really know what we were fighting about. He laughed, and then added, She gets like that sometimes.

What happened to your ear?

He touched it, as if to check what was wrong with it, and said almost in an apologetic way, When I was a kid, we had this dog and he bit a chunk of it off.

Was he vicious then, your dog?

Nah. I was just playing with him, roughing him up a bit. And he got a bit over-excited.

Dogs, hey!

He was a nice dog really. He looked away. Do you live here then?

Yeah. We live in the bottom flat. Me and my dad, Bob.

What's your name?

Zadie. She didn't miss a beat.

That's a nice name. He held the toe of his trainer and seemed to relax a bit more.

I know. It's my favourite name.

That's a bit of luck then. It being your name and your favourite name. Most people don't like their own name.

Sherrie-Lee nodded. Don't you like your name then?

It's alright. It's at school when you don't like it. No matter what your name is you'll always get kids making fun of it. You've got a mark on your shirt. Mark set go. Nonsense like that.

Sherrie-Lee considered what he said, thinking about all the times kids had teased her real name. Nobody makes fun of Zadie, she said. Which was true.

Is your dad in?

No, she said automatically. Then, because you could never be too sure of people, she added, But he'll be back soon.

He looked around the shed as though he was looking for something, and then reached behind him and produced an empty plastic bottle. One of those two-litre sized ones, though the original label had been torn off. Listen, Zadie. Can you do me a favour? Would you go and fill this up with water for me? I'm parched.

She took the bottle from him and went inside.

When she had given him the water and was back inside, by herself on the sofa, she thought how nice it felt saying Bob was her dad. How proper normal it made her look. Then she caught herself smiling. All that spying she'd done, and she hadn't even noticed someone was living in the shed at the back! No shit, Sherlock.

*

At the park, Sherrie-Lee took her notebook and pen from her pocket and flicked over to a new page. She wrote down the date and the time. There were quite a few people around, but that was the good thing about insects, they didn't seem to mind people the way some species of birds did. She took her usual route. Since the fifteenth of March, she had been doing a survey of insects in the park. She was good at this kind of thing. For two years, she had been monitoring birds, and had become an expert on the ones that lived around here. She had taught herself the names of all the ones she had seen and could tell a crow from a raven. A raven was bigger and when it was flying its tail fanned out in a kind of diamond shape, whereas a crow's tail was more rounded. Crows also liked to hang out by themselves, or in pairs. Rooks too, she could spot. They had thinner greyish beaks, and lived in groups, often alongside jackdaws. Jackdaws were the easiest to spot. They had grey heads and pale eyes. All the different kinds of birds had their own special habits. Their own special way of being. There was no end to all the amazing facts you could learn about them. Learning the names of different animals, finding out how to tell one from another felt important. Finding out about them, and finding a way in, opened up the world in a new way. This learning of names, this storing of facts inside herself. You'd be amazed if you took the time to find out. Like how crows never forget a face. Or how they are highly intelligent, and when they encounter a mean human, they teach other crows to recognise that human so they can avoid them. So now, when she saw a crow, she could think of its name and all the facts she knew about it. It was like a story in a way, and that's how she thought of it. Being drawn into a world created by the story of an animal. The library had loads of books about birds. Birds were what she really loved. Probably, there were just as many interesting facts about insects, but she was finding it more difficult to get drawn into their stories. She moved to insects because she had been learning about the insect population collapse. She had been so fixated on the birds that she hadn't noticed the insects so much. Though it made sense, and you could see that that was probably why a lot of birds were dying out, the insect-feeders anyway. The seed-eaters had problems of their own.

Everything was dying out and it was all happening a lot quicker than anyone imagined. They were losing their habitats on a daily basis. Sometimes it depressed her so much that she had difficulty getting out of bed. The creatures were powerless in it all. They just had to stand by as their worlds disappeared. Powerless and voiceless. They couldn't stand up for themselves. She had a secret wish that she would find an orphaned corvid baby, perhaps a crow, that she would raise it and teach it to talk. Though she knew too that if you found an orphan like that, it probably wasn't an orphan and you should leave it to its parents: they were the best at looking after it. Rescuing baby birds was a bit like giving bread and milk to hedgehogs. It was misguided. A lot of people didn't know that. That bread and milk is poisonous for hedgehogs and that rescuing a bird is almost definitely doing more harm than good.

She spent a lot of time back in March and April learning about the different species of insects, but all the time she still came across ones that she didn't know the names of, there were so many different species, and sometimes some of the ones she knew were hard to tell apart so there was a bit of guesswork involved too. A bit like looking at stars. She found it even more depressing than monitoring birds. All the stuff she had read. Farmers, gardeners, haters of ants, all of them were addicted to insecticides. She went to the garden section of the DIY superstore on the edge of town and hid all the insecticides. It took ages finding places to put them all, where they wouldn't be found so easily. She pushed some behind the grass seed. Some she put inside a kind of fancy metal bin dotted with round holes. Others she put in a trolley, or hid behind bags of gravel. It was not like other shops, because it was massive and there were not many shop assistants and they didn't seem to worry about shoplifters so they were not always on the lookout like they were at other places. Another time she took a roll of labels from school and wrote on each one – DO NOT BUY THIS PRODUCT!!!! IT KILLS ALL THE BEES AND EVENTUALLY YOU!!!– and stuck them on the spray canisters. People were short-sighted and could not see how bad killing insects was. At first, she thought they were just fucking stupid, but that was not fair, they just needed educating. And all the companies should not be producing the insecticides and advertising them in the first place. She was optimistic in this respect. People just needed saving from themselves. This phrase she had heard somewhere and thought of it each time she found herself thinking about this particular dilemma. Farmers ought to know better, though. Living in nature and being dependent on insects to pollinate their crops, and still they sprayed, even when they didn't need to. Neonicotinoids were the worst. She had been researching all about them in the computer room at school. They were a nerve poison. A nerve poison! And deadly. Just five maize seeds sprayed with the stuff was enough to kill a partridge. And that was just the start, if it got in the soil and the food chain. She could feel the rapid thud of her heartbeat.

All the way up to the folly at the high point of the park, she didn't see any insects. But that part was all rhododendrons and those big waxy-leaved plants with no flowers, so it was usually the deadest part, insect-wise. She probably could find some if she looked hard in the grass, but she didn't do that in this part of the park and she needed to keep to the same routine. Behind the folly was better. There was a kind of small meadow with grasses and tall, wild daisies. This folly bothered her, too. It was a kind of stone seat with four stone columns and a roof above it. It wasn't the thing itself that bothered her. The word was the problem. She looked the word up once, but it didn't seem right. It was a Victorian thing, this kind of folly. The dictionary had said. Sherrie-Lee thought it was a silly word for a silly thing, and that made it seem worse somehow. They had a lot to answer for, those Victorians. The sign to it saying folly also irked her. She sighed, seeing it now, as she always tried not to look at it. She always tried, but never succeeded. This was like a ritual. Always at the same section of the park she would begin trying not to see it, and then she would see the thing. It was mad, really. I mean, how hard could it be? You just needed not to look that way. But not looking at something was a lot harder than you might imagine. Anyway, the seat itself, when she got there, was a good place to sit for twenty minutes to count the insects in the meadow. The hill was steep. It made her breathless getting to the top, her poor heart working overtime. Made her legs ache, striding up. From the seat, she breathed in the warm air. A small breeze rustled through the pink heads of the grasses, making them all move in the same direction. There were a couple of white butterflies flitting together. She wrote down *two cabbage whites* – there were a couple of other butterflies they could have been but she plumped for cabbage whites. There was a six-spot burnet moth milling around the yellow flower heads of common ragwort. And a hoverfly near to that. She wrote them down in her notepad.

6

Although it didn't seem to have all that much going for it, the city at least had a good skyline. Bob looked at it from the wall of the cafe, high on the hill, next to the memorial. The sinking sun bled into the sky, reddening the edges of clouds and the sky beyond. The industrial relics of the city's architecture blackened up in the diminishing light. Factory buildings bolstered by rows of terraces, which spread beneath like trays of boxes in specimen drawers that he had seen in a museum as a child. He imagined the people inside like the insects collected and housed in the small wooden boxes – carrying out their lives, their hopes and burdens. Further out, the lines spread out and curved into cul-de-sacs of semis. The outline of the castle reached above, and the tower of the Priory, all of it reducing to silhouette in the fired glow of the sunset. Bob's thoughts emptied out and slowly repossessed him as he watched the progression of the sky. He was thirty-six years old and had long felt that things ought to change. The *how* of that change had so far eluded him. Had manifested only in a series of bad decisions. He tilted his head back to take in the uppermost reaches of the sky, high above him. At the zenith, a watery blue took back control over the colouring, resistant to the blaze of the sunset.

A memory pushed its way into his mind. Inside: the first time in the canteen. The nervousness he had felt seeing the rows of tables full of men sitting with their trays. Taking his place in the queue. Knowing nobody. The smell of men and boiled meat and cabbage mixing with the echoed scrape of cutlery and voices. How quickly he fell into the routine, the enforced hours in his cell, the mind-numbing boredom and idleness rebounding off all the white walls. He was grateful that his first cellmate there was quiet and easy to get along with. And then after he was released, perhaps it had taken him longer to adjust to that than it took him to adjust to being inside. Freedom was a funny thing. Everything had been difficult. Finding a job. A place to live. Readjusting to being with people. Deciding things for himself, even the basic things, like when and what to eat. What to do with his time when there seemed to be so many options. There had been so many things he needed to make up for. The sentence people got was for time spent inside, but there was all the extra time that people served when trying to get back to life on the outside. Like climbing out of a river and still walking around for months, years, with the river mud clinging on.

*

The evening had been advertised as a 'Lament for Lost Species'. There were about twelve people in the church hall when Sherrie-Lee arrived, all of them much, much older. They were sitting on chairs in a semicircle when she got there and the speaker stood at the centre of the circle, while the sitters shuffled and arranged themselves. Sherrie-Lee took a vacant seat between two grey-haired people. Her stomach growled, causing her a flush of embarrassment. The speaker looked at them before he welcomed them briefly and efficiently in a gentle, quiet voice.

We are joined here this evening in a confusion of our feeling. We are tossed into a sea of bewilderment in our loss of connection to what's happening to the world. In our collective sorrow for this world and our need to mourn all the lost species.

Sherrie-Lee hadn't known what to expect and was put off by the therapy-group arrangement of chairs, but when mourning all the lost species was mentioned she was gripped by a sense of the urgency of it all. Everything else could be put up with after that. That it was just her among a lot of old people. That there was no token food on offer. That it was just one person speaking, with everyone else having to listen. Though she was glad that everyone didn't have to introduce themselves, not only because she had a personal dislike of doing it, but also because it meant that it wasn't about them at all, it was about the animals. She wished that more people were there to listen and that younger people, people her own age, cared more about all the animals and all the stuff that was happening.

Grief was our innermost feeling and mourning was the out-ward show of that grief, he continued. Where are our funerals for all these extinct species? raising his voice just a little and looking off into the back of the hall. We must come together to express grief and protect species in the future, he said. We must trust the process of ritual.

He explained that he had written the names of some of the extinct species on leaf-shaped pieces of card and each of the thirteen people had to pick up three of them and place them in what he called the 'sacred space'. He instructed them to take turns placing a leaf in the sacred space and to pronounce each of the names of the lost species. He gestured towards a small circle of unlit candles behind him. People stood up and began to move towards an area at the back corner of the hall, which Sherrie-Lee had not noticed when she came in. A tall man in a brown waistcoat took the lead in collecting his three leaves.

There was a solemn feeling in the hall, that Sherrie-Lee had felt as soon as she arrived. The feeling had intensified as the evening progressed. They took turns, slowly, in placing their leaves in the sacred space. Pronouncing the names of the extinct species. Mexican grizzly bear 1964. Desert bandicoot 1943. Caspian tiger 1970s. Eastern cougar 2018. Saudi gazelle 1980s. When all the leaves were placed in the sacred space all the people stood around quietly before returning to their chairs and then, in silence, the speaker lit the candles, crouching down to light each one in turn.

A ten-minute silence followed. Only the odd shuffle could be heard, the creak of a chair, someone's breathing close to where Sherrie-Lee was sitting. She felt a deep burrowing sorrow in that ten minutes. She felt the sorrow of everyone around her too. It seemed from the beginning a kind of sorrow from which there was no return.

Walking back to Bob's place, she thought about all those animals that she would never meet. How all of them were gone forever, never to return. Never to exist or be born again. How real it made it all, having those funerals for them. That made it concrete and undeniable and terrible at the same time. Sherrie-Lee felt like she would never be happy again. As though everything had changed and nothing could ever be the same. And she felt, too, that the woman with the short grey hair, who had sat next to her in the semicircle, had felt the same as Sherrie-Lee. She saw that after the silence, the woman's face was wet with tears.

She walked an extended, convoluted route back to Bob's, feeling the need to walk and come back to herself. As she walked, bits of the evening played in her mind with fresh sadness until she tried not to think of it at all. She would put another thing in its place when the thoughts came. She would make herself think good things about Joshy, about the library, about Claire, about her nan until that filled her mind, with only the edges of it threatening to peel away, to let the sadness back in.

Already the creak of the floorboard just inside the living room door had become familiar to her. Coming in now it felt like a greeting, as though the room was welcoming her. She came into the room without turning on the lights and sat for a long time in the darkness.

7

When she first saw the poster pinned to the telegraph pole, it was from a distance. Only the word MISSING stood out in bold black capitals at the top. Her breath caught in anticipation and the arteries feeding her brain pulsed and throbbed as her heart rate quickened. The photo below it was out of focus, and it took a few steps of walking towards it before she could make it out. It had rained the night before, and this had made the plastic wallet that the poster was sealed into steam up slightly, adding to the blur. When she got close enough to see, she saw that it wasn't her after all. The thing that was missing was not even human, but a ginger cat. The photo showed it curled up on a white background. Missing since Saturday, she read. She immediately noticed that it had been missing for less time than she had, but there were no posters about her being missing. No posters for a missing twelve-year-old girl. Though, she supposed, that was probably a good thing, not something that she should feel sad about. If anyone was kicking up a fuss, she'd probably have to skedaddle back home. She read on. A four-year-old male ginger cat, answering to the name Tiger. Tiger is affectionate and will be scared while he's away from home. He has three legs. Please check your sheds and garages. Please call this number. She warmed to the cat after she read that it only had three legs, thinking that it wasn't its fault that it was being looked for and she wasn't. People were funny like that. They liked their animals. There was nothing wrong with that. She spent several minutes looking at the phone number to memorise it. 077 – pretty standard. 844 – eight is two fours. 725 – seven take two is five. Seven add two is nine, or that's nine digits before it – ending like it began with a zero – 90. She turned her back to the poster and recited it a couple of times. She would write it down when she got back.

Wandering around the streets and through town, the day expanded and felt vast and timeless. Noting the names of plants she knew as she passed: shepherd's purse and dandelion and pineapple weed growing from the cracks in the pavement, stunted and persisting everywhere. At the empty shop fronts, gutted inside, or left with old shelving and bits of counter. A4 notices still Blu-tacked to the inside of windows, advertising coffee mornings to fight cancer, the choir performing at the Priory, the circus coming to town. All the dates from months ago. There was a Bargain Booze on the corner, next to the ladies' underwear shop. Poundland between the pie shop and the RSPCA charity shop. She stopped outside the All-You-Can-Eat Chinese Buffet. It didn't look like much in the daytime, the big windows and the interior all dark. It didn't open until lunchtime. Below the windows the wood panels were warped and painted red. The sinter of dirt spattered up from the ground from recent rainfall. There was litter on the pavement outside. An empty fag packet and an old juice carton, from a brand she didn't recognise, squashed and scuffed and faded. Sherrie-Lee hoped one day that she would be the kind of person that ate out somewhere like this. She'd seen it when it was open, all the happy families and the groups of friends inside, their plates piled high, eating until they couldn't eat any more.

And walking further out, where the houses began, there was hardly anybody around. Across the oversized car park there was a brick-built theatre that always looked derelict, with layers of buddleia growing out between the bricks in the chimney and the upper part of the walls. Small terraced rows, tidily packed together, led to the bridge by the canal. Her footsteps resounded against the wooden floor of the bridge as she crossed. At the other side of the canal the houses swelled into themselves, stretching into semis with gardens. There wasn't much happening in the day, but in the evening she'd walked down these streets and seen the people inside. People living their lives like she might one day. Someone coming into a room carrying a tray of things to eat and drink. Someone leaning over to switch on a lamp or the TV. People sitting round the dinner table. She imagined them with their full bellies. Happy and content. She thought of the sardines she had been eating. How they had filled her up. She wished she had discovered them before. They filled you up much more than cereal bars, which no matter how many you ate never got rid of all the hunger, never got rid of that jagged knot in your stomach. The area was posher than any she hung around in: some of the houses had neat driveways and gardens. You could tell all the people had proper jobs. You could just tell from the orderliness of everything. That was a kind of life she used to dream of. Then, later, she worried that maybe all that wasn't for her. She thought that that was what she dreamed of, being part of a big, busy, happy family, but then she'd stayed over at Bernadette Stead's house for a few days. With her two parents and brothers and sisters. All the running about, all the noise and the laughing and the talking. She'd felt a kind of gaping loneliness. And then the sad thoughts afterwards of how maybe it wasn't for her after all. Soon after that she'd met the storyteller at school. He'd turned up at just the right time. She had started to think that that could be a new kind of dream. She just needed to collect lots of stories, collect them, memorise them, and keep telling them. Learn to tell them so well that everyone would want to listen. You could survive like that. She was sure. That and maybe a bit of shoplifting when things got lean.

Then she thought again how she had been gone for five days and there were no posters looking for her. Nothing. Nothing on the news. Nothing about her, anyway. When they'd heard the bank robbery being reported – the *attempted* bank robbery – there was no mention of her at all. That they were looking for two men was good, was all Bob talked about, because it meant that Dom had got away, so there were no real witnesses, which Bob said was a good thing too. That no one got hurt either. And he said that since there was no mention of her, she could go home. Nobody would be looking for her. She was offended when he said that. After all she'd done for him. She told him that they didn't tell about all their lines of enquiry because they didn't want to give the game away. Then, when that didn't seem to work, Sherrie-Lee had said that there were no witnesses except for her. And then they'd both gone quiet after that, and she'd felt like she'd said the wrong thing and that she'd like to backtrack so she could unsay it. But she couldn't think how she could do that. Once you said something it was very hard to take it back. Especially if you said something mean or something the other person didn't want to hear. The mind seemed to latch on to those kinds of things. The things that ruffled it. She wondered now if there was a story about the unsaying of something or if she could make one up. You'd have to start with the saying of some particular thing. Like a prophecy that some terrible thing would happen, a mistaken thing. And how it would have to be unsaid because people might do bad things because of the mistaken thing that was said. But how would they unsay it? The thought returned her to the original problem. She had the urge to hurry back and write it down and try to work it out that way. A heavy feeling of anguish came to her and then subsided.

Turning and anticipating getting back to her notepad made her think of the phone number on the poster. She said it to herself again, to make sure she could recall it. 077, 844 – two fours in eight. 725 – seven take two is five. Seven add two is nine – ending like it began with a zero – 90.

*

Grace had not always been a gargoyle of a girl. After Joshy was born, when their mam had been too poorly to look after him, Grace had spent a lot of time looking after him and teaching Sherrie-Lee how to change his nappy and hold him when giving him a bottle so that his head was properly supported. She had been patient with Sherrie-Lee, helping her put a cushion in the right place under her arm so that she could hold him in just the right way so that her arm wouldn't ache or slip when feeding Joshy. It was easy to forget all this in the storm of how Grace was now. Sometimes she would have to remind herself of this, and sometimes this helped her with the business of trying to be nicer to Grace. She would remind herself that once upon a time Grace was a human being. Though this would make it sting extra hard, seeing how she was now. Thinking that once they had clubbed together all their efforts in Joshy's first few years, before Grace had seemed to outgrow them all and lose interest in anything to do with them. Even the pitch of her voice had changed for the worse. It hurt that she sometimes said mean things about Joshy. It was a step too far for Sherrie-Lee. Joshy was the sacred space of their family and Grace was a fool for not knowing it.

In the earlier years, Grace had answered all her questions about their dad, had told her details about him that Sherrie-Lee had stored away and elaborated on later. She knew that he had a tattoo of the earth on his arm. The earth as a round globe with the moon next to it. From this, Sherrie-Lee had worked out for herself that he had been interested in space and the universe. She had wondered what else they had in common. She'd told Sherrie-Lee that he'd owned a dark blue Volvo and so she had started, later, to notice the makes of cars and learn to recognise them from their symbols. Once, when Sherrie-Lee had seen a dark blue Volvo parked outside the strip of shops near to where they lived, she had waited for the owner of it to come in case it had been him. But the man who had come had been a young man. Far too young to be her dad. Then Grace had stopped telling about him and started getting mad when she asked. Even the photo she kept of him disappeared and couldn't be found when Sherrie-Lee had looked for it.

*

Back at the house, before she settled herself in to anything, she went round to the shed. Looking in, she saw that Mark wasn't there, though his sleeping bag was. She pushed a tin of beans and a tin of sardines through the gap and sat for a while outside on the grass, thinking. A small black insect, less than a centimetre long, walked on her arm. It had long curled antennae. She didn't know its name and hadn't ever seen one like it before. It was like a line-drawing of an insect, just walking down her arm. Like someone had drawn a cartoon insect on her skin and now it was moving along between all the little hairs that grew there. Moving its antennae around ahead of it. It was so light and fragile she couldn't feel it as it moved on her arm. Amazing, really, how delicate a living being could be, even though it had all the business of life to do. Finding food, mating, finding a home. She felt it a shame that she didn't know its name. She thought of going to the library to look it up. She hadn't been for nearly a week and she still needed to know more names for all the insects round here for her survey. She knew lots already, but there were so many of them. Hundreds. Thousands of different types. Even when she wasn't doing the survey creatures just rocked up that she didn't know the names of.

She leaned her head back against the shed, and squinted into the sun's glare, so that only bubbles of suspended light were visible between her eyelids. Sun-warmed, she wondered about that other planet out there in another universe that was the same as the Earth. She wondered if there was another Sherrie-Lee out there, leaning against a shed, grass grown all around her and her head full of the same unfathomable stuff that she struggled with. A Sherrie-Lee with the same hair and even the same jacket, but warmed by a different sun.

8

From the window of the kitchen, Bob watched a magpie hopping along the apex of the shed roof. It hopped along like the hunchback in a video game he used to play. It was calling loudly – shouting, it seemed to him, as though it was angry about something. He peered more closely through the window to see what was going on. The magpie hopped again, down to the lower edge of the roof, before dropping down to the ground. It was only half-visible in the grass but he could see it crane its neck forward and open its beak to call again. A single call followed by a barrage of repeated sounds – loud and mechanical – churr-churr-churr. And then he saw, from beyond the shed, another magpie. It flew onto the roof, an arrow through a fan of wings. He had not noticed before how loud they were or how effortlessly they flew. Gliding on long tail feathers. They took off, one following the other, to the tall tree in a neighbouring garden. The words of the magpie rhyme came back to him – *One for sorrow, two for joy.*

He finished buttoning up his shirt and looked at the time on his phone before letting his mind drift to Gina. Sometimes she could be intense about things. She told him that it wasn't enough to have one feminist in a relationship, that both people had to be feminists, otherwise it didn't work. Otherwise, it was just a battle of the sexes. It was easier to agree with her, although he didn't really get what she meant. In truth, he did not feel like much of a feminist, and if you took that truth deeper, he'd have to admit that he wasn't all that keen on even the word itself. The mention of it made him feel uncomfortable. Made him feel guilty without knowing what he should feel guilty about. When he'd read in the local paper about the chaplaincy centre up at the university; about plans to restructure it in response to the months of vigil and protest about the phallic design of the roof, he had been truly bewildered. He sympathised with the chaplain who said that he couldn't understand the sudden offence at it, after thirty years of it not offending anybody. It had been built as a multi-faith centre and the design had been careful to respect all faiths. The building reached up into the sky towards God. The structure had been erected in this way, without using symbols that would favour one faith over another, so as to be inclusive and offend no one. A feminist spokeswoman had been quoted as saying it was high-time the building was changed. The roof was a phallus. A symbol of male privilege. It was unacceptable in an enlightened place of learning to have such a structure jutting out. He thought of the chaplain and shuddered at their shared incomprehension. He did not tell Gina about what he had read in the newspaper for fear that he would betray something about himself. She was sometimes, he felt, on the lookout for things that he couldn't see without her pointing them out for him. And even afterwards, when he thought about it, sometimes he still couldn't see.

*

Sherrie-Lee turned on the TV and laid on the sofa in the half-light of the living room. Jeremy Kyle was on. She switched the channel quickly. Shows like that made her furious. The way they mocked people. There was even one that was about people who'd bought stuff on tick and when they couldn't afford to pay for the rest of it they made a programme about taking it away from them. When she first saw it, Grace and her boyfriend were watching it. She looked at their faces when she realised what the show was about, just to see their reactions. To see if they were shocked by it too, the way she felt. But they were just watching it, staring at the screen. Really, just staring into it the way Joshy gets when he watches stuff on TV. It was fucking incredible how poor people were treated. Laughed at. These TV companies making money and TV shows from the misery of poor people and turning the TV watchers against them too. Because that's how it worked. If you laughed at people when they were mocked, you couldn't feel any proper sympathy for them. It was all round fucking degrading. A lot of people she knew watched them. Poor people laughing at other poor people. It made her really angry, enough to make her want to scratch the skin of her legs right through to the bone. She wondered if one day people would wake up to that kind of shit and see how bad those shows really were and take them off the TV once and for all. Or if in the future it would be even worse and nobody would even question such stuff, if they'd just accept it all as normal. It would perhaps become normal to treat poor people like that. She wondered if laughing and making fun of the misfortune of people would just be so normal that nobody would even think twice about it.

A pain shot up her left leg, making the lower part feel numb. She tried to stretch her ankles by scrunching her toes up and relaxing them. Then she walked around the living room a few times, before pushing her feet into her trainers and going out to the shed to see if Mark was there. It had rained in the night and the wet of the grass soaked the bottom of her jeans on the short walk to the shed. She knocked.

Who is it?

Zadie.

Just a minute.

She heard some shuffling inside.

Still here, then?

Yep. She noticed that he'd had a shave since the last time.

Mrs still mad?

Yeah. Sometimes it takes a few days.

Did you get those tins?

Yes, thanks. I had them last night. So what you up to? Must be the school holidays.

Yep. I'm gonna go home, get some stuff.

Home?

I mean my mam's house. My parents are divorced. I live with my dad, Sherrie-Lee said these things with a relish. It felt good to say, something like normal.

That's different.

It's the way I like it. It's good here just me and dad.

No brothers or sisters?

She was going to say no, but could not bring herself to deny Joshy, even among all the other lies. As though casting him there, in the debris of non-existence and untruths would be a betrayal too far. I've got a little brother but he lives with our mam. He's younger.

That's cool. So just you and your dad, then?

Yep.

Is your dad in?

He's at work. She smiled, just saying that felt satisfying too. Having work was a kind of distinction, she knew that much. It wasn't possible for everyone.

Where does he work?

He's a professor. A professor of astrophysics.

Astrophysics? That sounds clever.

It is. It's about all the stars and how they work and the universe and everything.

A professor, he repeated, looking up at the house.

She nodded, though something was shifting between them, something she couldn't quite pin down.

You don't get many professors around here.

We like it here. He works on dark matter. It holds everything in place. Without it, we wouldn't exist. Without dark matter, there would be no stars. No stars exploding and reforming and creating stardust, so we wouldn't be here, because we are made of stardust. Everything is. Stardust contains all the chemicals of life. It falls to Earth and makes life on this planet possible.

He looked at her sceptically, pulling his knees up in front of him on the sleeping bag.

It's true. We are all just chemicals. Without the big bang, there'd be no dust, no chemicals of life. It's all in the stardust. It's how everything started.

She looked at him to see if he'd understood. She thought not, though she'd explained it in the simplest way she knew how. There was a strange glint in his eye that she couldn't read, like he was thinking something else and hadn't been listening, but she couldn't be sure. He smiled at her vaguely. Maybe he couldn't understand – it was complicated for some people – or maybe he thought she was making it up. It did sound a bit daft, all that stardust stuff. If you didn't already know that it was true it must be like someone talking about fairy dust or nonsense like that.

Anyway, I've got to go. My dad will be back soon.

It wasn't true that people would believe anything, because there was a lot of stuff that people were not willing to believe. It was also noticeable that the things they were not prepared to believe were often real and true. That was the funny thing about people. They'd believe any old nonsense if it fitted in with the nonsense they already believed, but tell them something that was true and it was like, *hey, enough of that.* The way they looked at her sometimes when she talked about stuff like climate chaos and species extinction, as if she was making the whole thing up and they weren't going to be fooled into believing any of that rubbish. People had a low threshold for truth and even for words. People who lived around here, and where she came from too, weren't that big on words – they were just something like a rough tool, like a tin opener, made to function just enough for the practical getting on with things. That's how it was for most people. They didn't see any urgency to increase the amount of words in use or to find just the right word for the job. In fact, there was a kind of distrust of language precision and fancy words in general. These were things, in themselves, to be avoided. Better a few words for a lot of things than a lot of words for a few things. Sherrie-Lee had noticed often and given a lot of time to thinking about it. Apart from the occasional oddball like Dammo Taylor, who did use a variety of words that people weren't accustomed to using – he used them to show other people up, and for this reason alone was disliked by almost everyone. Disliked and not to be trusted. People teased him about eating dictionaries for breakfast and washing his mouth out to get rid of the excess of words. New words, out-of-the-ordinary words were regarded as suspect. This was why vocabularies were kept at a bare minimum and new words took a while to assimilate, if it was possible to admit them at all. They had to be accepted more generally among people first, they couldn't just be brandished about and thrown in whenever. Dammo Taylor could attest to that, if he cared to. More than once, she'd seen him with a black eye and heard stories that he'd gone overboard with his vocabulary usage and had not heeded any warnings. Though there were contradictions to this too, she'd noticed. Like the speed with which new slang was adopted, running wildfire immediately, especially those words that annoyed Sherrie-Lee the most.

*

She wondered what Bob was doing at his job at the call centre. She'd seen a picture of one. All the people sat in rows with computer screens and headphones. They spent all day calling people. One after the other. Each of the people in the rows endlessly calling people. The phone bills must be massive. And it wasn't just the place where Bob worked. There were hundreds of these places. Thousands of them. The telephone lines reaching into people's homes, people in the middle of hoovering, in the middle of putting the tea on or having an argument, and then their phones rang. She imagined them stopping what they were doing, looking over at the phone when it started ringing – even though a ringing phone never looked any different than a phone that was not ringing – going over to the phone, picking it up and then being disappointed. All those stupid questions and offers going from one part of the earth to another, when that could have been space for real connection. That's what it all seemed like from what Sherrie-Lee knew about them. Imagine if all those people, instead of pointlessly ringing people up who didn't want to speak to them, had something real or useful to do, like cleaning up habitats or teaching people to care about animals, or just making conversation with someone who hadn't spoken to anyone for three days, how much better the world would be. It seemed like a problem that would be easy to solve if people really wanted to solve it.

9

For days now, Sherrie-Lee had needed to go home to get extra clothes. She had worn her underwear inside-out, back-to-front, and back-to-front-inside-out, all the possible ways it was to wear them to get the most use out of them, and then started again from the beginning. There was other stuff she could do with too. She had been putting off going home, finding other things to do. But today, it was becoming urgent. Walking through her estate Sherrie-Lee didn't see anyone, which was unusual, she thought. As though it wasn't just Sherrie-Lee who had gone AWOL. She couldn't even see anyone in their windows and gardens, though it was a sunny day. She saw all the familiar things that she saw every time she walked through the estate. The house with the trampoline. The corner section of grass with the overgrown privet hedge. The gate that had come off its hinges. The pink bird house on a post in the middle of a lawn that no self-respecting bird would ever sink to using. Sherrie-Lee picked up a stone, ovalish and grey, with white markings on one side. She would take it for Joshy, for his collection of fossils. None of them were really fossils, except the ammonite she'd nicked from Courtney McKinnley. And even that didn't look like much more than a stone from one side, which meant that the stones could pass for fossils too. She picked only the ones that looked like real fossils. She had found most of them for him. She thought he liked them because they were creatures trapped inside something, a bit like he was trapped inside himself not being able to talk properly. Sometimes, he got frustrated because of that, especially at school.

He'd even been excluded a few times because of it. The markings on this one was a bit like the underside of a beetle, with lines criss-crossing like squashed traces of legs. That's what she'd tell him it was, the fossil of an ancient kind of beetle, bigger than the modern beetles. All the prehistoric creatures were giant, except the prehistoric horses. They were tiny. She put the stone in her pocket. She liked fossils because they were not what they appeared to be. It was incredible, really, that something alive could be turned to stone like that. And exist as a stone for all those millions of years, looking like a stone but having the trace of something else hidden inside it. A trace that could only be seen if you knew something about them already. So many things were like that. She thought of all the times she'd walked around with Joshy looking at stones that might be fossils. Sometimes he found one that didn't even look anything like a fossil, but if he fixed himself on keeping it there was nothing she could do to persuade him otherwise, even though it grated a bit to have one that wasn't even a good impostor in the collection. The collection felt like it was hers as well, she'd found so many of the stones.

She walked past her Aunty Susan's old flat. Someone else was living in it now. There was lots of stuff strewn over the front garden. Stuff waiting to be cleared away. She stopped and looked in. Among all the rubbish there was half of a vase. It was exactly half, broken down the middle as though it had been chopped in half. She'd seen a lot of broken things, but never something that had broken like that, so perfectly. Stepping inside the garden, she turned the half-vase with her foot to get a good look at the pattern. It was her aunt's sparkly vase. Sherrie-Lee remembered the summer before she died, how she had obsessed about this vase in one of the shop windows in town. As though if she could have it, it would have transformative powers. It was more than just a vase. Sherrie-Lee had thought at the time that if it had been smaller, she would have got it for her and then, with bigger things, how you just needed more bravado. Just pick it up, pretend to be looking at it in the light, then just walk out with it. Soon after that she'd saved up anyway and bought the thing. When she got it home, she polished up the table so she could put it there. Sherrie-Lee had helped her. A whole crowd of people went round and sat on the sofa and looked at that big vase, up there on the table, like it had some magical qualities. Someone had said that it was so shiny and smooth-looking, like glass. Someone else had asked how they got all those sparkles inside. Sherrie-Lee herself had wondered that, because all the sparkles seemed to be just under the surface. It's just a vase, someone else said, and they had a point. How much did you say it was? £14.99? And they made a huffing sound which meant *Jesus, I wouldn't pay half that for it*. Someone else reassured her aunt and said it was a bargain. That one day it might be worth something, even though nobody believed that, and everyone laughed. All its magic seemed gone then, and people started to leave. In all the time her aunt had had it she'd never seen any flowers in it and now, here it was. It would never hold anything now. All those dreams gone too. And although she was only twelve and it seemed crazy to put so much into one fifteen quid vase, she felt kind of slumped and out of energy. That some bought possession had seemed charged with all kinds of power and importance, and to look at it now, broken and useless and stripped of meaning, seemed appalling and terrible.

She didn't want to go back to her own house now, the way she was thinking. Everything felt drawn down and over. There was a kind of hopelessness about the place. Even walking down the street she felt it. She couldn't find the right word to think of the kind of sadness it was. It was more than just one sadness for one life unlived; it was wider than that – for all the unlived lives, where nothing ever happened and even the everyday ordinariness gets cocked up over and over again. For no real reason other than from being here. Of never being able to escape, or have enough money or hope or chance. She crossed the empty road towards the park. It seemed strange that there was no one around. She thought about all the past, and how sad it was that it was all gone. The people, their voices, all gone, because they were nobody important. All their stories gone too. There was nobody even to uphold the memories of them because people only valued the wrong kind of stuff. She sat on a swing. The metal chain creaked loudly and slowly as she began to move it gently, her foot pivoted against the special tarmac beneath. The sound made the hollowness inside her spread, threaten to overflow.

As she sat, Sherrie-Lee saw Keeley Downes, who was a year younger than she was, climb over the low fence of the park and come over to sit by her. Everybody called her Keeley Downes, never just Keeley, or Downes like everyone called her older brother. She didn't look at her, or say hello, she just came to sit by her. Sherrie-Lee was just glad to see another person, someone she knew.

Where is everyone? She asked.

Keeley Downes shrugged.

Shouldn't you be in school? Sherrie-Lee said to her.

Shouldn't you?

Keeley Downes took a phone from her back pocket, and dragged her finger across the screen in a practised way.

Thought you were proper missing, she said casually.

Sherrie-Lee looked at her.

That's what your sister said. She said you'd done a runner.

Nah, just been away for a while. That's a nice phone.

It doesn't work. She held it up so Sherrie-Lee could see the dead screen. I bought it from Derek for a quid. Keeley Downes was wearing a sparkly blue top with three coloured buttons on each of the shoulder straps. Sherrie-Lee used to feel jealous of her at primary school because of the fancy clothes she sometimes wore. And because she always got school dinners. When Sherrie-Lee had asked why she couldn't have them, the teacher said that your mum had to fill in an application form to get school meals for free. She didn't ask again.

Keeley Downes had a younger brother too who was an arsonist. He had burned down a number of sheds and small buildings before they took him away somewhere. Keeley Downes had said that it wasn't him that had done all that setting fire to things, but people had noticed that after he'd been taken away, all the fires had stopped – which in the eyes of everyone had been evidence enough. But Sherrie-Lee wasn't so sure. She'd always liked the way she'd stuck up for her brother. Arsonist or not. It was important to stick up for something.

She watched as Keeley Downes stopped looking at her phone. Then Sherrie-Lee thought, suppose she says something to someone. She didn't want stories of herself not being missing being told, not right now.

So, she said to her, stepping closer. Don't tell anyone you've seen me, Keeley Downes, that's very important, see. An' don't tell anyone this either, I've been taken by scientists. Who knows, they might just be from another planet. I don't know where they're from, but they're a weird bunch. Doing all kinds of research here, it's not just me. It's lots of other kids too. They keep us all in cages, in this long white room. I know what you think, that that's pretty fucked up, but that's just the best way to fit us all in for experiments.

What kind of experiments? Keeley Downes said. One of her eyelids was continually lowered like she had a lazy eye or something. Sherrie-Lee kept trying not to look at it.

I can't tell you that. But it's bad stuff. She looked off into the distance, for effect, so that Keeley Downes could see how serious and tragic it all was. Anyway, Keeley Downes, I've got to go now. Sherrie-Lee got off the swing and turned to face her in one movement. And remember, she said tapping her nose twice.

Keeley Downes just looked at her, her unafflicted eye was wide and incredulous, watching the older girl as she got up and began to walk away. How come they let you go, then? she asked, but Sherrie-Lee didn't answer.

Now, she thought, as she was walking off, if she told anyone, she'd tell them all the crazy stuff too and nobody would believe any of it. She knew Keeley Downes would be watching her as she walked away. She didn't look back. She didn't want to spoil the effect. She was planning something, though she was not quite sure herself what it would be, but she knew that whatever it was, it would be useful if people still thought of her as missing. She felt that it gave her some sort of power, and that was essential to the illusion of it, to stay one step ahead of everyone else.

She pulled out the stone from her pocket, turning it over, so the smooth part was under her thumb. She moved her thumb over the surface, thinking about the extinction of the planet, the fires burning in Australia, the doom awaiting just around the next corner. If all the animals died off, they could be preserved in the stones, like fossils – just like had happened to the dinosaurs, until the Earth had shaken off all the humans and recovered itself, and the animals could come out of their fossil hideouts. Though it made her even more sad to get to the end of this fantasy because deep in her heart she knew it couldn't be true, despite what those *Jurassic Park* films said. She kept thinking about it and trying to make a story out of it, but it was too depressing. And those fires would be burning all the fossils. She'd seen stones reshaped and melted by the heat. Stones from volcanoes melted and bubbled into different shapes. And the whole lot was just pointless nonsense. People would rather spend fifty quid on a handbag than pay 10p more for stuff that didn't at the same time kill all the bees and the birds and the polar bears. That's how fucked up all of it was. Sometimes it made her want to scream and cry and kick something or hold a bolt gun to her head and shoot the cool metal bolt right through her hot angry brain. People really stank, they deserved to become extinct, but all the other creatures, they didn't deserve it. They didn't deserve being burned alive. She'd seen the images on the news. The bodies of kangaroos piled up near the fences which separated the burnt out forest from the road, where they had tried to escape from the fires. Rows and rows of dead kangaroos. Why the hell didn't people knock down the fences? Or make a hole in them? The hollowness from that evening of the lost species came back. A wretchedness that could never be overcome by anything. She threw the stone as far as she could across the rec. She looked the other way so she didn't wait to see where it landed. So she couldn't be tempted to go and pick it up again. What was the use even of real fossils?

10

Bob realised now, as he walked along the edge of the park, that he was already looking forward to autumn, when the trees would start to change colour and the first of the season's cold would start to chill the air. Even as a boy it had been his favourite season. He liked going back to school. There was a point in the summer when the days seemed to get tired of themselves, ready for a change.

When he approached the corner where the mini-supermarket was, Bob thought again about what they could have for dinner. Though again the same things came into his head, even though he'd tried to think of something else that kids might like. He had been thinking about Zadie. It was time for her to go home. She'd had the same clothes on for nearly two weeks. He could offer to take them to the laundrette with his stuff, but no, that would be too much like inviting her to stay. This way she'd go home when she got too smelly. Not to be too mean about her, too personal, but she was heading that way already. You could smell the sweat when she was in the same room. Gina was right when she had said that he let himself get drawn into things too easily. He had defended himself when she had said it, but it was true. Gina was right about most things, he'd have to admit that, at least to himself, even if he didn't always want to admit it to her in person. It was not that he didn't feel sympathetic towards the kid, because he did. But there was a neediness about her, beneath all the show, that he didn't like. It unsettled him. He didn't like the weight of other people's needs and expectations. He'd let too many people down. His own mother, especially. And he'd never really had the chance to make it up to her. He'd imagined, while he was inside, taking her to nice places, showing her that he was doing good in things, that he was making things right. She was a nice lady. The best kind of person, really, and didn't deserve the kind of shame he'd laid at her doorstep. She never said anything like that, but he knew she would have felt the shame of him being inside. What all her friends would have been saying behind her back. He thought of that last letter he'd had from her. The straightforward humbleness of it.

Dear Lester,

It was nice to see you on Saturday. Me and your sister thought you looked very well. Better than last time. Just to say that you are always in our thoughts and that we will see you next time. Keep your spirits up.

Love, Mam.

He could still remember it, he'd read it so many times. He sometimes wondered if he would always remember it, like his prison number. If both were permanently etched into his brain. See you next time. But there wasn't to be a next time, her heart had given up. And then, at the funeral, when he'd been handcuffed to a guard, he'd felt the shame of that too. He was glad she didn't have to see that, with all the mourners seeing it, all her neighbours and friends.

He'd let Gina down too. But it was different with Gina. Gina wasn't needy. She was her own woman. Whatever came her way, she just dealt with it. She was a pro at life. She'd stuck by him, even though they'd only been together four months when he got arrested. When she came to see him and he'd tell her how sorry he was, she'd shake her head and say, *Lester, it is what it is. We can get through it, we just have to stay calm.* She was practical and this was one of the things he loved best about her. She'd be up in arms if she knew about that last bit of trouble, even though it was for her he was trying to get the money together, so they could live together. He'd lose her for sure if she knew. He couldn't stand thinking about her reaction. Her practical self wouldn't let her forgive him a second time.

Walking in, he turned the oven on and got the pizza and chips out of the bag. He didn't hold with that waiting for the oven to get to the right temperature business, it was a waste of electricity. Just a way for those energy companies to get more money out of you.

Hungry? he asked.

Yes, she said, coming to stand at the kitchen doorway. How was work today, then?

Jesus. I've got to get another job, that place is killing me. It's soul-destroying, Zadie. Call centres have their own special time-zone. The clock goes two minutes forward and one minute back. So the bosses can get more work out of everyone. He put a few tins into the cupboard and looked into the darkened corners of it.

Sherrie-Lee hovered near him and it made him feel obliged to ask her, What did you get up to?

I was keeping a look out in the street this morning. It was bin day. A woman from the end of the street came up shouting and pulling the recycling bins up the street behind her. Someone else came out from one of the houses, and she started shouting at her too.

Bob laughed. That's Debbie, she's nuts. It happens every fortnight. They always leave the bins outside her house, the bin men, and she thinks people leave them on purpose to aggravate her. Don't have nothing to do with her. She's just bonkers, and we don't want any attention drawing to ourselves, do we? Know what I mean, jelly bean?

She'd also been keeping watch of the shed, but she didn't share that part with him.

Have you eaten all the beans? His face was red from the effort of bending down into the cupboard.

Must have. She said it quietly, because today, deep down, she felt tired of lying, of making things up.

She watched as he emptied the fat white chips into a black metal tray and stuck it into the oven. He bit the edge of the plastic wrapping and pulled it away from the pizza. Is that why you wanted to rob a bank, because the call centre's so bad? she asked.

He slid the pizza onto an oven shelf and looked at her and sighed. Probably, he said. If we had a place close to her mother's, Gina and me could live together and she could still look after her mam.

What's wrong with her mam, then?

Alzheimer's.

That sucks.

Once you have a place to live, you know, permanent and secure – somewhere where you don't have to spend nearly all your wages on rent and the electric metre – it's easier for everything else to fall into place.

She was quiet for a while, and looked down, as though she didn't know what to say, then she piped up, I did a jigsaw puzzle too, but there were a couple of pieces missing, the puppy's eye and half the girl's smile. Four-hundred and ninety-seven pieces with the missing three. They are easy to do once you have a strategy. My nan taught me.

Bob nodded, which she took for interest, so she told him in detail, First you find the corners and all the straight edges. You have to look at the picture too. Look at it really carefully, and then organise the pieces from all the different parts of the picture. After that, it's a doddle. You can't go wrong, because there is a place for every piece. You know that, so you just have to stick with it. Even Joshy can do them. Not with this many pieces, but he can do them. He's smarter than everyone thinks. Deep down.

She started to break the jigsaw up, gently so that large parts of it would stay intact as she put them in the box. Joshy really was smarter than people thought. Just because he couldn't say much, people thought that he didn't have much of a mind. She remembered Luke asking her once, What do you think he thinks about? It was just her, Luke and Joshy in the room. It was nicer when Grace wasn't around. She told him that he was thinking about what he was watching. About the cartoon character.

Which one, though?

He's the mouse one, trying to get away.

How do you know, though?

Because if you switch it off when he's watching something, he gets mad because it hasn't finished, because he hasn't finished thinking about it. That's why he gets mad. Sometimes when we go out, he wants to get back to the TV and what he was thinking about before we left.

She didn't mind when Luke asked questions. It was better to ask if you didn't know. It was when people just assumed stuff about Joshy that she minded. Just assumed that he didn't have a brain, or any mind of his own. They just ignored him or talked over him. Sometimes they wouldn't even look at him, like they were trying to pretend he wasn't there. Sometimes people made her feel embarrassed on Joshy's account, which annoyed her about herself. After feeling embarrassed about Joshy came a hurt, restless and taut. A play of guilt and humiliation. And the people who'd made her feel like that would never give it a second thought. Probably didn't even notice it, so entitled were they to their own obliviousness. But it was them who should be ashamed for making others feel bad about being different, about being with someone who was different.

She put the jigsaw box back in the cupboard under the TV and went to sit on the sofa. She looked crumpled, sitting there with her shoulders hunched.

Bob came and sat on the chair nearest to where she was sitting.

You know what this place needs? she said.

Books, she answered for him when he didn't reply.

He looked around the room as if contemplating the lack of books.

You could join the library. I know the librarian there. I could introduce you and she'd find you the right books to read.

I've never been one for reading. But my dad used to have a lot of books. My mam used to complain about all them dusty books he had in the house.

That doesn't mean you can't be one for reading now.

And what about your stories? he said. You should write your stories down. You could make your own story books.

No, that's not for someone like me. Writers don't come from where I come from. Nobody has anything to say there. It's all just stuff to hide. I would be embarrassed. Anyone would be. Pen pushing. It's not proper work. It would be almost as bad as becoming a do-gooding social worker, no one would stoop that low.

She really meant it about social workers. She knew enough about them to mean it with knobs on.

That's not true, he said. Anybody can be anything.

Yeah. Sure they can, she mocked, looking up at him.

They both laughed.

Yeah, he said, sighing.

Anyway, her name's Claire.

Whose name?

The librarian. You'd like her. She's cool.

Bob was no looker, that was for sure, but there was nothing actually wrong with him, and it was a mystery to her what some women went for. She didn't mention Claire's blue hair. People were superficial and made up their own ideas about even little things. And there was nothing to say that Bob wasn't in this category. Even bank robbers had their prejudices.

78

Bob was looking at the screen of his phone.

Most of the kids I know just want to be celebrities – not famous for doing anything. Famous for doing nothing, going on one of those dumb shows sitting around talking about nothing – but, that's a kind of empty way to be. What I'd like to do is drive around in a beaten up old car thinking up all kinds of crazy stories and collecting stories from different places. She laughed and fell into an awkward smile.

The smell of pizza expanded in the room as Bob opened the oven door. The oven was smoking so Sherrie-Lee went up to the doorway of the kitchenette to see what was going on.

Is the pizza okay?

It's good.

I thought it was burning with all the smoke.

Nah. it's fine. It always smokes like that when you use the oven. It wants a good clean.

Sherrie-Lee watched the pizza as it was brought out of the oven and put on a plate. It was perfectly round with reddish-pink circles of pepperoni dotted onto the surface. It was too big for the plate and the edge on one side folded down to the counter-top. With a knife, Bob lifted all the cheese from one side of the pizza to the other. Strands of it glistened and stretched as it was pulled up, steam rising, carrying the glorious smell.

Sherrie-Lee thought about her storytelling, about why she didn't share her ambitions with anyone. People felt stuck and squashed by other people's expectations of them, but that wasn't the worst of it, and it was something she was thinking of more and more, that people were constrained too by the straight-jacket of no expectation, that nothing at all was expected of them. You could be marked by all the millions of things that didn't happen, all the things that would never happen.

11

Courtney McKinnley was one of those kids who always got driven to school every morning. Whenever Sherrie-Lee had caught sight of her, she would be sat upright in the front passenger seat looking forward as though removed from everything else that was going on. She never acknowledged Sherrie-Lee even though they had known each other since primary school. Sometimes she wondered if Courtney suspected the truth about who had taken her fossil all those years ago. She still wore her blonde hair tied up in neat plaits around her head like some kind of crown. She had once told Sherrie-Lee that she wore her hair like that so she wouldn't catch anything from the other kids. But that was in the days when she still threw the odd comment in her direction. When she reminded herself of these facts about Courtney McKinnley she felt glad about taking the fossil.

Bob hummed while he busied himself in the kitchen. She'd noticed that he often hummed, never a particular tune, just a kind of jumble of humming sounds, put together. It never seemed to be any tune really. He must just draw a kind of comfort from it, from doing it rather than producing a nice tune. And although it was tuneless she found it comforting too. Though the man in the shed was starting to worry her. He was asking a lot of questions about Bob. She wanted to tell Bob about him, warn him just in case, but she knew he'd be mad as a wasp in a jar if he thought she'd been chatting about him to some stranger in the shed, furious that there was anyone in the shed at all. All day she'd been thinking that she never saw the face of the other bank robber. It could be him for all she knew. When she'd asked Bob what the other robber looked like, he'd just said that he had brown hair. When she'd asked about his ears, he'd just looked at her funny. And when she'd asked if his ears had any distinguishing marks, like earrings or tattoos or bits missing, he'd laughed and said that he thought he just had two regular ears. But maybe he'd not noticed the missing bit. Why else would Mark be asking all those questions about Bob?

She thought about the storyteller who had visited her school, when she was in her last year of primary. She'd never imagined anything like it. He looked like someone from the *Lord of the Rings* or something crazy like that. He had this coat that he'd had specially made for him. It wasn't a coat exactly, more a kind of cloak, with long, exaggerated sleeves, and it was kind of padded so that the designs that were sewn onto it looked almost 3D because they stood out a bit. On the coat were sewn 700 different creatures or things or places, and he told everyone as they sat around him in the hall that each of these creatures or things or places stood for a different story. He didn't patronise the kids when he talked, he didn't say, So then, how many stories would that be? Like the teachers often did, always trying to teach you what you already knew. And then smiling, looking pleased with themselves and whoever had been stupid enough to answer, as though some real gem of wisdom had actually been communicated. As though they were all fuckwits or something. He chose a few different children to point to something on his coat, and when they had chosen, he told the story that went with it. When someone chose something from the back of the coat they had to describe what they had chosen so that he could recognise it and tell the story that went with that too. He said the coat had been specially made for him and that it had cost £2,000 and then he said that he knew what everyone was thinking. *How does a scruffy old man like him have £2,000 to spend on a coat?* Then he told how he had got the money. It was from a special grant so he could go round schools and libraries in it, telling the stories of all the pictures.

Sherrie-Lee was amazed by it all, that there was such a job as a storyteller and that somebody could actually earn a living through it. She had felt excited by the idea. That's when she started to collect stories and memorise them, and make them up too, because that's what she wanted to be, only she hadn't realised it until the man came into school. Seven hundred stories, that was a lot of stories. She thought of that number and how long it had taken him to learn them. He had laughed when she asked him how long it had taken. Not because he was dismissing her, but because it was an important question. He took it seriously and thought about it for a few moments before answering, as though no one had asked it before. He said it had taken him forty years to learn them. More if you counted the years he had spent listening to them. He said the stories came from all over the world, that they already existed and that he hadn't needed to make any up. When she worked it out it was seventeen-and-a-half stories a year, which didn't seem that many, though it was really because you'd have to keep remembering all the other stories that you'd learnt from the years before. She had decided from then on that that is what she was going to be, but she kept it to herself. She wasn't stupid enough to tell anyone. She didn't want anyone laughing and spoiling her dream because she knew that that was what would happen if she told anyone. And instead of a special cloak, she would have her collection of special artefacts, that she would take around with her in a beautiful wooden trolley, with drawers with special compartments for her desiccated frog, moth and gull's skull and all the other precious things she'd collected, and she would open it out so people could choose something and she would tell the story that went with it. She wanted to make up some of her own stories too, add her own special slant to them. She felt good when she thought of it all. A whirling of excitement that began in her stomach and made her feel warm. She felt eager to be getting on with it. Like everything was going to be okay.

*

She wasn't tired when she laid down on the sofa and spent a long time staring at the ceiling. She followed the familiar cracks in the woodchip wallpaper, the part of the ceiling where it bulged down slightly, near the light fitting. The spherical paper lamp shade with the thin ribs of dust on the uppermost hemisphere. The five black dots inside the bottom half – the deceased bodies of flies. She turned on the TV but, after only a few minutes, the electricity ran out. Out of instinct, she quickly turned the telly off so it didn't seem like her fault that it was all used up. She didn't want it bursting into life when Bob put more money on the meter. Giving the game away. She went over and kneeled by the window, opening the curtain a little so she could watch as the swifts finished for the night and the darkness dropped. She thought of a riddle she knew. When you talk, I stop. What am I? It usually took ages for people to get it, if they were bothered to try to answer it at all. Bothered to try and work it out and guess. She would have to tell them after a while – silence – because hardly anyone guessed right. An upended fly began to buzz on the windowsill by her elbow, buzzing itself faintly into unconsciousness. She thought she had heard it earlier, but then it had stopped. She flicked it so it fell back onto its feet, but it just buzzed itself onto its back again and fell silent. She could wait for the stars to come out and probably she would get sleepy by then.

When she looked over at the steps leading up to the front door, she saw a ginger cat crouched on the bottom step, looking out at the street. She couldn't see how many legs it had because of the way it was sitting with its back to her, but somehow she knew it was Tiger.

She opened the window and called to it. Tiger, she whispered. She put out her hand towards the cat and made soft beckoning sounds to it. Rising, it stretched itself up the steps and slinked over, jumping onto the windowsill. Her heart jumped to see that he had a missing leg. It really was Tiger. He moved as gracefully as if he had four legs, only wobbling slightly when she stroked her hand against his side too firmly. It was one of his front legs that was missing. She went into the kitchen area and brought Tiger a saucer of milk to coax him in through the window. He jumped in and purred loudly. He must be starving, missing since Saturday. She went back to the kitchen and opened a tin of sardines.

When he was eating the fish, she closed the window. She knew that Bob had an early shift in the morning, but it wasn't late, she could get him to call the number. She grabbed her notebook with the number in and went through to find Bob, explaining about Tiger through the closed door. She had to convince him that they needed to call about Tiger because he said that he was already in bed. She emphasised the bit about Tiger only having three legs, to maximise sympathy and urgency.

Bob was fully dressed when he came into the living room. He stood by the cat and watched as it ate.

What is it eating? he asked.

Oh, just some leftovers.

He raised an eyebrow. Okay. Let's get the number rung and then they can come and pick it up.

Him. It's a boy, not an it.

Bob began to hand over his phone, pausing and holding his stare for emphasis, as he said, Don't get into any nosey conversations.

She dialled the number and informed the woman who answered that she had found Tiger. Well, when can you come and get him?

Can't she come now? Bob gesticulated exaggeratedly next to her to compensate for his lowered voice and when she came off the phone he threw his arms up. What's happening? His voice rising in irritation.

She's coming to get him tomorrow, she can't come tonight because her son is asleep and she said she can't leave him on his own.

Where will he stay until then?

He'll have to stay here. We can't have him getting lost again.

Bob shook his head, taking back his phone, and left the room.

When Tiger had finished his food, Sherrie-Lee lifted him onto her blanket and stroked his neck until he settled down to go to sleep. It was nice having another living creature next to her. An actual furry animal. She pulled her fingers through his thick fur and felt the soft beat of his heart, listening to the gentle rumble of his purring. After a while, he got up and went to lay down in the chair. She was too tired to go and bring him back. She liked falling asleep here, falling through that hole in sleep into endless layers of deeper sleep. At home she would often be woken up by her sister, who she shared a room with, and told to go sleep somewhere else because her boyfriend was with her. Sherrie-Lee would have to share Joshy's room and bed down on his bean bag, curling up on it like a cat. He would always be asleep by then. She would watch him sleep. There were no curtains so the room would be filled with a half-light from the street lights outside. He had the same nose that she had, slightly too wide and short, but his eyes were different. His were big and brown. Soulful and like pools, them eyes, their nan had said.

*

How can it not be Tiger? It's ginger and it's got three legs. She stared at the woman with a mixture of contempt and disbelief as she looked down at Tiger and shook her head. The woman had a round face and was wearing a flowery sun dress. The dress had no sleeves and you could see red pimply rashes on her plump upper arms.

Tiger has more white on him than this cat. And the wrong leg is missing.

They both looked down at the cat in disappointment.

He probably just got a bit mucky, being missing and everything and not having a home to go to.

And the leg? No, she laughed. It's definitely not Tiger. And seeing the disappointment in Sherrie-Lee's face, she added, Thanks for looking for him though and going to all that trouble. This one probably has a home round here.

The poster didn't say which leg was missing, Sherrie-Lee said, as if blaming the woman for the mishap by not being more specific in her descriptions.

She knelt down to give Tiger a final stroke and said, It's a good job I didn't tell Tommy about coming here. Building his hopes up.

Fuck Tommy, Sherrie-Lee thought to herself. How many three-legged ginger cats can there be?

She sat down on the sofa when the woman had gone and looked at the cat, who had jumped up on the chair opposite and was now curled up, asleep. It slept a lot, she'd noticed. Must be tiring having only three legs, having to learn to balance in a different way.

You'll have to stay here, Tiger. Me and you, we're both strays. The shed man too. House full of strays, she sighed.

The cat ignored her.

12

Well, he can't stay here, Bob said when he came home and found the cat still in the living room. He was sniffing. His nostrils flaring. It already smells catty.

I can't smell anything, and where will he go? Sherrie-Lee asked, kneeling down beside the cat, stroking him. All by himself, with no one to look after him.

If he's not the missing cat, then he has got somewhere to go. Whoever he belongs to is probably worried about him and wondering where he is. Come on, let him out so he can go home. Bob said as he went to the front door. When he opened it, the cat quietly padded out on his three legs without even a backward glance, as though he seemed to sense that his time there was up.

Sherrie-Lee went out after him, deliberately not even looking at Bob. The cat walked down the steps and up the road. Walking on the pavement, like he thought himself a little person. If Mark wasn't there he could live in the shed, but she didn't want him drawing Bob's attention to the shed. He moved at a walking pace for a block and then he ran across the road without looking and into a driveway. Sherrie-Lee ran after him. There was no sign of him, but the door had a cat flap and she supposed he must have gone in there. The curtains in the downstairs window were half drawn so it was too dark to get a decent look inside.

The pains in her legs had started up again. Good, she thought to herself, a feral feeling of wretchedness scraping at her insides. She didn't even try to do the stretching exercises she normally did when the pains came on.

She thought briefly about what Bob would be doing and hoped he felt bad about poor Tiger. If he looked out of the window, he might see the shed man anyway, even without Tiger living there. Well, too bad. She didn't care anymore. Even if he told Bob that she'd been helping him. The way he'd just walked off, Tiger had seemed to sense Bob's words turning against him. As though he knew he was unwanted. That it was his time to go.

Walking through the estate towards town, Sherrie-Lee looked around for someone she could say hello to. Someone with a dog. You could always strike up a chat with a dog walker. All you needed to do was say what a nice dog it was. They were always up for a conversation about their dog. She liked meeting people that she didn't know. Having little conversations. You could be anyone and it would be alright. There was a nice feeling about that. That's how she'd like to be always. Skipping through life, having a chat here and there. Not having to worry about anything. Not letting other people in to throw the spanner into things or just up sticks when they felt like it. But, looking around, she could see that nobody was about.

The sun baked down on the top of her head, warming her.

It got busier as she approached the centre of town. People going in and out of the shops. Pushing prams, carrying shopping. The door of a small clothes shop opened as she passed, the music beating, making her quicken her step. She could smell weed at the corner and looked round to see where it was coming from. Every-where and nowhere, she answered herself, saying the words out loud. When she got to the bottom end of Hope Street, where the incline of the town began to rise, she looked up at the street sign, as she always did, so she could see where someone had graffitied NO in front of Hope. It was written in white paint, twice the size of the writing on the street name plate. It was always satisfying to look at. It made her smile every time. She looked into the dark interior of a pub, slowing her pace down. She could hear all the voices inside joining together, and laughter rising above it. A slot machine could be heard too, dinging and whirring in an attempt to sound exciting, like game shows do. She saw her reflection in the windows of the shops, and pulled her shoulders back to stand taller and look more substantial. Consciously, she put more purpose into her walk, more of a stride into her steps. The smell from Mr Chippy wafted from across the road. It made her realise that she was hungry. Her stomach rumbled in confirmation. She was thinking about what to do about the hunger, and then forgot all about it, as she approached the art gallery and saw a dark blue banner above the front entrance. ARCTIC. In thick white letters. She walked up the steps, touching the big rounded bronze sculpture with a hole in it as she passed. It had been polished to a golden sheen on the part that she touched, polished by all the hands that had smoothed over it over the years. She liked that about it. The trace of everybody passing by and touching it. She liked it more than the sculpture itself. It seemed to hold something of the city, a brief unthought moment in all those lives it came into contact with. Somehow it seemed to hold them. All the connections. The rest of the sculpture was a dark, dirty brown.

The art gallery felt like something special immediately because of the high-ceilinged, glass entrance and the hush of the place. She walked through the entrance hall. On the doorway of one of the rooms that led off from the hall was a label saying Polar Bear. As she walked in and saw inside the room, she thought she must have made some mistake. There was no polar bear in there. She faltered and asked a man walking out if it was the room of the polar bear. He nodded and gestured into the room. The room was a massive white open space, empty except for a big rusted metal cube in the centre and a wide wooden bench next to it. She wondered if there was a picture or something of a polar bear on one of the other sides of the cube. She went in and walked around the cube. There was nothing. She sat down on the bench next to the cube and looked at it. It was just a box in a big white room. She wondered if the polar bear was inside the box, but that was ridiculous. It was just nothing. Just a big good-for-nothing rusty box. She put her head in her hands, feeling tired and bored and cheated. More than that, she felt angry. Her vision, blocked off by the nest of her hands, held traces of the bright lights from the room. They wobbled and jumped about when she closed her eyes. She looked at the cube again. She wanted to kick it. She stood up and walked out. She didn't want to go into any of the other rooms after the crapness of that one. She'd had quite enough let-downs for one day. She went back through the entrance. On the steps outside a woman handed her a flyer. She read SAVE OUR ART GALLERY on it as she walked away. She screwed the flyer up and shoved it into her pocket.

She walked back up the main street. The buildings were tall and grey and old, so that you could only see a strip of the sky. From outside Wetherspoons, she saw a man walking in her direction. One of the legs of his jeans was cut off above the knee. She saw that he was walking towards her, holding the cut off leg of his jeans, and so she moved to the edge of the pavement. He stepped to that side too.

Look, he said to her, pointing to his jeans and holding up the separated leg. Someone has cut the leg off my jeans.

He had short ginger hair and stubble. A woman in a leather jacket and short skirt ran up behind him, laughing.

Take no notice of him, love. He cut it off himself. The man turned slowly to look at the woman, a look of glazed astonishment on his face. He was drunk, Sherrie-Lee thought, disapprovingly.

She walked round them and was on her way. *Everyone was just fucking weird. Everything. Fucking wild.* She wished she could just wander off, without thinking of where to go or needing to make some place up of where she needed to be, and just fall through a crack in the pavement and be somewhere else. Somewhere where everything made sense. She thought about all the senseless conversations she had had, or had overheard. All the nonsense. It was better when conversations were left inside people's heads, when it came out it was all nonsense. That's what people liked. Fucking nonsense. That's what they fixated on. Even though they knew it was all bullshit. That's what they wanted to stuff their heads with. As though if their heads were all stuffed with nonsense, they'd have no room for anything real. Because that's what people couldn't bear – anything real. She'd noticed that, whenever she'd tried to tell people about what was happening to the planet, or that the hedgehogs would soon be extinct. All they cared about was *Love Island*. People were being groomed to be thicker and thicker with all the constant nonsense they were being fed. That was how to keep people powerless, stuff them with nonsense, that way they don't question anything or stick up for anything or anyone. They don't even stick up for themselves. They stay docile and stupefied. It wasn't the real stuff that Sherrie-Lee couldn't bear, it was that nobody cared about it, nobody was even really aware of it. And that they made out that she was weird for caring made it all worse. She would tell someone she knew about how the planet was heating up and how most of the animals would die out. And they would just look at her in an odd way and say to her *Sherrie-Lee, what are you like?* Like it wasn't real what she said. Like it was just something in her head. All the things that really mattered in the world got pushed aside by the nonsense. It would only get any attention when it was too late. She thought about the lament for lost species. And the candles they had lit. And the silence. A hollowness filled Sherrie-Lee and spread inside her with the urgency of it all.

13

Oh shit, Sherrie-Lee said, stretching to see further out of the bottom corner of the window.

What is it? Bob moved towards the doorway of the kitchenette. He rushed to the other side of the window when he saw that she was looking out.

There's a cop car, pulled up across the street. Two cops are getting out. There's that girl that lives there talking to them.

Make sure they don't see you, Bob said, looking at Sherrie-Lee from the other side of the curtained window. He lifted away the edge of the curtain with his little finger to peer out again.

They watched the cops going with the girl to the door, knocking. There was a figure behind the net curtains upstairs, one of those wide windows with two small opened sections at the top. There seemed to be some kind of conversation happening between the cop and the person inside. After a few minutes, the door opened, and the girl pushed in past the boy, who Bob now recognised as her brother. The policeman was talking to the brother. The girl came back talking on a phone, one hand on her hip. Even from across the street, you could tell that she was enjoying the defiant posturing. She passed the phone to the cop. The cop took it, looking embarrassed at his colleague, who nodded approval. He spoke on the phone for a few minutes. The cop passed the phone to the boy who also spoke briefly on it. He handed it back to the cop and brought something out of his pocket which he also handed over.

Why don't you go out and see what's happening? Sherrie-Lee said.

Yeah, sure. I am on the run, remember.

Not really. Go over and find out. It makes you look innocent and that way you'll find out what's going on.

No way. Bob walked the length of the room, biting at the edge of his fingernail.

Look, they're taking him to the car. I'm gonna go.

You're not going anywhere, he said, standing to face her.

I am. She moved towards the door.

Stay out of sight. I'll go.

Outside, the night was just starting to get dark and the air still smelled of sun-warmed earth and cut grass.

Is there a problem? Bob asked when he reached the scene.

Who are you?

Just a neighbour.

Do you know the family?

Bob nodded.

It's just a family dispute. It seems the parents are on holiday and, well, I just spoke to the mother. They say that Liam has got to find somewhere else to stay until they get back.

It's okay, I can stay at my mate's, Liam interrupted, as though anxious to let Bob know that he had somewhere to stay.

Liam seemed nervous, as he shifted his glance from Bob to the cop. It's all her fault, he said, nodding aggressively towards the sister. She should have picked me up. Instead, I had to walk here and then when I got here she'd locked me out and gone out... He was rambling and fighting back tears. Cost me 120 quid, he added loudly so his sister could hear.

Come on, then, the second cop said, gesturing towards the open door of the car. The parents asked us to get the key off him and make sure he gets to his friend's house so he doesn't cause any more trouble.

Bob watched them get into the car. He watched as the car started up and drove off. He had the sensation of going under water in the swimming pool. Of chlorine stinging his eyes. Filling his nose. Filling his ears. Blocking sound. Making the world feel far away and on top of him at the same time. The girl was shouting something he couldn't make out from the distortion, the simultaneous echoing and muffling. His blocked ears. Then the odd high pitch of the front door slamming as the girl went back inside. Then the bubble popping in his ear canal. The seepage, but in the wrong direction, not out but into the brain. Then the sounds coming to, TVs through open windows, music from somewhere, and arguing starting up a few doors down. Everything pouring back into auditory focus as his brain readjusted to the sounds.

He looked up at his own window and saw Zadie standing in the middle of it, in full view, gesturing for him to come back inside with rapid beckoning movements of her hand.

He felt a stab of annoyance. The kid was really getting to be too much. It was high time she left. This run-in with the cops only stood to prove the urgency of it.

She opened the front door just as he reached it. What did the policeman say? I saw you talking to him. Why was the girl shouting at you? What did the boy say?

Why were you standing at the window? Anyone could've seen you.

Sherrie-Lee about-turned in front of him and walked on through to the living room. He thought she'd go into a mood or one of her sulks because he'd been cross and criticised her when she didn't like any kind of criticism and sometimes took even random and casual remarks as a personal attack. In the living room she sat up brightly, cross-legged on the sofa, looking at him in an expectant, engaged kind of way and not in the slightest bit sulky.

So, what happened? she repeated at Bob as he sat down on the chair.

He looked across at her and recounted everything that the policeman and the boy had told him. How the girl hadn't turned up to pick him up like she'd been asked to by the parents and how he had to walk miles to get home from *Home Bargains* where he worked, the one just out of town, and then how she had not left the key out for him and how he'd had to get a locksmith and get a new key and change the lock, which had cost £120. Then, how the girl had come home and called the cops when she couldn't get in. The parents were mad about the fighting and the changed lock and blamed Liam. They told the police that he must go somewhere else until they came back.

And then what? Sherrie-Lee was eager to hear every detail.

You shouldn't have made me go out there. I think that copper wanted me to take that Liam in.

She looked at him as she listened, hardly changing her expression, and then pushed herself into the sofa so that her back was stretched and flush with the back of the sofa. She hadn't said anything since he had stopped talking. She narrowed her eyes and bit on her lower lip. He thought only briefly about what she might be thinking and then thought about the cops being called out to such trivial nonsense and wondered at them turning up at all. No wonder they couldn't do anything about real crime. He was forgetting himself. It was just as well, really; he had the sense that, in a smaller way, it was a lucky escape. Joining up with the bigger lucky escape. Like dots connecting the lines of a web. Only the dots were closing in on him. And the next time might not be so lucky.

*

Sherrie-Lee's eyes had grown accustomed to the dark and she'd made a game of going through all the things in the room, imagining what they looked like in the light. The colours of them and the details. Now when she looked at them they had begun to take on these details and colours, as though imagining them had left a trace imprinted there. But the darkness that hung in the room felt like something, almost like she had trained herself to see dark matter, even though she knew that was impossible. She remembered the first time she had learned about dark matter. How it made immediate sense to her. She had always imagined something holding everything together, making everything possible. Not God, like some people said at school, but something more physical, more there in the real world, there and everywhere at once. The thing that kept the sofa and the table in place, as well as all the planets. Looking around the room now, that thickness of the dark, of the air. It seemed like dark matter becoming visible, for a brief time, letting itself be seen by those who cared to see it. Though she knew that that was just an illusion because the thing about dark matter was that it couldn't be seen. Only the effect of it could be seen, and only then if you knew about it already. No wonder it took so long to be discovered. Probably it had already given up on ever being discovered. She wondered if it was in bodies too, if it held all the bits of body together and was able to squeeze in amongst all the other stuff in there. The lungs and the kidneys and the heart, and all the stuff between. She wondered if it held people together, if, without it, all the different parts of the body would be separating and moving about, impossible to keep track of. The way her body sometimes felt. When the different parts of her body sometimes felt separate and not connected to each other. Like she was one of those *Funnybones* characters, with limbs all over the place. It started sometimes with the pains in her legs. Sometimes, it just seemed that way without anything bringing it on. It came on just by thinking about it.

14

On Sunday, Bob was supposed to visit Gina, but she called him to say that her mam wasn't so well, and that it wouldn't be a good idea. So here he was when Sherrie-Lee was supposed to have the place to herself. She could tell he was all downhearted about it. For over an hour he had been sitting at the table, staring at the wall. She'd tried a few conversation openers but he hadn't really been interested. He had been saying how much he was looking forward to it all yesterday, up until he got her call. He hadn't seen her for over two weeks, he'd said. Two weeks didn't seem that long a time to Sherrie-Lee, but it must have for Bob, for him to be so down in the dumps about it.

She decided to use some reverse psychology on him, like she'd learned from watching *The Simpsons*, when Homer tried to practise it on Bart to get him to do something, but it all went wrong and he ended up using it on himself and doing the job himself.

She's probably gone off you, that Gina has.

Nah. Not Gina. Me and Gina, we're for keeps.

You sure? Nobody is ever really for keeps. Things happen all the time. Maybe she's getting fed up of you. You think you know someone and then the next day they just up sticks and disappear forever. That's just how people are.

He shook his head, smiling. He looked happy whenever he talked about Gina, which sometimes annoyed Sherrie-Lee. Sometimes it was all Gina this and Gina that, and always when he talked about her, he told Sherrie-Lee that she would be coming to visit soon and that she'd have to be gone before that because Gina wouldn't be putting up with anyone else around.

Anyway, what makes you so sure about Gina, then?

He shrugged. I just know. He stood up, picking up his mug and scratching at his chest through his t-shirt.

How do you know, then?

Well, it's hard to explain. It's just, you know, when you know, you know.

Is that how people feel when they get married?

I suppose they do.

Why do so many people break up then?

He didn't answer, and instead just looked ahead of him. It was his sign that he'd got fed up of the questions.

Will you and Gina get married?

Suppose we will.

How long has she been your girlfriend for?

Six years.

That's it, then. That's the problem. That's too long a time to be waiting for anything.

Nah. We are good, me and Gina. He smiled again. A broad, goofy kind of smile, like he was smiling because he couldn't help himself.

She's getting tired of waiting, you know, to get married. It happens all the time. She had stopped with the reverse psychology thing, now she was digging at him for real.

Nah. Me and Gina have talked about everything. He looked awkward, before adding, We'd be married or living together now if it wasn't for her mam.

How do you know, though? That might just be an excuse.

He gestured with his hand half-swiping the air, brushing away the conversation. His face took on a knotted, irritated look.

We should go for a walk, a big one. Up on the moors. We can take some sandwiches and have a picnic and everything.

He smiled, sitting down on the sofa. At least he wasn't looking out for coppers or anyone who might be the bank job people.

It'll be fun. You should do something with your day off. Then when you talk to Gina, you'll have something new to talk about. Must get boring having the same conversations all the time.

He raised his eyebrows and breathed in deeply, his elbows on his knees and his hands clasped together.

*

They were lucky with the bus, they didn't have to wait too long or walk too far when they got off. She didn't know why people complained about buses so much, them never turning up or bus fares being too dear. Sherrie-Lee liked them. She liked sitting on them and watching other people. People were different on buses, they sat in a kind of passive way, glad to sit down and give up the responsibility of getting somewhere to someone else for a while. She liked too, the way people kind of glanced at each other in that same passive way, never looking at each other too long. There was a kind of togetherness that everyone understood. Just being alongside each other. No conversation necessary. It lasted only as long as you were in the bus, but it was something real and special all the same. It was a special connection between people just because everyone understood the rules without having to be told.

The day was heating up. They could smell it in the air already when they stepped outside of the flat, but up here on the moors, the wind seemed to snatch much of that away. The air, even when it was still, felt abrasive in the lungs and thin at the same time, as though the layers of peat beneath where they walked had sucked the fullness out of it. They could smell the peat and the sweet scent of the long grasses that clung to and entangled their feet. The sky accosted her senses, it was so big and open and blue, like it had been hidden from her in all its magnificence all these years and she was seeing it properly for the first time. Down there, in the town, everything crowds it out, all the buildings reaching up and claiming a piece of it, but here the sky was free and the way the air felt as though it took the breath from inside her lungs seemed a part of it. There was a map on a sign as they entered the area and they spent a while looking at it and deciding which direction they would head off into. There was a tarn towards the middle where they agreed they'd stop for their sandwiches.

They walked for the first hour more or less in silence. In all directions, the whole landscape looked the same. The purple-pink of the heathers and the rough grey of the limestone boulders that jutted out through the foliage here and there. And the red-tinged green of bilberry bushes with their shrivelled black berries. All of it grew thick and kept you to certain paths as though it knew you were the sort that had to be contained and kept out. There were hardly any birds to be seen. Only as they walked they heard a strange trilling call and tried to look to locate the source of it.

That bird is a curlew, she said like she knew what she was talking about even though the bird itself was nowhere to be seen. She knew the names of a couple of birds from moorland habitats and just aimed at the curlew, feeling that somehow it was the most likely one.

She had been excited to get to the moor when they had been on the bus, but now, walking in it, the excitement was worn bare and had been replaced by a numb emptiness.

There's ferns everywhere. Look how green they are. Bob bent down to inspect the foliage.

Sherrie-Lee looked around at all the ferns poking up through the heather and scrub. Long and graceful leaves stretched out and bent over towards the ground, showing a bright, fresh green colour where the light caught them.

Some of them are just starting to open, Bob said. They look like those fossils, the spiral ones. The fronds are all curled up in a spiral. Do you know the ones I mean? Bob stood up and glanced towards her just in time to see her roll her eyes.

I thought you'd be interested. These ferns were around when the dinosaurs were around. It would all have been forest then. Thought you liked all that stuff. The tone of his voice fell flat on the last sentence.

He seemed hurt. She was annoyed too by her own meanness. She wondered why she was sometimes mean like that. Just automatically putting in a mean word or gesture, when it was no benefit to anyone. She tried to make a joke to make up for it. It'd all been going so well, staying at Bob's, and she didn't want to blow it just because she was a bit narked. Was it all forest then when you were a kid? All forest and dinosaurs?

Nah. It was already owned by his lordship then. It was already grouse moor, like this, when I was your age.

They walked on again, each in their own thoughts, following sheep trails and worn tracks through the overgrown scrub when they lost the path.

I'm hungry, she said. The tarn was nowhere in sight.

Bob stopped and looked around. We have been here before, he said. Remember this broken tree, with all the bark missing. We must have walked in a big circle.

Oh yeah, she said, staring at the tree. All of it looks the same, just bushes and grass and more bushes and grass.

We must've turned back on ourselves at some point. That's the thing about grouse moor, the landscape is on continual repeat. What we need to do is keep something in sight, when we walk, some pointer that we can use. Like dead reckoning.

Good luck with that. She was beginning to regret suggesting coming here.

On the map, the route was pretty straight, so if the path seems to bend we have to make sure that we bend back at some point. He looked around. His confidence in what he said seemed to grow as he went on, convincing himself more and more of the certainty of it. Further on we'll see something we can use as a pointer.

They walked on. Bob was walking ahead of her. Her legs were getting tired and she was thinking about the *Penguin* biscuits that she'd seen Bob put in the bag. She hated it when products used animals on their logos or in their adverts when they had nothing even to do with the animals. They were just using them. The animals got nothing in return. She would never buy anything that used an animal like that, but now that she had seen Bob putting the biscuits in the bag, she really had to fight against wanting one.

It seemed like they had been walking for hours. Sherrie-Lee had stopped trying to keep up with Bob, it was too exhausting. She sat down on a small boulder. In the far distance she could make out two giant cuboid buildings and the stretch of bay just by them, made visible by the change of light falling into it.

Hey, Miss san fairy ann, what yer doing? Bob had walked back to where she was sitting.

What are those two big blocks over there? She pointed them out for him.

That's the power station. Come on, keep up, he said walking off.

She stood up reluctantly and followed after him. What time is it? She asked, but he was already too far away to hear.

I don't believe it. Fucking hell. I don't believe we came back to the same spot again, Bob said, stepping into the clearing and looking round.

I'm fucking hungry, she said.

Don't swear.

You did.

That's different. It's not nice for girls to swear.

That's sexist. She was getting more irritated the hungrier she got. And the sun was so hot now that it was baking her brain for sure.

Well, it's still not nice. It's not nice for a whippersnapper like you, anyway. He looked at her for a minute, she was really out of breath. Have you got asthma or something?

She glared at him.

Kids are unfit these days, he said, shaking his head.

Unfit for what? she said, trying to irritate him by deliberately misunderstanding.

He ignored her.

Get the sandwiches out then, she said suddenly. She had her eyes wide and looked as though she was on the verge of tears.

They sat down on a flat hunk of limestone and he brought out the bag with the sandwiches. He handed hers to her first and watched her bite into it. She had this way of wobbling her head, slightly, when she went in to bite something, the way a baby does when it follows a spoon. He smiled to himself.

Why're you smiling? Aren't you having yours?

She took a swig of her drink and wiped her mouth with the side of her hand.

I know a good story about getting lost, she said chewing the last bit of her sandwich.

Hansel and Gretel? A sarcastic tone filtering into his voice.

No. It's a Japanese one. Or Chinese. Anyway, it's from one of those places because there is an emperor in it.

Is it a long one? He looked around and sighed heavily. He was tired of her stories and wasn't in the mood for one now. He wanted to get back.

No, it's short. Once, in days long ago and almost forgotten, there lived a poor man. A man so poor that he would often go to bed with so much hunger in his belly that the sleep that would come to him would be poor and broken.

She got this kind of look in her eye when she told stories, like she was heading somewhere or she could see the story forming and playing out way off in the distance. It was all part of the performance. Part of the act. She seemed to enjoy all the performing and telling stories. He felt like telling her he wasn't in the mood for a story just now. He'd noticed she was a good liar too. When those people had asked if they knew where Coronation Tower was, she had just reeled off some directions though he knew this was her first time here. Watching her now, leaning against the rock in the old grey jacket she always wore, strands of her hair lifted and blown about by the wind, he saw how it was something like bravery, standing there, in the middle of nowhere, her little voice rattling out one of her stories, even though there was no one around who really wanted to listen.

He was so poor he couldn't afford a wife, so he lived alone and often found himself day-dreaming from loneliness and the lack of sleep. He would invent a better life for himself in his dreams – he would have a house to live in, with a garden where he could grow vegetables. He would find himself a good wife and have many children.

Bob took out his bottle of water and took a swig of it. He looked about, only half-listening. He was glad he didn't tell her that he wasn't really in the mood for a story. Perhaps she needed to tell one. He noticed she told them when she was anxious, like they calmed her down or something. He walked a few steps towards another boulder and sat down, his back towards Sherrie-Lee.

She didn't care that he seemed to be ignoring her. She was telling it anyway. This was her show and it was Bob's loss if he didn't want to listen. She looked away from him, smoothing her hair behind her ears, and continued. He couldn't find a proper permanent job, instead he worked here and there for different people whenever he was needed. He found himself working in the gardens of the emperor, a job he liked very much because the emperor had a great variety of gardens, with many kinds of flowers and birds that came to visit. One day, after hours of tending the vegetable gardens, he found himself walking back through the flower garden where the emperor had spent the afternoon reading. He was greatly excited by this because he had never before seen the emperor. In fact, hardly anybody saw him because this emperor was reclusive and liked to spend time on his own in his great library. Beside the pond he saw that the emperor had left behind the imperial pillow, which was said to be enchanted and make the dreams of anyone who laid their head on it come true. If only he had such a pillow, his own dreams would come true. There was not another soul around and the temptation was too much. He hid the pillow under his smock and walked home with it, telling himself that he was just borrowing it and that he would take it back the next day.

That night, he spent a long time trying to get to sleep, wishing for it so that his dreams would come true. When he finally slept, it came about that his dreams did come true, and he woke up to unimaginable riches and splendour. His bed was covered in the finest silks and precious jewels were encrusted into his golden bed frame. A servant brought him the most delicious food when he woke, and tea in a golden cup. Another brought him the finest clothes he had ever seen. When he walked among the people, he recognised many of them from his former life, and he saw, to his amazement, that they greeted him as the emperor. And he was much loved by the people because he walked amongst them and listened to them and did what he could to make their lives better. Soon he found himself a beautiful wife, who was as kind and gentle as she was beautiful, and they had many children together. He ruled like this for twenty-five years, until one morning he awoke, with the enchanted pillow still beneath his head, and found himself returned to his old sleeping place, beneath the eaves of an old bakery. Coming to his senses, he found that the whole thing had been a dream. The riches, the wife, the family. He had gone to sleep as a young man and woken up as an old man. When he got up and walked around the streets, the people he recognised had also grown old. But nobody recognised him, his hair and beard had grown long and white, his clothes were even more ragged, only just holding enough of their shape to cover the skin and bone beneath. He had watched them all in his dreams, but nobody had seen him for twenty-five years. He wandered around for only a little while, until his legs tired, his muscles wasted and weak from lack of use. He was more alone than ever. He went back to his sleeping place on his old tired legs and waited for the bakers to leave. When they had gone, he took the enchanted pillow and stuffed it into one of the fires of the great ovens.

They were silent for a few minutes after the story.

Did they even have bakeries in China? You never get bread or cake in Chinese places, Bob eventually asked, turning towards her.

She looked at him, eyes widening. A moment of fury flushing into her face. Did I say bakery? I meant tannery.

He should have just gone back to sleep.

And slept forever?

Why not? He'd had twenty-five happy years like that. And what was there in the real world?

But he'd missed out on his real life. Isn't that bad?

Who's to say? It didn't sound like the real world had anything to offer him.

Maybe it was the waking up bit that was the dream. Maybe he dreamt that he'd woken up? A bad dream.

How did he survive for so long without food and water?

You need less when you sleep.

Yeah, but twenty-five years?

Does that matter? It's the story that is important. She picked up a little stone from near the rock where she was sitting and looked at it as she rolled it about in her hand. You have to give stories a chance you know. You have to be prepared to listen. Be open to what they have to say. She pulled her arm back and threw the stone as far as she could. Narrowing her eyes to follow it. Three pheasants rose up in alarm, one of them making a loud vibrating alarm call, half-clucking, half-bark, that seemed to speak for all three, echoing above the heather as they flew off. They watched as the birds disappeared into another stretch of heather further off.

You nearly got one, he joked. We could've had it for dinner. He smiled and waited for her to respond. When he saw that she would not, he changed tack. Seriously though, I can't see anything like this place in that story. He started to pack the wrappers from the picnic into his bag and zip it up.

Because we keep coming back to the same place, like he did. He came back to the beginning to find that it was all a dream. She didn't tell him that she'd chosen it too because Bob was too poor to have Gina as his wife, so he'd feel sympathy for the story. To give him a foot into it so he could understand it better. So much for that!

It was an illusion that all those great things happened. He never got anywhere. Just like us, we keep coming back here.

I didn't like that one. It was too fucked up.

Oh, you didn't? She was fuming. The ingratitude of some people was astonishing.

Why do your stories never have a happy ending? Fairy stories always had a happy ending when I was a kid.

That wasn't a fairy story. She scowled at him. Not all stories have a happy ending. Only childish people expect them to. Let's go back. I'm a bit fucked off with all this countryside.

Don't swear. Thought you liked the countryside, with all the animals in it and stuff.

It doesn't feel like countryside. It's just all this. She threw her arms in the air and looked across the landscape. There's only pheasants. We haven't seen any other animals. Even the sheep have fucked off. There's nothing else here. She pulled the *Penguin* out of her pocket and tore the wrapper without looking at the picture. She bit into it quickly and crunched it.

He shook his head.

She walked off ahead of him. He'd put her into a mardy mood. She stomped off, not even waiting to see if he was following. She was only trying to be entertaining, with her stories. Trying to cheer him up a bit. Now he was even more fed up with himself. Why did he have to say that he didn't like her story, when she had been so looking forward to coming here? She wasn't used to the countryside, he thought. You had to grow up with it to really appreciate it. You had to come to terms with it and know what to expect. It could be overwhelming otherwise.

15

That night, when Bob had gone to bed, Sherrie-Lee went to the kitchen window. Turning the light off so that she could see better and not be seen herself, she looked out at the shed. There was a faint light inside it. At first, she thought Mark had got candles out there. But there was a different quality to this light, it didn't move gently like candle-light, it was steadier than that, holding in one place. Once, it had moved across to point in a different direction and had been blocked out entirely, as though someone moved in front of it or it had fallen against something. Then she saw Mark's head rise up in the little side window as though he were looking out at the house. Spying on them. What if Bob was looking out of his window? His window looked out at the back garden too. Daft bugger, that Mark, if he wanted to do some spying, he should turn that damned torch off. But maybe that was his game, maybe he wanted Bob to see him, then Bob would go out and confront him and whatever Mark was after could come out into the open. She turned and went back into the room. She turned on the TV with the sound off so she could think what to do next, but her mind was running all over the place. Each time she tried to herd her thoughts into some kind of order, they kept breaking ranks and running off.

A blue light flooded onto the carpet from the screen. It was some drama. People kept coming into rooms with serious faces and then the camera would cut to a close-up - more serious looks - and then the camera would cut again to some other scene entirely. She was curious about what Mark was up to, but more than that she just wanted him to go away so it could go back to how it was before. She would just go and tell him that he had to leave now. If he refused, she would tell him that she had called the police. But if he really was the other robber that wouldn't scare him. And that seemed a bit of a harsh thing to do. Especially if he wasn't the robber Prince Charles after all. She got up from the edge of the sofa where she'd been sitting and went to the kitchen window. The shed was in darkness now and as she watched it for signs of movement, she decided that she would leave it until tomorrow before telling Mark he had to leave. Enough was enough.

She tried to fake feeling relaxed by laying back against the rise of the sofa, though she could feel the rapid beat of her heart in her chest, the throbbing of her pulse in her temple, without even having to use the flat tips of her fingers to feel for them. She had read in a book that the human heart beats at the same rate as those grandfather clocks from the olden days. She imagined the slowness of that ticking with ease because she had heard it in old films. Seeing the image that went with it, when the camera panned into the clock face and the loud slow tick was the only sound that could be heard. Echoing. She knew that even when she wasn't stressed her heart rate was much, much faster. More than double the speed. Probably because her heart had some small defect. Not defective enough to have any effect in the present, but a ticking bomb for the future. She knew too that she might only live about half as long as the average person because every creature has approximately the same number of heartbeats to spend in their lifetime. She was unable now to recall the source of this information, but she remembered in detail the facts of it. That every creature lives for the same number of heartbeats, and the little animals, like birds and mice, only live for a few years because they have a very fast heart rate, but elephants and whales and tortoises live for a very long time. More than a hundred years, the slowness of their heart pacing it out, stretching their lifespan.

Morning dew clung to the grass at the back of the house, drenching the bottom of her jeans. She reached the door and called through, Hey, Mark. She used her most authoritative voice. Because she knew that sometimes you had to organise people; they couldn't ways be relied upon to do it themselves, and if you were not careful, you could get sucked into their apathy.

There was no answer. She looked through the door and then put her hand through and lifted the rough, plastic string off the nail.

The door swung open. There was nothing of Mark to be seen. His sleeping bag was gone too. Even his water bottle and empty cans, which she'd noticed he sometimes left behind, were gone. Just the empty space where he'd pushed away the other stuff in the shed to make room for himself. She felt sorry now because it surely meant that she'd been mistaken all along about him being after Bob. She should feel relieved, and she was sure that she was feeling this somewhere, but mostly she just felt sad. She'd avoided going to see him and now he'd gone. She'd been suspicious of him in his hour of need. That's what having stuff to hide does to you. It makes you suspicious of everything. Maybe, she thought now as she walked back to the house, maybe that was why he'd left. He didn't even say goodbye. Not even a thank you note. She thought again of something she had thought of before. About how everyone was distrustful of everyone else. Of each other. Of the differences each brought with them until those differences could be passed over and put away as harmless and in no way existing to mock or threaten or undermine. So off he'd gone. Just upped sticks and left. Just like how he'd arrived. No announcement. That's what people did. They just left when they needed to. Like they didn't like goodbyes. It made her feel sad though, the sadness kind of mingling in with all the sadness of other times that it had happened.

She knocked on Bob's door, even though she knew he was out at work. Looking inside, she noticed how tidy everything was. The bed was neatly made. And inside the wardrobe, the clothes were either hanging on coat-hangers or neatly folded at the bottom of the wardrobe. In the far corner of the wardrobe was a shoe box, which she pulled out. Inside was a clear plastic bag full of letters. The envelopes were torn open at the top and addressed to someone called Lester Johns. The address, Her Majesty's Prison Forest Bank, Agecroft Rd, Pendlebury, Manchester M27 8FB. Dear Lester, some of them began. She read through a few of them quickly. They were signed, All my love, Gina. XOX. So Lester was Bob's real name. She read them, wanting to find something in them that would confirm her negative thoughts about Gina. Gina had rounded handwriting, with circles above the lower case i's for dots and diagonals crossing the e, a bit like the Pac-man character from that old computer game. Reading through the pages, if anything, Sherrie-Lee thought how Gina seemed like a good person. She wrote about when he got out. How it would be a new start for them both. How life was just beginning, and for him to stop writing that he was sorry. He made a mistake, that's all. That was all in the past. She wrote about her job and about how she thought of him all the time and counted the days now that they'd finally given him a release date. As Sherrie-Lee read, she began to feel like a trespasser. Reading the letters, kneeling there on the floor by the wardrobe, she felt she was intruding on something very personal that was none of her business. She also realised that those three that she had just read must be near the end of his sentence. She looked at the date stamp, and then at the date stamp of the one at the bottom of the pile, there was a three-and-a-half-year span between them. She looked through the other date stamps, squinting at the ones that were smudged or illegible. Maybe it was for robbing a bank or something like that. Maybe it says in one of the other letters, but there were a lot of them and she felt now that she shouldn't be looking at any of them. *And forgive us our trespasses.* The words of the prayer she was made to chant in school assemblies came to her. *As we forgive those who trespass against us.* She put the letters back carefully in the plastic bag and folded it into the box. *And lead us not into temptation.* She replaced the lid and put the box exactly where she had found it in the back corner of the wardrobe. *Amen.*

Sherrie-Lee walked through to the living room. She stood there in the muted semi-darkness not quite knowing what to do with herself. She opened the curtains. She wasn't supposed to and this was the first time she had broken the rule. She screwed up her eyes and turned her back to the window. Filaments of dust floated in the air. The light showed a furred layer of it on all the smooth surfaces. She had become used to seeing the room only in artificial light or in degrees of darkness. She decided it looked better that way. The sun lit up things that were sometimes better left in the dark. She re-closed the curtains, tugging at them when one of them caught on a notch in the rail. The smell of them was old and dry and dusty, just like how they felt in her hand. She sat down on the sofa, bringing her knees up in front of her and hugging them close to her body.

So many things were running in Sherrie-Lee's brain that she jumped up and went out for a walk. She could think things through better if she went out. She didn't know why she felt shocked by the letters, by the fact that Bob had been in prison. When she met him he was robbing a bank, after all. And so many people she knew had ended up doing time, including her own brother. Maybe it was because Bob hadn't told her and she wasn't expecting it. Somehow she felt let down and disappointed and sorry for him at the same time.

She walked through the estate and then out towards the fields that led to the canal. The day was bright and warm, though there was some cloud off to the west. When she was half-way through the first field she noticed that she hadn't seen any birds, or heard any birdsong. The whole time she had been walking she could not recall seeing a single bird. She stopped now in the middle of the field and looked up at the sky. There was nothing. Not even a crow or a seagull. She thought back to all the lost species they had lit candles for. And how, with each passing month, there were more and more of them.

The line from that book about the train picking up all the animals that were dying out came back to her. *And soon there would be none of us left.* She'd read it again and again to Joshy. *None left,* Joshy would repeat. That look in his eye he got when he was becoming fixed on something. The twitch, when his focus was taking a new direction. She felt a kind of longing for him then, a kind of need to be sitting close alongside him on the sofa watching some dumb TV programme. Or walking with him, looking for a new specimen for his fossil collection or going to one of those IDAW meetings she used to drag him to.

She had always wanted to be kidnapped, or to discover she had been accidentally switched at birth, and be returned to her real family, who were nothing like her own haphazard family, or for her real dad to come and claim her. Her sister either had a face on her and had nothing to say that was nice, or else she was pouting and wearing skimpy clothes and telling Sherrie-Lee to get out of the way. Nothing good ever came out of Grace's mouth lately. Nothing that wasn't an insult. That's what words were for. A ricochet of hard consonants flying out against people. That was the function of words at home. There was never any real communication to be had there. Her older brother was always in trouble or prison for drugs and robbing things. Maybe, she should write to him, like Gina had written to Bob. Her mam was short, mousey and freckled and had a lot of missing teeth. She felt sure that she never wrote to him. Sherrie-Lee was embarrassed when her mam opened her mouth in front of anyone and showed all those gaps. She sometimes used to work as a cleaner, and wore a blue and white check nylon apron, with pockets in the front where she kept her packet of cigarettes. Sherrie-Lee had never once been on any kind of outing with her mother, the way that proper families do. Not that she expected it. There was always something dulled about her mother, like she lacked energy for stuff. It made it worse that she wasn't quick with her mind either. Sometimes Sherrie-Lee thought that she'd jump off a bridge or drown or something just to make her mother upset, or go missing just to show her, but the older she got the more she realised, that she would be non-plussed even about her own death. When Nan died, who was her own mother, and Aunty Susan, who was her sister, she didn't see her cry even once.

She thought again about those IDAW meetings. The hall. The sound of the plastic chairs which creaked when you sat on them and every time you moved. The scraping of the legs against the wooden floor. The shuffling of feet when the meetings were over. IDAW stood for In Defence of Animal Welfare. Sherrie-Lee had been to four meetings, two of them with Joshy, and one protest outside the town hall. Joshy had liked his animal warrior badge, the yellow circle with a black and white badger's face on it. But the meetings had been a bit of a problem for Joshy who didn't always like being around groups of people, especially in unfamiliar places. She'd taken him home early from both of the ones she had taken him to. But the last one she had been to alone had been interesting. The main speaker in each meeting had been a small woman with short black hair, which was pulled up at the front a bit like the hairstyle of Tintin. She wore an oversized army jacket and black boots. She was a good speaker, Sherrie-Lee had thought. She stirred up everybody's feelings and made people feel motivated to join in. That's how Sherrie-Lee had felt, anyway. She had talked too about a time when there'd be no animals left, no bees, no hedgehogs. We were sleepwalking into extinction after extinction. We were going to wake up one morning and they'd all be gone, she said. She paused for effect when she said something motivational. We needed to wake up now and if people wouldn't wake up we needed to shake them up to make them wake up. She had this habit of leaning forward when she spoke, with one foot in front of the other, like she was ready to take off somewhere. People cheered their agreement at her, even though there were only ever about fifteen or twenty people at the meetings. Sherrie-Lee had signed up to help. She couldn't go door-to-door because of her age, but she could collect signatures at the stall in town when they needed to do a petition. And protest, of course. Anyone could do that, all you had to do was turn up.

As she walked that stupid advert kept coming to her mind. *Compare the Meerkat. Compare the Meerkat.* It really annoyed her. And what did the meerkats get out of it? She walked, trying to think of other things to get it out of her head. She wished she had more control of what went on in her mind. It was like dropping a box of marbles and all those marbles running off everywhere. At least when you told a story or read one there was some kind of order to things there.

She saw the silhouette of the factory in the distance across the sloping field of dried out grasses, which had had all their colour stripped out of them. The chimney rose at one end, the huge block of the rest of the building over-sized and derelict. Behind it, narrow streets of red brick terraces ran towards the back end of the town. One after the other, squat beneath the single block of flats that rose, unashamed, into the blue of the sky. She walked across the field towards the old factory. The heads of grasses bashed against her knees as she walked. The dust from the seed-heads falling as her legs hit them. There was a single-storey building next door. You could go inside it because all the doors and door frames had been removed. There were three rooms, but all were separated from each other. You had to enter each of them from the outside. There were no internal doors to connect them. Each room had a large metal-framed window, rusted, with most of the glass panels shattered or missing. All the wiring had been ripped out too, only a single boxed light switch remained, painted a metallic grey and, in one of the rooms, there was a broken coat rack on the wall. It had all its hooks knocked off. The bottom half of the brick-walled interiors had all been painted a green colour. Not dark or light, but somewhere in between. Not like any other green colour she had ever seen. Old-fashioned, she concluded, touching the flaking edges of the paint as they peeled away from the mortar joins between each brick, feeling the dry paint crack and crumble beneath her fingers. In the corner of the room that had its doorway nearest the factory there were some plastic carrier bags crammed with stuff and covered with a dark blue towel. Near the bags was a white mug with no handle. Sherrie-Lee retreated when she saw the stuff. She thought briefly about Mark, but rejected the idea of it being his stuff as soon as it entered her mind. She felt then that she was in someone else's private space and was scared that they might turn up. She skirted out of the building and round the back of the factory. The windows began high up so she couldn't get a look into the building. Strong roots from a bush grew out from between the bricks a few feet from the ground. Wedging her foot on top of the knot of roots, she tried to reach up and pull herself up to the window. She could reach the ledge but lacked the strength to lever herself up. Sherrie-Lee gave up after a few attempts and leaned back against the outer wall. The sun shone against her face, making her close her eyes against its brightness. A terrier kind of dog ran up to her and jumped up at her, sniffing at her crotch and scratching her legs through her jeans with its claws. She patted its head to get it to stop. She needed to go home and get new clothes and other stuff. She looked round but could not see its owner. The dog didn't try to follow her as she headed off towards the canal. When she looked back at it, it was sniffing the ground, cocking its leg up against a large blue plastic drum.

16

Sherrie-Lee had once been shown a kind of drawing joke about a boy who'd made a drawing of a pig for his teacher. The drawing looked like this:

That's a nice drawing, the teacher said, but the pig looks a bit square. Can you make it look round? The boy took the drawing back and made it look round.

Sherrie-Lee had shown the drawings to a lot of people – well, kids mainly – but nobody had found it funny. That was a problem sometimes with jokes. That was the risk. It was a tricky business. Even more so than with stories. With stories people just had to listen, but with jokes they had to listen and find it funny enough to laugh. There was more at stake. She had thought about it a lot. Most of the kids she knew were rubbish at drawing. They still drew stick people and if you asked them to draw a pig, they would probably do it like that, all straight lines and so wouldn't see anything wrong with the joke drawing. So she'd shown it to the traveller kid in her class, whose name was Jimmy, to see if he would get it. Jimmy was brilliant at drawing, but he'd just looked at it all serious for a while and then said that maybe it looked a little bit like a polar bear, if the head was a bit smaller. People were hard to please.

Sherrie-Lee was on her way home. She was just going to go there, nip in and out, but even thinking of her home made her feel like she was stuck in some far-off place. Like she was blocked off from everything, trapped behind glass or stuck in a kind of fog, and unable properly to do anything. She just had to go home, get her stuff and get back. Keep on track.

The house looked just the same as it always did. Even the bits of litter in the garden looked the same. It disappointed her, this did, as she had thought that because of her absence, it would somehow show itself differently when she went back. Although people didn't seem to realise she was missing, she thought that the house might realise, like some silent watcher. The way that buildings sometimes know things and hold onto the sadness of things that happened inside them. She walked past the house a couple of times wondering who might be inside. She hoped Grace and Luke wouldn't be there with smelly old Pearl. What you up to? Luke'd always ask Sherrie-Lee. Not in a mean way. Friendly. Sometimes he'd look at her as though he was sorry when Grace said something nasty. She looked up at the room they shared. The curtains were open but the window was closed, so probably there was no Pearl in there, with the way she always stank. She turned into the path. There was an empty can in the overgrown grass near the fence. The grass feathered into grass versions of flowers at the ends of some of the stalks. The rotating clothes hanger that stood in the front garden had been broken for months; the bars holding the washing line were pointing downwards, like a broken umbrella; and the rows of yellow plastic line were stretched out and hanging limply to the ground. By the door, when she reached it, a cereal packet innard had wedged itself between the back step and an upturned recycling box. The door was always unlocked. Her mam said they had nothing to nick anyway, but she suspected that it had more to do with never been able to find the key. People would nick anything. They didn't have keys like normal people. She always thought it was because they never had a car. Car keys held everything together in a big bunch. With car keys you always needed to know where they were. You couldn't just leave a car open and hope for the best the way you could with houses.

The idea that she could just take a quick look at her stuff in the shed came to her as she was about to enter the house. It wouldn't take a minute and she felt a need just to check on her collection, now that she was thinking of it. She walked through the tangles of grasses and clicked open the shed door. She smelled the familiar mushroom smell of damp and rotten wood as she went inside. The interior was dark except where light shone in through the spaces between the boards. Near the gap where a window had once been and was now boarded over, a dusty 3D shape of a trapezoid stretched into the interior of the shed. It seemed to hover like something lasered out of existence in a sci-fi film. Sherrie-Lee stepped into the lighted shape and reached into the corner, swishing away at a cobweb that had fallen across her bag of stuff. That was a good sign, she thought. It meant that nobody except the spiders had been here. She pulled the black bin bag toward the light that came through the gap in the window and untied the knot at the top. The bag deflated against her as she opened it, the air rushing out and making her hair blow upwards. Inside was her cardboard box. She was tempted to take everything out and have a proper look at all her special stuff just for the pleasure of looking at it, but she thought better of it, thinking she didn't have enough time. She pulled back the flaps at the top of the box and looked in. Everything was in good order. The hedgehog skin she'd found. The severed bird's wing, which she picked up and unfolded to check it still stretched out. The long seed pod her aunt had given her. Carefully, she picked up a smaller box and checked that her dead moth was still in there. She didn't touch it because touching it made all the colours dust off. She smoothed her finger over the skin of her desiccated frog though, to check that no damp had gotten to it. It was one of her favourites. She had found it dried out by the side of the road. You could see all the bones that stuck out beneath the skin. You could even see the whiteness of them, the skin had gone so thin and transparent. She stroked the beak of her seagull's skull from base to tip, before putting everything away. She folded the flaps of the cardboard box back in place so that each was interlocked with another and pulled the bin bag over it, tying it into a knot and placing it all back into the driest corner of the shed. It felt good closing the door, knowing that it was all safe.

She looked through the kitchen window at the back of the house to see if it was all clear. Once inside, she could hear the orchestrated violence of cartoon characters beating each other to death coming from the living room. When she peered in through the door, she saw Joshy on the sofa, watching TV. The music and bangs and crashes were blaring out. Sitting there in his underpants, watching the drama of the cartoon unfold, he didn't notice

Sherrie-Lee. He should be in school at this time, she thought to herself. She wanted to go and sit next to him and never leave. She had brought a box of cereal bars with her and a tin of sardines and put them on the end of the sofa for him. Still, he didn't notice her. She wondered what he would make of the sardines, and whether he would be able to use the ring pull to open the tin. From upstairs, she heard her mother's voice calling her sister's name. She froze when she heard that voice. The dry call of it. She retreated slowly from the doorway, and edged up the stairs to her bedroom. She peered in first, to check her sister wasn't there. Their bed was unmade and there were piles of clothes all over the place. On the wall was a small poster of some pop star she didn't recognise; there was a crease down the middle from where it had been folded in a magazine. The bottom corner had been ripped off. There were broken fags on the chest of drawers and the black blobbed marks left by mascara brushes against the white veneer. Some dark pink powder from some pot of makeup was dusted on the surface and smeared in places.

Is that you, Grace? She heard her mother's voice coming from the bedroom next door. A slightly slurred, having-an-after-noon-nap kind of voice.

She pulled open the drawer and stuffed some clothes into a carrier bag. From under the bed, she pulled out a pad of A4 paper with some posters she had started to make and put those in the bag too. Shifting the chest of drawers, she leaned behind it and pulled out a small drawstring bag that held all the photos that her nan had given her. She felt at the thickness of the pile of photos inside but did not open the bag. She grabbed her pile of animal pictures, too, before she pushed the chest back against the wall. A bottle of her sister's perfume fell over.

Her reflection in the mirror above the chest of drawers caught her by surprise. She never looked how she expected. She thought of herself as tom-boy-tough but the reflection that looked back always showed a pale, frail-looking thing, too pathetic-looking for her liking with thin mousy hair and thin blotchy skin to match. She liked the way she thought of herself, but the mirror had something different to say. She never looked in mirrors intentionally. She didn't like the double they showed. Waiting to contradict everything with an image of another Sherrie-Lee that she didn't recognise. The mirror seemed to hold something final against her, and the only thing to do then was to struggle to get back inside herself, to her real self, without the mirror interfering.

Sherrie-Lee, is that you? her mam called when she heard the stairs creak. Sherrie-Lee looked up to her mother's bedroom door to check that she hadn't seen her. To check that she was just casting about for who might be on the stairs from the interior of her room.

As she was leaving, she had another quick look in at Joshy. She was filled with an overwhelming sense of her old self. A dogged gnawing at the edges. If she stayed another minute, she wouldn't be able to leave. A sense that she was abandoning her little brother began to creep in. Walls of guilt struck up in all directions. Veils of it falling all around her. The whole of it threatened to entrap her.

She wanted to have a train like in that kid's story, and drive off in it, with all the endangered animals in all of the carriages, with everything they needed. Her and Joshy driving it, and the polar bear, too, one of the ones she had seen on the telly, scavenging on discarded crates and rubbish, crawling over them, degraded and starving.

Outside, on the estate, she walked around for a while, with her hood pulled up so no one would recognise her. She went to sit near the club. She thought she could keep watch on the drug dealers that pulled up in their cars by the park, not take notes or anything stupid like that, but just keep an eye on them, memorise number plates and stuff like that, but there wasn't much point in that since the police knew everything anyway. And, even if they didn't, she would never snitch anything to them. She went instead to sit on a bench by the club. A male house sparrow picked at the ground underneath a bush. Another one was in the bush watching.

There were things she supposed she missed about being at home. Not just Joshy, but the familiarity of everything, of everyone. Even Grace. Like when they argued about whose turn it was to do the washing up, when there were no clean cups or plates left. They'd argued and then Luke had come into the room saying that it was okay, he'd found a big glass on the windowsill, and Grace and Sherrie-Lee had looked at him and laughed when they saw that he was drinking from a glass vase. Grace had said to him that she didn't know how he could do that, that there was even a green mouldy line on the vase where flower water had once been. And Luke had shrugged as if to say that he didn't care and he'd just gulped all the water down and the three of them had laughed together and forgotten all about the problem of the washing up. And the way, when Grace came into the room and she'd try to hide her book under a magazine because Grace would always have something to say about it. And even her nan, who had always approved wholeheartedly of everything Sherrie-Lee did, sometimes seemed to disapprove of her always reading, when she complained that she always had her head in a book. What you always reading for? she would ask as though it were depriving her of other things. What other things she couldn't imagine. And when she'd bumped into Luke and his brother and his brother had said that he could get her some good coke. That they'd had a shipment of organic, fair-trade cocaine so even the Sherrie-Lees could buy it, and Luke had pushed him away, protective of her. There were a lot of things to like about where she lived. Those comforting things that seemed on the surface to be things you wouldn't like, but to the truly initiated were often the things to really like. To really feel like home.

People began to arrive in small groups; the women had their hair done up nice and some of them had jewellery on and makeup, and the men were a bit dressed up too, in jackets or cardigans. She recognised some of them, but nobody noticed her with her hood pulled down over her face. There was a sign for *Karaoke* chalked in blue fancy writing on the chalk board outside, and in pink writing underneath it said *Pints £2*. She'd been a couple of times when she was younger with her nan and Aunty Susan, both of them had enjoyed a good sing-a-long. You chose which song you wanted to sing. Her aunty could sing *Ruby, Don't Take Your Love to Town* better than Kenny Rogers, everyone said. It was her speciality. She chose it each time they went. She could picture her now, small behind the mike, closing her eyes as she sang *Oh Roo-o-oo-ooby, for God's sake, turn around*. Her nan could sing anything and chose different ones each time, sometimes four or five in a single night if there weren't many takers.

Sherrie-Lee couldn't resist looking through the window. There was something nice about how seriously they took doing their songs. It wasn't really a performance. It was just them, the words on the screen, their song. Which they sung like the song they chose was something deeply special to them. She had enjoyed the times she'd gone with her nan and aunt. She wanted to be back in those times. Sitting between the two of them and drinking orange cordial through a straw. She would've paid more attention to it all if she had known how soon it was all going to end.

17

Sherrie-Lee woke to the sound of roadworks, somewhere off in the half-distance. The continuous thread of the noise, not loud enough to have woken her up, but noticeable immediately in the first moments of being awake. The noise rumbling, dulled and swallowed into the ground. It made her, in the half-light of waking, seem remote and distinct from herself. She sat up and felt numbed, listening to the sound, which was also not loud enough to be immediately annoying. In this darkened room, she thought how it was the quiet that she liked here. There was a special comfort in silence. You could just be yourself in it. She traced her finger along the pattern in the bark cloth of the sofa, the orange and brown bobbled lines. She noticed dirt on the skin between her fingers and licked and rubbed at it to remove it. She laid down on the sofa with her head hanging over the side and observed the familiar stain on the carpet by the edge of the sofa. It was paler than the rest of the carpet, as though the colours had been partly drained from it. It was like the shape of a dog's head seen from the side, a proper dog's head, with a proper snout, not like a bulldog or a pug. A snout even an old dog could breathe through. She wondered if the noise was getting louder, if the rumbling was getting nearer, or if that was just the impression made by its continuation. All the furniture was old – not just old, but ancient like the room of an old person. She got up and turned the TV on to drown the roadworks' noise, pulled out the poster she had been doing, and picked out a red gel pen to finish colouring in the bubble writing, trying to colour with all the lines going in the same direction so it would be neater. A blob of gel had dried at the nib. She scratched it off with her teeth, tasting the metal of the pen tip, so that when she brought it to the paper it wouldn't scratch through her poster. The tip of her tongue poked out of her mouth as she concentrated on the colouring. When she was done she held it up and read it to herself. *Stop Killing Bees.* Underneath she had drawn a spray canister of insecticide inside a circle with a big red cross over it. She wished she was better at drawing and that her bubble writing didn't look all uneven and straggly.

*

A couple of times while waiting for Bob to come home, she'd imagined the conversations they would have together. All the thises and thats they would talk about. And sometimes, while they were having an actual conversation, she would try to say something to trigger the exact same conversation that she'd imagined them having. Only it never worked out like she'd imagined, and the real conversations would seem disappointing in comparison. She thought too that it was somehow Bob's fault for not playing his part in the conversation. Then she felt bad for thinking that. Disloyal. When he'd only ever been kind to her. Often she found conversations were hard work. She nearly always had to do most of the work to keep them going or make them more interesting. Most of the time she didn't mind. It was good practise. She practised her storytelling voice too. Especially since the time she had heard her own voice on a tape recorder at school, when everyone had to record pretend interviews of each other. It was a high-pitched, thin sounding voice. An insubstantial child's voice. It wasn't like she imagined it sounded. It wasn't how *she* heard it when she spoke. And it wasn't the tape recorder making it sound bad because everybody else's voice sounded like them and when she'd asked the teacher why her voice sounded like that on the recording machine, the teacher had laughed. She practised making it sound deeper and slower so the consonants sounded less clackety. The kind of voice people would want to listen to. It was no good having great stories to tell if the voice was no good. If the voice was squawking away like a parrot, putting everyone off. She thought of that old musical she had seen with the man dancing in the rain. When they learned how to put sound with film, some of the actors had such terrible voices that people didn't want to watch their films anymore and who could blame them? Voices could be very off-putting.

From her drawstring bag she pulled out her nan's photographs. She shuffled back on the sofa to sit up straight and placed them on her lap. She liked to spend time looking at each of them, savouring all the details, the memories, the way that she had done each time her nan showed them to her. She liked the ones of her nan as a young lady, in her smart plaid coat. Her hair all neat and waved. The photo of her in her wedding dress. The lace of her dress, the big bunch of roses that looked dark grey in the photo but which she knew to be red, because her nan had always talked of her bouquet of red roses. And the photo of the whole wedding party. The granddad whom she had never met. How her nan had said that he was the most handsome man on the whole street and that everyone wanted him. Though it was hard to see that from the photo. People must have had a different idea of handsome back then. Everybody looked so serious in the photo. Nobody was smiling. That's how you had your photo taken back then, her nan would tell her. You dressed up smart and you didn't smile.

There was one with serrated edges. Nan sitting on a back step, older but still with her dark hair, with her head thrown back against the door frame, her eyes closed. Sunbathing. Framed by the shadow of a rose bush arched over the wall next to her. There was a photo of Sherrie-Lee's mother and her aunt and uncle as kids, sitting on some grass with some other kids, dressed in dungarees, tank tops, flowery dresses. The colours all tarnished and faded. In the background, another child leaned against the ropes of a gala tent. There was one of her nan pushing a pram. And one with nan's brother on a motorbike in a back yard, wearing gloves and a flat cap, with the bottoms of his trousers gathered by a clip. Photos of people sitting on sofas. Another photo showed a child in a hat standing in a photographer's studio. The studio stamp indented into the bottom right-hand corner, *Crossthwaite and Heap's, 14 New Briggate*. The writing slanted to the right with fancy lettering. The bottom of the P in Heap's extended and stretched back to underline Crossthwaite and Heap. Even before her nan was losing her memory she couldn't remember all the people in the photos. No one knew who the child was. The photo seemed to be from before Nan was born. A nameless child from a nameless time. Sometimes Sherrie-Lee made up names and stories for the ones that had no names attached to them. The photographs were slowly fading. Like memories, Sherrie-Lee thought, taking away all the small histories of families and people. The front door clicked open. She jumped up, putting her photographs back into the cotton bag and grabbed the notepad she had been jotting in earlier.

Look, she said, walking to the front door as Bob was closing it, holding the notepad above her head. I've been keeping watch of all the comings and goings. She began to read from it. 10.32: man walks dog along the road, 11.17: man walks dog in the other direction. Only this time he's wearing a hat. That's weird, isn't it?

You probably didn't notice the hat before.

Maybe. But I doubt it.

You're gonna have to be getting off home, Zadie. Gina is coming to stay for a week, Bob said as he entered the front room.

Why?

Her sister is going to stay with her mam so that she can have a break.

No. I mean why do I have to go? She had her hands on her hips in protest.

She's not gonna like that I've got some weird kid staying here. He smiled apologetically.

I'm not weird. We'll get along. I'll help her with the cooking and cleaning.

You haven't done any cooking or cleaning so far, he laughed. Anyway, you can't stay here forever.

Why not?

He just looked at her, shaking his head. He let out a short, tired kind of laugh.

Why is she coming anyway?

She's my girlfriend.

Why doesn't she live round here then?

I already told you. She had to go stay with her mam because she's sick. Are you hungry?

No.

We had a laugh at the call centre today.

Sherrie-Lee had moved to the sofa and wrapped herself in the blanket.

Don't you want to hear about it? He turned his head towards her as he put his bag of shopping on the table.

Sherrie-Lee shrugged.

Someone called this bloke and he got mad, shouting for being interrupted with nonsense.

Heard that one before. She yawned a theatrical yawn and switched on the TV.

No. This time we all took down the number and called it. The man went ape-shit, the first few times anyway. Then he stopped answering. It was funny though.

Hilarious, she said, pulling a half-hearted mock-laughter face.

Daft, really. Anything to relieve the monotony.

Sherrie-Lee didn't respond.

Oh, come on sulky-britches. What's up?

I'm not sulking.

He came and sat next to her. Let's have a look at your spy notes then.

He picked up the notepad and read the notes. What does that say? Woan walls past. Kid on skitbod. Your writing is terrible.

It's not. She grabbed the notepad from him.

He stood up and walked to the window and peered through the curtains to have a look for himself.

Maybe we should open the curtains. It's like someone died in here. Gina's not gonna like that the curtains are closed all the time. She'll wonder why.

Gina's not gonna like... she mocked in a whiny voice.

He went into the kitchen and Sherrie-Lee could hear him opening and closing cupboards. Usually, she hovered about watching to see what shopping he had brought, commenting on this and that. But when he looked back, he saw that she had not moved from the sofa.

18

Sherrie-Lee had been dreaming that she had been driving a car. Inside the car was her nan and Joshy; they were on their way to Whitby for a holiday. Her nan was singing and she was joining in and so was Joshy, but they needed to stop because Joshy had to go to the toilet. She wished she could still be dreaming it, going away on a trip together, and felt annoyed at being woken up by the hoover coming into the room.

Quick sticks, she was out of the flat and headed in the direction of the library, trying to put some purpose into her walk. She'd show Bob. An ice-cream van drove past her, its mechanical music loud and fast and over-jaunty, like an oversized wind-up toy. It was the tune of *Teddy Bear's Picnic*, over-loud and intermittently sped up, then slowed down to a distorted version of itself. It took her a few moments to work out what song it was, it was so mutated. The music stopped abruptly when the van came to a halt. A woman with two kids walked up to the little window and bought two cones. Sherrie-Lee paused and waited, pretending to tie her laces. She didn't want the ice-cream seller to think she was a potential customer. The van even looked like an over-sized toy, garishly decorated and improbable. The van took off again. The music began as soon as it started up, until the van and music grew distant, then disappeared altogether.

When she arrived at the library, she wanted to go inside, but didn't want to be seen by Claire, whom she had grown to know quite well over the years. Looking through the window, she saw her behind the main desk. It was easy to recognise her because of her blue hair. She was sitting at a desk doing something on a computer. Claire knew what kind of books Sherrie-Lee might like and she always had one or two to recommend to her. Even when Sherrie-Lee had mislaid her library card, she said that it didn't matter and still let her take the books out. At school, when they had drawn their 'Happy Places' and everyone had drawn play stations, or Pokemon cards or the park, or their holidays or favourite food, she had drawn herself with a book in the library. Then she'd felt embarrassed when the teacher had asked what it was. She wasn't as good at drawing as she was at other things and she often had to explain what her drawings were, which was more than annoying. She had thought a few times already about going in in disguise and just borrowing a few without taking them out in the usual way, but always in the end she had decided against it. It had been two weeks since she had read anything proper.

There were a couple of winos on the bench outside the library in the little garden area, and further down, on the bit that sloped around towards the back, there were two teenage boys. One of them had a skateboard. He stopped skating because the other one said something. He stepped off the skateboard, picked it up and placed it under his arm. The other boy said something else, and then the skateboard one started pushing him, and then the one who had said something started pushing back. He pushed hard, and the boy dropped his skateboard and fell over on his backside. The boy without the skateboard went red in the face, straightening himself up. He folded his arms. His Adam's apple stuck out and kept bobbing up and down. He didn't look like he wanted to fight, but kept saying things to the skateboarding one, provoking him, until they started pushing each other again. Sherrie-Lee wanted to shout over to them. *Stop. This is a library.* She felt so angry that she imagined herself grabbing hold of each of them and bashing their heads together. Then she wondered why she wanted to do that and thought that it was because she'd heard her nan say so many times – *They want their heads bashing together* – whenever she saw or heard of people behaving badly. She wondered if it was the same on the other planet, universes along. The one that, by the rules of infinity, was just like ours. If people there had the same problems. If they too needed their heads bashing together.

Walking away she thought something must have got to the one who kept saying things even though he didn't seem to want to fight. Something must have upset him so much that he just had to let it come out. She'd seen a lot of fights in her time. She'd become an expert watching them spark up out of nothing and flare up. Emotions building up inside people until they were just under the surface. People trying to let them come out gradually, or keep them inside, but this only having a knock-on effect on what showed itself above the surface. Brushing up against it like some invisible energy was at work. Fights were always starting up over nothing. Over misunderstandings. Like the time they'd been allowed to bring games in at school, as a reward for collecting all that money for *Children in Need*. Jimmy and Kane had been playing a game where you rolled two dice and Jimmy had said that he didn't know that you could split the dice and move two counters in the same roll. And Kane had said that he didn't know that he didn't know and that was it for the game, probably forever, although Jimmy was usually the reasonable sort. And she'd once seen a fight between two men, in broad daylight, on the pavement near her house. One of them knocked the other one down and the man just lay there, not moving. One of the people who'd come to watch said he was dead. The fight was all over a kid's bike. He wasn't dead, though. He got up eventually, but he was in a bad way.

She thought about the self-help section of the library. There were books in there that could cure anything. If only people knew. There were books to help you stop over-eating, quit smoking, lower blood pressure, give up drinking or gambling. Books to help you become a success, grow your confidence. Use the power of your mind. Everything from thinking yourself thin to winning love and influence and making better use of your time. There were no limits to the things books could help you with.

That's why people need stories, just like they need dreams. She thought of the storyteller man, about what he had told her about India. How the Hindus use fairy stories to calm a deranged mind. It made a truck-load of sense, that. In fairy stories you always had to help yourself, bring yourself to safety. There was a kind of wisdom in them that applied to the world beyond themselves. A deep kind of wisdom that you felt would keep on resonating into the future. She had seen too many people cave in from the lack of these wisdoms, even though she was only twelve. Look at her older brother. Then all that trouble with the police, with drugs, and now look at where he was. Though, somewhere along the line, telling stories must have meant something good for people. People must have known how good and important they were, otherwise there wouldn't be so many of them knocking about.

From the town hall clock, Sherrie-Lee saw that it was just past six. The IDAW meeting was not until seven, but that was okay. She liked walking round town when everything was closed or closing up. It gave the city a behind the scenes feel to it that felt good to be a part of.

People sat on rows of plastic chairs in the hall. She looked around at them and saw a few faces she recognised from the other meetings. There was the man with blonde dreadlocks who she'd seen a few times. He was stood near the front, putting up a poster with the IDAW symbol of the badger's face inside a yellow circle onto the noticeboard. A woman who she hadn't seen before was standing on a little wooden platform. Sherrie-Lee sat behind a couple she had seen on a demonstration outside the Town Hall and nodded at them when they turned to see who was shifting into the seats behind them. They smelled of some kind of musty scent, like spices. She looked around for the woman with the Tintin hair, but she wasn't there. Someone dropped a coin onto the wooden floor, she heard it roll about before it fell flat. Someone else coughed. The woman on the platform introduced herself and talked about the new agenda. She had a gruff voice like she smoked a lot of cigarettes. She did a lot of gesturing with her hands. She kept repeating the lines *The time is now* and *The time for action is now*. She wasn't as good to listen to as the Tintin lady. Sherrie-Lee wouldn't be learning any tricks for her storytelling listening to this one. She was trying to pay attention, but she found her mind wandering. The woman in front of her had long faded pink hair, with darkened roots. It was kinked and wavy like she had just taken it out of plaits. The man nearest to where she was sitting wore a pale denim shirt with the sleeves rolled up showing a tattoo and Sherrie-Lee leaned forward to see what it was. Some kind of animal baring its teeth, but she couldn't see if it was a bear or a wolf or something else. The notice-board above the poster was strung with triangular fabric flags. She sat there on the hard plastic chair, trying to sit upright. Her thoughts lifted idly as her mind detached from registering what the speaker was saying. She wondered what other people were thinking, whether their minds were drifting like hers was. She imagined all their thoughts drifting above them. She imagined these thoughts as little thought clouds floating above them. *Did I leave the oven on? The dog needs walking when we get back.* Random thoughts. *I need to be a better person. I need to try to be kinder. I don't like any of my friends.* She looked vaguely around the room, from person to person, trying to match each of these imagined thoughts to the person they might belong to. The smelling-of-spices couple were the ones thinking of the dog waiting for its walk when they got home. Only when she heard the line, *The time is now*, did she get caught back with the speaker. It sounded good and even though she didn't understand exactly what it meant, it made her feel a small line of excitement running inside her body. The same excitement she'd felt on the demonstration she'd been to. She could even imagine herself saying it. *The time is now.* Repeating it to others. The woman was shaking her head when she spoke. There was a ceiling light that pinged and went out just in front of her. She looked up at it to acknowledge its passing. She held for a moment a kind of smile that humanised its going out as though it had made some kind of comment. A quiet murmured laughter rose briefly in the room. You could only partially see the smile, because although she was only four rows away from her, the light bulb had provided half the light in that part of the room. When the man with the dreadlocks came to stand on the platform next to her, you could hardly make out his features. He looked out at the audience before speaking. Only his hair seemed to stand out. The outline of it was lit up from the shadows. The blonde contours showing up bright in the light. It was the first time she'd heard him speak. He repeated the words *new agenda* and said he would be handing out leaflets with a list of companies that would be targeted first. We start with boycotts and then move on. The time for direct action is now, he said. Companies that continue to do violence to the natural world in the name of profit. Nature is not for sale. They make it sound like the agenda of slash and burn and pollute is inevitable. Part of the progress of mankind. It's a lie they continue to prop up to push their own agenda for the profit of the few. Nature has no voice. We must speak out for it and be a voice for the voiceless. He looked out at them after he had finished speaking, like he was making eye contact with every one of them, but only an occasional glint in his right eye was reflected. Sherrie-Lee looked down at the legs of the chairs when his gaze was moving towards her. And then he stepped off the platform and went to stand at the side of the hall as the other woman spoke to close the meeting. She thanked everyone for coming and said without everyone's support the planet was done for. She said there was a mug coming round for donations to be made. Every penny counts, she said.

They knew her as Zadie. At least that's how she signed petitions, and how she sometimes signed in for meetings, which, she supposed, was the extent of how they knew her at all. It was where she'd first invented her new name, Zadie. The name was good, it suited her more than her real name, and said something. It belonged to the kind of person Sherrie-Lee wanted to be, not the Sherrie-Lee that lived in the mirror, but the real one. The kind of person she would be one day. A woman at the end of her row stood up and came towards her with the mug.

I don't have any money, Sherrie-Lee said.

The woman closed her eyes and smiled, shaking her head slightly in a kindly way to indicate that it didn't matter. Just pass it along, she told her.

She took the mug and stood up with it, passing it along to the man with the tattooed arm. She felt bad about not having any money to put in when all the animals needed their help.

19

Bob was remembering a fragment of himself from childhood. Walking behind his sister, trying to catch up with her. Every time he would catch up, she threw her bag over her shoulder and upped her pace so he would be left trailing behind again. She resented having to walk back from school with him and she made this known to him. Her disapproval of him. When he arrived home his mother was standing on a chair cleaning out a high kitchen cupboard, singing along to a tune on the radio. Jars and tins were stacked on the kitchen counter while she wiped at the interior of the cupboard. She had jumped when she realised he was standing next to her, and then smiled at him and ruffled his hair and called him Chip, which she often did. He felt content to be thinking of this happy memory of his mam, wearing her pinny and getting him to pass the jars and tins to her so everything could be put away again. Until recently, whenever he thought of her at all it would be overshadowed by the realisation that she was dead, that she had been let down by his bad choices without any chance for him to make it up to her. Perhaps that was the trick to remembering her in a happy light: come to thinking about her in an indirect way, through thinking of something else.

Bob thought that Zadie had finally left. He supposed he was relieved, though the flat already seemed quiet without her. Quiet but not unpleasant. He wished she hadn't been so sulky the night before. He wondered too, where she might have gone. She said she had no home to go to, but then she talked about her little brother at home. She made too much stuff up, and it didn't add up, really, when you thought about it all together. When you tried to map it all out to see how it fitted together. He flicked on the TV and scanned to a news channel. It had been over a week since the robbery was mentioned. He wasn't thinking of it so much anymore, and since the reports had said there was no money taken, he wasn't really worried about anyone else trying to find him, though he knew too that that's when it happened. That's when someone got you. When you let your guard down.

Gina would be coming soon. He hadn't seen her for three weeks. He hadn't told her anything about Zadie. He knew she wouldn't like it, though. Some kid who he didn't even know, coming to stay. It wouldn't make sense to her. It didn't make any sense without the bank incident. And if she knew about that ... He'd had a lucky escape, he told himself. He wouldn't do anything that dumb again. All the stress he'd had over it, and for nothing, really. He wanted to push on with his life. Move forward, after the wasted years inside. He wanted to move in with Gina. Maybe start a family. Settle down. Though he hadn't told her any of this. He didn't want to sound pushy or needy or anything like that. And then it all cost money. To do it properly, anyway. To do it right. Then he thought of the bad luck that had come his way and then he pushed it away with the thought that he'd trained himself to have when he was in prison. That things might have looked like bad luck, but you never knew what worse luck that bad luck had saved you from. And most of the time it pulled him out of himself and stopped him mulling over things too much.

From his position on the sofa, he could just make out Zadie's head bobbing along the bottom of the window as she walked along the pavement outside.

So you're back then, he said, greeting her as she came into the room.

Yeah. I haven't got my marching orders yet, have I?

Where've you been all day?

I've been to the library.

What did you do there?

It's the library. What did you think I did? She sat down next to him

Well, anyway, Gina's coming in two days, so you'll have to skedaddle by then. Shall I make some scrambled eggs? He got up from the sofa.

If you want.

*

No stories tonight? he said later on when he had cleared away all the stuff from tea.

Nah, she said. She pulled the blanket, which had taken permanent residence on the sofa, up over herself. By which she meant buzz-off. Bob had learned to read her well in the last weeks. When she came to stand near him when he was in the kitchen, even when she stood there and didn't say anything, it was a sign that she wanted to chat. When she watched TV she didn't want to be disturbed. He called her Lady Muck sometimes, she'd got so used to him waiting on her hand and foot. But he didn't want to upset her this evening.

Today I was thinking about this job I had selling uPVC windows, before I started at the call centre. I thought it was a bit like what you said about telling stories. How you have to gauge people. Work out which story line was going to work on people when you went door to door. If it was a middle-aged lady, I'd flatter her a bit. If that didn't work, when I asked her name, I'd tell her it was my mother's name. With guys, I'd tell them their neighbour was taking advantage of a new deal that was on offer. If the neighbourhood was a bit rough, I'd try the security angle.

She raised her eyebrows but said nothing and didn't look at him to acknowledge the gesture.

When he stood up to leave her in peace, she looked up at him and said, Sometimes there was no point even in a story.

She looked sad when he said goodnight. As he closed the door he felt like he'd let her down, somehow, but quickly told himself that was daft. He'd let her stay for too long already. That was all, and really, he couldn't imagine anyone else he knew putting up some mad kid that they didn't know from Adam for a couple of weeks. Even a nice kid like Zadie. She needed to get back to her own life, and get on with stuff. Get on with her own things. That's how life happened. You got on with stuff and it all came together.

20

The school Sherrie-Lee went to was separated from the centre of the city by the river and the snaking of a couple of major roads that seemed to loop around it. These simple topographical facts seemed to say something true that she already knew – that school had nothing to do with the real world, making as they did a disjuncture to all that was going on in the rest of the city. Even though the city was small and didn't seem to have much that was going on in it.

Last year they had put up a block of student housing, which could be seen from the school yard. The block towered above everything else, but beyond that nothing had changed. All the people who lived in them were hardly ever seen. They were just there occupying the big building before moving on to elsewhere. Where they were going, Sherrie-Lee didn't even try to imagine.

The school had seemed novel to her in the beginning. It was a two-storey building where her old school had been all on one level. The wide staircases had seemed exciting and daunting at the same time. Always they seemed to be thronging with children. Hundreds of them keeping to the left so that the squash of bodies could move in both directions, up and down the stairs without impeding either direction. Always she had felt a nervousness about what would happen if she took a wrong step. Long after the novelty of the school had worn itself out, the fear on the stairs remained.

*

Beyond the fencing she could make out a number of men in orange fluorescent jackets and trousers and white builders' helmets, standing or moving slowly about here and there. Inside the woodland it looked dark, a bit like that painting she'd seen, by somebody called Margerette or Magaritte, where it is a sunny day but beneath the trees it is night-time, and the house beneath the trees has to have its lights on. Among all the ribbons, a kind of poem was tied to the fence. It was written in black marker pen on a big sheet of white paper and had been laminated. It read,

> They hang the man and flog the woman
> Who steals the goose from off the common
> Yet let the greater villain loose
> That steals the common from the goose

> (Seventeenth Century Protest Song Against Enclosures)

Sherrie-Lee read, and wondered what was meant by 'Enclosures', then, looking at the fencing it was tagged onto, decided that it must be something to do with that. Obvious, really. Enclosing off an area. There were a few other signs that had been tied to the fence, some of them were just drawings of trees or the earth with RIP written above them. She was drawn to a sign that was written onto a square of brown cardboard, the kind that looked like it had been cut from a packaging box. It was next to a metal sign warning that Trespassers will be prosecuted.

The cardboard sign was written in capital letters in green marker pen. It read,

> IF YOU THINK THE ENVIRONMENT IS
> LESS IMPORTANT THAN THE ECONOMY,
> TRY HOLDING YOUR BREATH WHEN
> YOU COUNT YOUR MONEY!

Looking through the metal grid of the barrier, she noticed other people. There was a blue tent in a gap between the outer edge of trees, a banner flapping about and a few camping chairs near the tent. She had read about it in the list of forthcoming actions handed out at the IDAW meeting. The woodland had been bought by a property group based in Bermuda. It wasn't a massive woodland but it joined up two other wooded areas so it was important as a nature pathway. A group of tawny owls used it to breed and fledge their young. And there were a lot of bats that roosted in the trees. They were important, these pathways. A lot of animals needed them to get from place to place. It had been fenced off a few months ago and they'd blocked off a badger sett. A group of protesters had already been camped in there since then. A few trees were occupied too. The people needed supplies, food and water. A few had already been arrested for trespassing. Sherrie-Lee looked for people up in the trees but couldn't see anyone in the canopies from where she was standing.

She walked through the entrance where a fence panel had been removed and laid against another part of the still erect barrier. There was a group of four people standing together. She thought she might recognise someone from IDAW, but nobody looked familiar.

A woman with very blue eyes broke away from the conversation she was having. You here on your own, love? she asked Sherrie-Lee.

Sherrie-Lee nodded. The other three people with the woman looked at her, as though expecting her to say something.

I've brought some food supplies. She took a can of beans from each of her pockets. I thought there were people in the trees?

They're in there. They're in the middle of the woodland. The eviction team has gone in for them. You can put the food by the tent. I don't think people'll be here for much longer though. The end will come quickly now. She looked over towards the woodland.

Nobody said anything else for a few moments and then they resumed talking to each other.

Sherrie-Lee stepped back and moved towards the tent. She put the beans on the seat of one of the camping chairs. There was a kettle on a tall metal stand next to a circle of stones with ash and the charred fragments of twig in the centre of it. She heard the swish of static and looked over her shoulder to see one of the orange suits standing quite close behind her. She looked at him, but he didn't seem to see her. There were voices too coming from further towards the centre of the woodland. More orange suits were standing about, and there was some kind of small, tractor-crane machine with two men in the basket at the top. Some kind of conversation was going on with a man high in the tree, who sat with his legs astride a wide tree branch. Planks had been tied between that branch and another one to make a platform, on which a woman sat. A curtain of blue tarp was draped at the back of the platform, close to the trunk of the enormous beech tree. Two ropes were hung to the ground, strung from higher up in the canopy.

Two men were watching from the ground. One of them was filming the tree people with his mobile phone. Sherrie-Lee stood near the other one and asked him what was going on.

They're trying to get these guys out of the trees, the man who had a thick ginger beard said. The one with the phone stopped filming and looked round at Sherrie-Lee.

Are the press finally here? He nodded in Sherrie-Lee's direction.

Take no notice, ginger beard said. You just came at the right time, that's all. Nothing has happened for months.

Two orange suits came up to them. You're gonna have to be leaving here mate.

Okay, the man who she'd been talking to said, but nobody moved.

Sherrie-Lee looked up at the trees. Not just the one with people in it but all the trees. How tall they were. Most of them looked very old. With thick bark and moss and ivy growing all over them. Only a reduced amount of light came through the leaves in the canopy above. She had read somewhere that a single tree could support a thousand other species. She thought about this now as she looked at all the doomed trees and felt a sadness swell in her stomach. All those creatures just gone, like that, just because someone who'd probably never even been to this woodland wanted to flatten it to make money. It was true that all those creatures had no voice, that they were powerless in the face of all the destruction. People had to stand up for them.

The crane's basket was raised until it was almost at the same height as one of the branches in the occupied tree. A man climbed out of the basket wearing a climbing harness strapped over a yellow fluorescent vest. He fixed his ropes over the branches above him.

The four people who Sherrie-Lee stood with at the beginning came to join them. Nobody said anything for a long time. There was a sense that everyone was biding their time. Waiting. A sense that even time was suspended, waiting to move forward.

Occasionally, someone would break the long silence to say some brief, inconsequential thing, but nobody responded to it. No conversations were started up, she noticed, as usually happened when people were grouped together, waiting. People just stood about, patiently looking up at the trees as though they all understood some essential thing about the moment and wanted to show respect for it. It was a feeling that Sherrie-Lee had not experienced before. And, even though she had only just tagged along with this group and had never seen any of them before, it swelled inside her this feeling of connection with everybody and everything. This feeling of being united for something that was bigger and more important than just themselves.

The man who had tied his rope to the trees earlier, and had come back down in the crane in the meantime, now walked back to the area with another man. The crane operator came to join them and the three stood together, talking and looking up at the occupied tree. After deliberating for some time, the three men went to their positions on the crane and the crane basket was again lifted into position. The group of four began singing some kind of ballad-like song. There was a beautiful voice rising among them and Sherrie-Lee looked back to see who it belonged to.

We come in peace... To dig and sow.
We come to work the lands in common
and to make the waste grounds grow.

The beautiful voice belonged to the woman with the very blue eyes; it seemed to lead the other three voices. Her face looked calm and serene. They all looked up at the tree as they sang.

By theft and murder they took the land.
Now everywhere the walls
spring up at their command.

The singers looked as solemn as any choir Sherrie-Lee had seen.

The man with the yellow vest helped the woman who was sitting on the platform get into the basket of the crane. People cheered for her as she was lowered to the ground. The singers finished their song as she climbed out onto the bare earth. A man standing with another group shouted across – You're a tree hero.

The woman gave a short, circular, theatrical wave and bow and everybody clapped. She went to stand with the man who'd called her a hero. He put his arm around her and kissed the side of her head. They all watched as the crane went up again into the tree to bring the man down. The man who had, up until that point, been sitting astride the tree branch, stood up and attached himself to a rope and lowered himself to the ground.

There was clapping and cheering and cat calls as the man descended.

The man who had been filming when Sherrie-Lee first arrived got his phone out and was again filming the scene. One of the orange men asked him to put it away.

Why? He's not doing anything wrong, the man with the ginger beard said.

You've been asked to stop filming.

And we said that he wasn't doing anything wrong. He's just recording what's going on.

Put your phone away. Another hi-vis jacket stepped across, making a grab at the offending phone.

Hey. Watch what yer doing, mate.

The phone man stepped out of the way, holding his phone high up out of reach, but another security man knocked it from his hand.

The ginger-bearded man stepped forward. Hey, you can't do that. His face reddened with anger.

He was pushed back, but, in response, pushed forward again, standing his ground. Everybody else had stepped back, instinctively. Blue-eyed lady came to stand near Sherrie-Lee. There was more of a scuffle, and ginger beard was knocked to the ground and pulled face down by a man in an orange jacket, who held the man's left arm behind his back. One of his knees was placed on the right side of the man's neck. The side of the bearded man's face was visible and Sherrie-Lee could see that it was reddening from the pressure. He tried to shout out and coughed low into the earth. Someone else was filming now but nobody seemed to notice that. The blue-eyed woman came up close to Sherrie-Lee then and suggested that she should go home. She said it in a kind way, Sherrie-Lee could tell from the way she crouched down so she was at her level when she spoke to her.

Perhaps you should be getting off now. She smiled at her, holding her gaze as Sherrie-Lee started to say something, only half-formed, about just wanting to help.

Get yourself home love, the woman said.

And as Sherrie-Lee walked away she couldn't be sure what she herself had said to the woman or if she had said anything at all. She felt certain that she had not said anything coherent, at any rate.

The woodland was only a few minutes' walk from the river and that is where Sherrie-Lee found herself, walking idly alongside it, in the opposite direction to its flow. A few gulls called out, their wings held rigid as they glided above. The surface of the water was murky and did not mirror the stretch of their wings the way that the canal did. She thought of the man pressed down on the ground and then she looked out at the wide grey stretch of river. Near to her, the water came up high against the concrete, but further down at the outer stretch, where the river bent and widened, there was a tide mark of darkened slime that covered the rocks. She sat on some steps near the wharf and looked out at the water. The man had been very red in the face when the orange suit was kneeling on him. It wasn't the violence that shocked Sherrie-Lee when she pictured him now, it was the way it just happened. It came out of nowhere. Even the tree people had come down calmly. There had been no trouble. She pulled her knees up in front of her, holding her legs tightly in place against her, as there wasn't much room on the step to get a proper footing. She held that position until her thigh muscles felt balled up and painful from the effort of supporting the rest of her legs. Her right foot slipped onto the lower step, and she placed her other foot next to it to ease the strain on the backs of her thighs. She checked her heartbeat, placing the flat of her middle and index fingers in the places where she usually found it, but this time, even when she closed her eyes to concentrate, she couldn't find it. Maybe the shock had reset it to normal. Sometimes she looked into the palm of her hand at the lines. She didn't believe in that stuff but when feeling ruffled she checked on the length of the bottom line, which was supposed to be the life line. Just to check that it hadn't got shorter. It seemed to change every time she looked at it, especially the one on her left palm, which was supposed to be the most important one. She thought that man with the knee on his neck was going to choke. The security man was on him for so long. Even when he was struggling and coughing, he didn't get off, and another protester had rushed towards them to help the man on the ground but he'd been shoved out of the way by another guard. The guard had run at him with his arms folded and knocked the man onto his back. He hit the ground hard then jumped back up, ready to go again, but his friend had stepped in, putting his arm around him and leading him away. The words 'excessive force' came to her, words which felt like an understatement as she said them. She must have picked them up from a news programme. A woman had then run at the kneeling man but she had been grabbed by the arm and swung round onto the ground. She yelled and someone else was demanding to know the name of the security man who had swung her, but he just shrugged and half-smiled and walked away from them. As she was leaving, Sherrie-Lee heard one of the orange suits at the periphery making chain-saw noises, and another one standing next to him laughed. She watched a pair of swans swim by, together with seven fluffy grey cygnets. They were swimming up river. One of the parents led the group, and the other swam at a short distance behind them, as if checking for stragglers. The one at the front held its neck straight up. Sherrie-Lee felt tears prick at her eyes witnessing the calm grace of it, leading the way. The one at the back dipped its beak in the water now and then, as it moved against the ripples. She thought how nice it would be to be one of those cygnets, to be part of that family and snuggle up with the rest of the family when they stopped to rest.

The sun was round and bare and white, and appeared above the modern line and curve of the Millennium Bridge, a white blur surrounding it as it began its descent over to the other side of the world.

21

Sherrie-Lee thought she had misjudged Bob, that he didn't really like stories that much after all. Thinking back, he seemed bored by most of the ones she had told him. She thought of that day on the moor. How ungrateful he'd been when she'd tried to cheer him up. And another time when she'd made beans on toast when he worked a late shift. She'd put all that effort in and waited up especially, and he'd just said he didn't like to eat that late and didn't touch any of it. More than ungrateful. She had thought they were a team and now it was all Gina this and Gina that.

The pains in her legs had started up again. Her nan had said they were growing pains and that she didn't need to worry about them, but Sherrie-Lee wondered about that. So much pain, when she didn't even grow that much. She was the smallest in her class, except for Tom Taylor and he was so short he didn't even count.

She got her writing pad from her bag behind the sofa and tore off the top page to reveal a fresh, unmarked page. She smoothed over it with her hand and bit her top lip. She pulled the lid off her best gel pen and began writing.

Dear Police Officers, she wrote. We have the girl Sherrie-Lee Connors. If you would like to see the girl safe and in one piece, then it is necessary to follow these instructions. She looked at it and read over the lines a few times. She pulled it off her pad and screwed it up, putting the crumpled-up piece of paper in the front pocket of her jeans. It didn't look right. She wished she had an old typewriter. If she could get to the library, she could do it on the computer. She couldn't just turn up at school for the last few days either. Then everyone would see her and she couldn't claim to be kidnapped then, could she? She took the letter out of her pocket and straightened it out again. It looked like it was done by a kid. A kid trying to sound grown-up. She should go at it the other way. Since she couldn't pull off sounding like a straight-up grown-up, she should make it sound like a grown-up trying to sound like a kid. She started, Dear Policemen and Policewomen, we have that missing girl. Sherrie-Lee Connors. It gave her a small feeling of satisfaction writing that she was a missing girl. That'd show them. She was missing. They'd have to take some notice then. She read it again and sighed, tearing it from the pad and screwing that note up too. She closed her eyes and tried thinking about it, but she couldn't think straight. The scenes from the woodland protest came back to her, the man struggling on the ground, the woman being swung round. A surge of anger rose when she remembered the man making the chainsaw noise. She couldn't focus on the letter and all of a sudden it seemed that it was a stupid idea. Silly. Irrelevant.

She turned the light off and pulled the blanket around her. She lay back and waited for her eyes to get used to the darkness. She'd been working on a new story. She'd try to think about that instead. It was going to be one of those genie stories. Working it out helped her keep control of stuff. Helped her feel organised. Whenever she felt herself going towards an edge, it helped her feel centred. It worked for other people too. Some other people, anyway. Whenever Joshy seemed agitated, it worked for him, taking him somewhere quiet and telling him a story. Well, it seemed to work. It was hard to tell with some people. She didn't care that Bob didn't seem to like them anymore. Well, too bad for him. Other people could take them or leave them. It was up to them. There was no helping some people. She liked stories and that was the main thing. One thing that was for sure was that when other people were agitated, she felt agitated too, and what calmed her was telling herself a story. Organising her thoughts around the story and the telling of it fast-tracked her into a kind of rhythm of being quiet inside. It was a way to keep the chaos of the world at bay. To dilute the messiness that threatened to smother everything. To keep a bubble of order around herself where she could breathe and redraw the lines. She thought about the new story she'd been working on and started to tell it to herself.

A poor fisherman was having no luck with catching any fish, so he threw his net in one last time before giving up for the day and going home, even though he didn't like to go home empty-handed. When he pulled the net out again, he saw that there were again no fish, but in the net was an old jar. He lifted the jar into his boat and saw that it was an old clay jar, stoppered at the top with a wax seal. He took his knife from his pocket and dug out the seal. When he had broken the seal, he was astonished to see a genie coming free from the bottle. Where am I? the genie asked. The fisherman rubbed at his eyes and looked around him and told the genie where they were. What year is it? he asked. The fisherman told him this also. The genie looked sad and thoughtful at this and then said after a while that he had been trapped inside the bottle for almost a thousand years. They talked for a while about the passing of time and how it waited for no man or genie. Then the genie said that he would grant three wishes to the fisherman, as it was the custom with genies, but first he was impatient to see the world that he had not set eyes on for so long. Away he was gone, leaving the fisherman to wonder if what had happened had really happened, and if it had happened if the genie would ever come back.

After a week, the genie did come back, but had aged so much in that week that it was a pity to see him. His hair was white and he had deep wrinkles around his sad eyes. The fisherman was where he had been the week before. Fisherman, I beg you, where is the bottle that was my home for so long. The fisherman bent

155

towards the back of the boat and from under a piece of cloth, he pulled out the bottle. The genie said, Unstopper the bottle for me. I have seen enough of this world. How out of joint everything is. The fisherman was astonished. Why, when you have been a prisoner for a thousand years inside this bottle, do you want to return there?

The genie looked at him sadly, saying that he had in the last week travelled to all the four corners of the world. I have seen things that have made me shiver with despair. Most of the forests have gone and the animals too. Rivers and lakes full of nothing but rubbish, plastic bottles, bags, all kinds of rubbish. And where have all the birds gone? There is so much sorrow and pointless destruction in the world that I would rather return to my blind existence inside this bottle than to live among this creature called Human and see what has become of him. It is pitiful; I only wish that I had never been found and had been left with the images of the world from a thousand years ago.

That is sad, the fisherman sympathised with the genie. But, as he was about to open the bottle, he remembered the three wishes that were owed to him. The genie laughed, loud and booming. He smiled and then became furiously angry. Give away wishes to a human being when you are only capable of doing harm? The genie shook his head. With this, the fisherman was so cross he threw the bottle into the rocks, where it smashed into many small pieces. The genie roared and took off at great speed, leaving a great wind that rushed across the water, which swelled and heaved in its wake. If you listen out sometimes, you can hear him still, wailing and howling and crying into the rush of the wind.

Sherrie-Lee moved over to the window when she had finished the story and looked out. She thought about how words created worlds. She had become more aware of it since she had begun training herself to be a storyteller. She supposed words in books created worlds too, but having the word printed there on the page made it seem a fact too as well as a word. When you said a word out loud, the world was created as you said it. The hot day, the tree, the shelter beneath did not exist before you said them aloud. And now they existed, came into existence in the listener's ears, in the speaker's mouth, in the spaces between. Even our thoughts are made like this. Word by word. She thought about it for a long time and it seemed true enough, but some renegade part of her wanted to find a chink in the reasoning. It was too neat an idea. Too sewn up in praise of itself. She thought of Joshy. Words didn't work for him like that and she thought of her love for him too. That didn't depend on words. Caring for someone didn't depend on words. It had a meaning deeper than all that. It was not made by words and didn't need words in order to exist. She looked outside. There was no wind at all. She tried to imagine the wailing wind fetching up outside, like at the end of the story, but it was so still and dead out there that imagining it being any different seemed impossible. She was tired and slunk back to the sofa. She sat still for a long time, thinking and not thinking, until all the light had been sucked from the day and there was only the dark left in the room.

22

They looked at each other when they heard the knock at the door.

When the second knock came, Bob stood up and went to the door. Sherrie-Lee followed him.

Surprise, the woman said. Her own initial look of surprised happiness faded. Well, aren't you gonna let me in? What's up? You don't look too happy. What's up, Lester?

No. Of course I'm happy. It's just that... He looked down towards his feet as though looking for the right words. His cheeks had flushed red. You're early, was all he could say, looking back at Gina as she watched his reaction.

And who's this? she said, noticing Sherrie-Lee as she stepped through the doorway.

Gina, this is Zadie. Zadie, Gina.

Sherrie-Lee reached out to shake hands.

I am Lester's niece. He's looking after me for my dad. She smiled, genuinely pleased with herself.

You're Steve's daughter? Gina said. Then to Lester, I thought Steve's daughter was younger?

I've just arrived today too. Problems at home. Uncle Lester wasn't expecting me either, were you, Uncle Lester? Pleased to meet you. She stepped forward. Shall I take your bag? A huge grin on her face.

Gina handed her bag instead to Lester and followed him into the bedroom. She didn't seem too friendly. Sherrie-Lee noticed that she wore sandals and that the heels of her feet looked cracked and yellowed and rough. Very ugly feet, she thought to herself. Except for her nan's feet, they were the ugliest feet she had ever seen. And big too.

I'll make you a cup of tea, Sherrie-Lee called after them. She heard them talking in lowered voices inside the bedroom but didn't want to risk going closer to the door to listen and being caught out. No. That wouldn't go down well. She could already tell that she'd have to be on her absolutely best behaviour. She wasn't going to get anything past this one.

She made three mugs of tea and set them on the table, waiting for the other two to join her. She wouldn't call them when their tea was ready. Couples – and she knew this for a fact – didn't like to be bothered and nagged by other people. She would try to stay in the background as much as possible until Gina left. At least she got to stay a while longer.

Gina came in and sat opposite Sherrie-Lee. So, you got problems at home, have you? She looked suspiciously at Sherrie-Lee. And how is Steve? I haven't seen him for, well, it must be over a year now.

Oh. You know. He's the same. Got a few problems, that's all. She put on a sad face when she said this but Gina wasn't having any of it.

What kind of problems? She raised her eyebrows and leaned in towards Sherrie-Lee.

I don't know. Grown-up stuff. She shrugged and tried to look apologetic for not giving the kind of details that she knew Gina was after.

There was a questioning look on Gina's face as she looked at Sherrie-Lee. And what about your mam? She sucked in the air after she said 'mam', – like a reverse sigh, almost like she was angry. Like she was onto her, but she was trying to contain it until she'd got enough stuff on her. Until she made absolutely sure that she was a fraud.

Lester broke in, putting a hand on Gina's shoulder. Let's leave the kid alone. She must be upset.

She doesn't look upset, Gina said. A half-scowl was still on her face as she looked back at her. Gina seemed to be turning out to be the type to have dim views about everything. Sherrie-Lee felt a small wave of satisfaction at this. That she let herself get so narked by a kid. She tried smiling at the woman, a big smile full of feigned generosity, but couldn't hold onto it. Gina could dig all she liked, she wasn't going to get anything from Sherrie-Lee.

She could feel Gina's long stare on her cheeks even after she had switched her own gaze to Lester. It wasn't going to be easy, that was for sure. She would have to play it cool, give her as little information as possible. She'd been lucky so far not to say anything that contradicted the facts that Gina knew.

*

She thought of the giant heart poster in the science room at school. She could almost see it in her memory's eye, she'd looked at it so often. The cross-section with the different veins and arteries in red and blue. The big red one that looped over the top was called the aorta and a blue one that came out of the other side of the heart was called the superior vena cava. When she saw that one, she would always look for its partner in crime, which came out at the bottom of the heart. It was called the inferior vena cava. She liked the names. The implied hierarchy. The valves between the atriums and ventricles looked a bit like fallen cobwebs in the poster because they were painted a grey colour and stretched downwards. The aorta was the biggest artery; it took oxygenated blood from the heart to all the rest of the body. She sometimes studied the poster to work out what might be wrong with her own heart. She thought that maybe it was something to do with the aorta, maybe it was twisted or had a kink in it so that the heart had to work extra hard to pump all that blood out. It didn't bother her thinking that she had only half a lifespan to live. People lived an average of about seventy-five years, so probably she had about thirty-seven which was ancient enough, she thought, and was more than enough years for anyone to endure.

23

Sherrie-Lee was listening to the conversation, crouched down outside the living room door. She knew that Gina was going to be trouble. Too much of a smart cookie for her own good. They kept their voices low, but she could hear fragments of what was said. Who is she? Something's not right. She's not your niece, is she? Then Lester's voice, low and difficult for her to hear enough to make out what he was saying. Then Gina. What's going on, Lester?

She should've set him up with Claire instead, when she had the chance. You can't go wrong with a librarian. Especially one with blue hair. She would've been perfect for him. They would have got on together, all of them. And the two of them would have been grateful to her forever for helping them find each other. It would be like being in a Disney film. She leaned her head against the wall, and pictured the three of them walking off together. She stood up and tip-toed to the bathroom, where she flushed the toilet. She looked down and watched the water churn, then listened to the water refill the cistern until the last drop had poured in. In the mirror above the sink, she mimed being Gina. *What's going on, Lester? Something's not adding up here!* She put her hand on her hip, elbow sticking out, and shook her head and pulled unimpressed faces, the way she had seen Gina doing. A slight turn of the head, an exaggerated closing of the eyes. *What's going on, Lester? She's not your niece, is she?* No shit, Sherlock.

*

Gina came into the room and opened the side window, flaring her nostrils. It seemed nicer without the curtains drawn all the time. The fresh smell of outside came in.

It's gonna be a warm day out there today, Sherrie-Lee said, breathing in the current of air from outside. Isn't that nice? She smiled as wholesome a smile as she could muster.

Gina made that noise again, like a quick, low humph. She had started it yesterday, Sherrie-Lee had noticed. Making it towards the end of whatever Sherrie-Lee was saying. It was more than annoying. If you had any sense of manners, you could say it was rude.

Lester brought in three plates, each with a sandwich. He had piled the plates on top of each other to make carrying them easier. The top one, he gave to Gina.

Look at that, Sherrie-Lee pointed out. The pair of them followed her gaze to the stack of plates. Sandwiches, sandwiching the plates, she said. They looked back at her as though she had a screw loose.

Sherrie-Lee ate her sandwich in silence. At each bite, she tried to imagine which part of her body the food would be going to, coaxing it along, anxious to keep all parts of her body adequately nourished. Her heart. Her brain. Her legs. Perhaps she did have a screw loose somewhere.

What are you going to do today, then, Zadie? Lester said, leaning forward on the table when she had finished.

Do you play cards, Gina?

Gina shook her head. She ate with really small bites, keeping her mouth closed as she chewed, slowly and carefully. Even though they were small bites she took ages to chew them, wiping the corner of her mouth with a paper napkin after each bite. It was a weird way of eating, Sherrie-Lee thought.

She noticed that Lester was eating differently too, slower, with his mouth closed, which he didn't always do. And it was the first time they had ever used paper napkins. She looked at her own untouched napkin on the table in front of her. She wasn't sure about Gina. Ever since she had arrived, Bob seemed to have a worried expression on his face.

Zadie is really good at telling stories, Lester said, after he had finished his sandwiches. Aren't you, Zadie?

Sherrie-Lee flared a patched red, thinking of all the fairy stories she knew about wicked step-mothers. I like fairy stories, she said, turning to Gina. Do you?

Gina was still eating and made them wait while she finished chewing. Dabbing at her mouth again with the paper napkin before replying. No. There's enough fairy stories around here. Gina gave her a long look and placed her hands flat on the table, readjusting her position into the back of the chair. She gave Lester the same long look before she spoke. Life is too full of made-up stories. Politicians make enough up for everybody. Saying they will do one thing and then doing the opposite.

That's not stories, Sherrie-Lee said. That's just lies. There's a difference.

Doesn't seem like much of a difference to me. There are two ways of looking at something. Either something is true or it's a lie, or it's a half-truth, which is also a lie. What do you think, Lester? She turned towards him as he was just standing up to go to the kitchen.

Technically that was three things she had just pointed out, Sherrie-Lee thought, but kept it to herself. Instead, she just looked at her with something like pity on her face. Adults had a weird idea about what truth was. They saw truth as a fixed, unchanging thing. It was the wrong way to see it, she thought. Truth could be one thing and then another. Like people believed one thing one time and another the next. To her, stories were above all that. They were full of little truths just waiting to happen. Waiting to be seen. You could go back to them, remember parts of them, and find new things in them. New truths and meanings.

How old are you, anyway? Gina turned to face Sherrie-Lee.

Twelve.

Twelve? She made that humphing sound again. Isn't twelve a bit old to be telling fairy stories and what-not?

She hated that phrase *what-not*. Above all, it just sounded thick. She would add it to the list she was making of all the words she didn't like. The top three lately were retard, which really made her mad when she heard it, preggers, and then banter. But what-not might just go straight to the top of the list.

Gina had thick black hair, not long and not really short either. She wore big round glasses, that were kind of tinted a purple colour like sunglasses. Sherrie-Lee could see herself, miniaturised and doubled in the reflection of each lens. Gina was not a smart cookie, like she had thought in the beginning. Just difficult to charm. Impossible to charm, in fact. She had tried for a couple of days. The day before, she had put a ribbon on the eyeshadow trio she'd stolen. I don't wear makeup, she'd told Sherrie-Lee. No thank yous. Nothing. Charmless as well as impossible to charm.

Sherrie-Lee stood up and gathered the plates. With an exaggerated effort she brushed the crumbs onto the top plate, even where Gina had been eating and there were no crumbs. Going to take these out to feed the birds. Thanks for making the sandwiches, Uncle Lester. She smiled as she turned away.

The rats will eat them, more like, she heard Gina quip.

Well, they need to eat too. And we should look after all of God's creatures, don't you think?

Sherrie-Lee went to the front steps and sat down on the bottom one, brushing the crumbs on the grass verge to the side of the step. She didn't know why she'd said 'God's creatures', she never said that kind of thing and didn't even think of them as having anything to do with God. She had just said it, she supposed, to

165

lord it over Gina, the way some people did when they referred to God and to let her know, at the same time, that she was nice and cared about all the animals. She didn't even know if she believed in God. At school, people just said God things automatically, they didn't even think about what they said. If someone were to ask Sherrie-Lee on the spot whether she believed in God, and she had to take one side or the other, she would go with her instinct and say no. She should try to be nicer to Gina, though, because Lester would like it and, after all, Gina was just an animal too. All people were.

Lester and Gina were sitting in silence when Sherrie-Lee returned to join them. She looked at Gina to smile at her, but she wasn't looking. A blow fly buzzed over them, cutting across the room in repeated straight lines, visiting the table on each of its rounds until it was wafted on its way, first by Lester's hand then by Gina's.

I bet your mam is missing you. You being away and everything, Sherrie-Lee said.

Lester rubbed his hands flat over his face, emerging red from the rubbing.

My sister is there. I've only been here a few days, she said. Then, licking the back of her spoon before putting it back in her mug, she added, How long are you here for, Zadie?

That reminds me, Lester brightened up. I spoke to Steve this morning. He said you could go back tomorrow. Things are looking up at home. Isn't that good news? Lester was smiling back at Sherrie-Lee.

I didn't know you spoke to Steve? Gina said, leaning towards Lester. There was no pleasing some people. The fly buzzed by again, Gina swatted it with her hand but missed. The bang of her hand on the table made the mugs jolt.

Good news indeed! Sherrie-Lee responded. But you know Dad, he can change his mind in a heartbeat. She looked pointedly at Lester and then at Gina, who looked between the two of them, measuring, before resting her gaze meaningfully on Lester. Her mouth was twisted as though she was trying hard not to say anything. There was something a bit bitter about Gina, which made her seem older than she was. And all the sucking on her lips that she did made them look wrinkled. If she'd been more friendly towards her, Sherrie-Lee would've shared these useful pieces of advice, but as it stood, there was no helping her.

*

She walked along the wooded ridge at the back of the estates. The sunlight fell in lines and patches as it made its way through the trees. The ground was hard and dry from the lack of rain. At the edge of the path, it crumbled as small stones broke free from the cracks in the parched mud. She had tried everything she could think of with Gina. She had been kind. She had tried to be clever and funny. Nothing washed. Maybe it was true what people said and three really was a crowd. And there was nothing you could do about it. It was as simple as that. She'd always had a bit of envy for people who had someone to nag them. It always seemed to carry some suggestion of normal people about it. People caring for people. Caring enough to nag and give all that advice and instruction. Sherrie-Lee had always wished she'd had someone to properly nag her about stuff, so she too could be normal. Feel what it was like to be normal. She'd imagine then her mother snapping up to it, telling her to hold her shoulders back, or pick her feet up when she walked, or not eat with her mouth open. Things that she'd heard other mothers say to their own children. But now having had the experience of Gina, she wasn't sure that she would like that at all.

She didn't come to these woods as often as she would've liked to. There were never many people around and she'd heard stories from a few different people about a man in the woods, stalking people, getting his thing out. Today, she was fed up and didn't much care. She quickened up her walk and at the top of an incline she had to stop because she was out of breath. As her breathing calmed, she could hear the sound of traffic from the main road below, rebounding from the trees. Like the sound of marching, the quick succession of sound rising and falling as it hit the trees and then fell, like the sound of some army – left, right, left, right – way off in the distance. She used to come here a lot when she was just getting into nature, years before she knew anything about the man in the woods. In the early days she liked being on her own looking and listening out for things, but had thought at the same time, how all that nature spotting was probably not for short girls with mousy hair and no special clothes or equipment. But then she had heard this loud call, a kind of bird call, like a demented blackbird, she had thought at first. Then she had seen it. It was just there, poking out from a hole high up in a tall dead tree. A little black and white bird with a patch of red above its beak. It hadn't even tried to hide when she stood there looking at it, though she was sure that it could see her. It was a young greater spotted woodpecker calling to its mother for food. But it seemed like more than that to Sherrie-Lee, it was as though that call had been a message for her too. Telling her she should keep looking and listening, that nature was there for everyone. It didn't care who it was that saw it. Maybe she should tell Gina about it, see if she wanted to come and look for woodpeckers, give her another chance too.

24

Sherrie-Lee made a list of all the things wrong with Gina. Her voice was harsh, like she smoked a lot, even though she didn't smoke. Some people were just unfortunate. She wasn't friendly. She never laughed. She made annoying noises and had annoying habits like sucking in her lips. She had ugly feet. Not just ugly, but fugly. Fucking ugly. She drew a line down the middle of the page, and wrote Claire at the top of the second half. There she listed all the good things about Claire. Top of the list was that she was a librarian. Next, she knew the value of stories. Third, very kind. Fourth, smiley, with blue hair. She also listed her nice feet, even though she'd never actually seen her feet.

What you doing? Lester said, as he came to sit on the sofa next to her.

Sherrie-Lee pulled her notepad towards her chest. Nothing. She shrugged when she saw that his expression was still asking what she was doing. It was kindly meant, though, the way he was raising one eyebrow, looking at her sideways. She would've laughed if it had still been just the two of them. But Gina's presence spoiled all that. She couldn't relax and be herself.

The front door clicked open.

Gina came into the room with a face on her. Look at this! she said, holding a newspaper up in front of her. The headline said, MISSING SCHOOLGIRL. There was an old photo of Sherrie-Lee underneath. It was grainy from being enlarged. Sherrie-Lee felt a buzz of excitement. So, it had worked. Her ransom note. They'd believed it. Then the excitement, as quickly as it had flared up, seemed to fall, hurtling downwards. Like falling in a dream, never hitting the bottom but expecting it the whole time. She recognised the photograph. It was an old school photo from a couple of years ago. When she looked up from the paper she noticed Gina giving her one of her scowls. She'd lowered one of her eyebrows so there were two lines between her eyebrows that looked like the number eleven.

Don't you think this Sherrie-Lee Connors looks a bit like our Zadie? Gina said.

No shit, Sherlock, thought Sherrie-Lee.

Lester took the paper from her and began to read aloud.

Sherrie-Lee leaned across and looked at the photo. She noticed it was yesterday's paper. There is some resemblance, Sherrie-Lee said. She'd have to admit that. The eyes are different though and the mouth. A lot of kids look similar round here. There's a lot of inbreeding.

Lester read from it. The police suspect that she has been kidnapped. Though it is not clear exactly how long she has been missing. A ransom has been received asking for £50,000 in exchange for Sherrie-Lee's safe return. Sherrie-Lee stole a glance at Gina, who was still staring at her, looking mad and something else too. A kind of *what-did-I-tell-you*-look.

Probably a hoax, Sherrie-Lee said.

Lester looked over at Sherrie-Lee. She couldn't read his expression only that she knew she hadn't seen an expression like that coming from him, ever. She'd never seen him looking anything like cross before. Even the skin on his face seemed to look darker. His whole face. It stopped her going on with the hoax thread, folding it into the falling feeling inside her.

Gina took the paper from him. It says here that her family didn't realise she was missing at first. They said she often took off. That she was unruly and wilful and defiant. Gina stood there looking at Sherrie-Lee. Unruly, wilful, defiant, she repeated. A strange look on her face. A look that might have been simply a look of triumph. What's going on? she asked.

Lester stood up, shaking his head. First, he walked towards the window, rubbing his chin. Then he turned round quickly and walked in the opposite direction. Fuck, he said, putting his hands up to his face. He kicked the edge of the sofa on which Sherrie-Lee still sat and walked out of the room. The whole place shook when the front door was slammed shut. Somewhere from the street a dog barked.

Through the window, Gina watched him leave. What the hell's going on? she repeated.

Sherrie-Lee just sat there. If she had a room to go to, she would've slunk off too. She felt just about as bad as when she stole the fossil that Courtney McKinnley had brought to school. It was a small black stone with half an ammonite showing on one side. She said she found it in Whitby. When she took it she didn't think it'd be such a big thing. It was just a stone, even if it did have a fossil in it. The headteacher had different ideas. She came in to speak to the whole class. She described it and then she did a little speech about how special it was to Courtney. At which point, Courtney burst out with heavy, impossibly loud, sobbing. Wailing like you've never heard. It made everyone look down at their shoes embarrassed. Even the kids that hadn't taken it. Which had been a relief to Sherrie-Lee, that the other kids had somehow seemed guilty and sorry too. That way her own shame and regret didn't stand out too much. That's how she felt now. Full of regret for what she'd done. Full of shame. She wasn't expecting things to get so out of hand. She got up to go to the toilet.

Where do you think you're going? Gina said.

While Gina kept talking at her and asking her questions, Sherrie-Lee looked down at the brown and orange swirls on the carpet, all the comfort she'd found in that pattern was long gone. She'd have to leave now, that was for sure.

She wanted to tell Gina that it was all her fault, coming and poking her nose into stuff that was none of her business.

You're very quiet for someone so full of stories, Gina said, after a while.

I want to go to the toilet, Sherrie-Lee said. Gone was her usual confident way of speaking.

What's going on? She put her hands on her hips. Come on. I want to know.

Sherrie-Lee shrugged.

That's you, isn't it? That Sherrie-Lee? What kind of a name is that anyway?

Sherrie-Lee stood her ground and remained silent. *What kind of a name...* That'd done it. What kind of a name is Gina, she wanted to say.

After a whole minute of staring at each other. Gina muttered Jesus under her breath and went into Lester's room, closing the door behind her.

Sherrie-Lee sat on the sofa and put her head in her hands. It wasn't supposed to turn out like this. Now he'd never want to be my friend again, she whispered aloud into her hands. All the thoughts in her head raced each other around, like spinning marbles, making it difficult to think in a straight line.

It had all come to an end. She wanted him to know that she was Sherrie-Lee, but it wasn't what it looked like. She began to write him a letter to tell him the truth. She had planned to give him the money to buy a house for him and Gina. She originally wrote, *though I think you could do a lot better*, but she screwed that up and put it in her pocket so that they wouldn't find it after she'd gone. He liked Gina and she supposed she was alright. Nice of her to look after her mam like she did. It probably meant that she was caring and stuff. She'd stood by him while he was in prison. And apart from all her faults, Sherrie-Lee couldn't help but notice a kind of dignity about her. A reserve. The way she held herself and didn't jump in when she'd tried to provoke her. She began the letter again, telling him how things were. She thanked him for looking after her. Said that these were probably the best eighteen days of her life (so far anyway) and that he needn't worry, his secret was safe with her. That she was honest and honourable and would never grass on anyone to anyone. Especially not a friend. She underlined the second anyone so that he would know that she hadn't told Gina about the robbery. She wanted to write a whole lot more, but she couldn't think what else to write. So she ended it by saying sorry for the terrible handwriting, that she hoped he could read it, because she wanted him to know the truth, and that she also hoped he wouldn't be too cross with her, as real friends were hard to come by. She signed her name as Zadie. She thought about taking the letter with her and posting it so that nobody but Bob could read it, but then she thought how she wanted him to read it sooner than that, so that he'd know straight away that he was safe. She could just hide it in his room, or in the packet of crackers, but how could she be sure that he'd find it and not that Gina, who had turned out to be quite the bloodhound already. She read the note back to herself. There was nothing in it to give him away. Gina might think he was doing a favour for someone he knew from prison, say someone who had taken his daughter on a bank job, and then asked Lester to keep an eye on her for a few days, until things died down. Maybe she'd even take pity on her and ask her to stay. Maybe they could adopt her as their own daughter or something. She chastised herself for her childishness. *Enough of that sentimental nonsense, Missy. That soppy stuff is just for little kids.* No doubt she'd wonder what someone was doing taking their kid to a bank job. She'd agree with her. I know, Gina, she'd say. People! They're just so irrational. She picked up the pen and added a PS, writing slowly. My dad will be grateful too, he always said a friend made in prison was a friend you could turn to. And he said that he was glad to have met a friend like you there, Lester.

She knocked on Lester's door. Gina opened it. She didn't look cross anymore. She'd been crying and her cheeks were red. She had taken her glasses off and had panda eyes where the mascara had run, and the hair at her temples was slicked back. She saw too that she had her case closed and placed on top of the bed.

I just wanted to say that I am really sorry but it isn't what it looks like. I didn't mean to cause no trouble.

Gina just looked at her in a kind of wounded dog way.

She gestured towards the bag and said, I hope you're not going. I hope I've not made you mad with Lester.

Gina sucked in her cheeks and looked back at the bag. It's hard to find somebody you trust in this life, she said, then she sat down on the bed. All the badness Sherrie-Lee felt inside doubled back on itself.

It'll all be okay. You can trust Lester. I'll leave and nothing will get back to you. You were right. I am Sherrie-Lee. Lester was just doing my dad a favour. He'd got himself into a bit of trouble taking me to the bank robbery and Lester was just looking after me until it all died down, and then I had the stupid idea of sending a ransom note. Lester had no idea about that. That was all my idea. Sorry I lied too about Lester being my uncle. I was just protecting my dad. I didn't mean to cause no trouble. Lester met my dad inside. He was just being kind. You know Lester.

Gina sniffed and then said, trying to catch up with what Sherrie-Lee was saying, Your dad robbed a bank?

Tried to. It went wrong and he had to run off.

The one on the news the other week?

Yep, she said in an exaggerated way.

The news never said anything about no kid being there. Why did your dad take you to rob a bank?

Sherrie-Lee just shrugged, trying to look pitiful and sorry at the same time. She was going to say that sometimes he took her to the park, sometimes to the pictures, sometimes to do a bank job, but it didn't feel like the right time to tell one of her jokes. Even at the best of times people didn't laugh at them and she didn't want to end up in more trouble.

I've written this note for Lester, to say sorry. You won't get no more trouble from me.

She handed a folded piece of paper to Gina, who took the note, listlessly.

Sherrie-Lee had stuffed her things in a carrier bag, and she turned and walked out of the front door, the bag scrunched up in her hand.

25

The door clicked shut behind her. Outside, the brightness of the day seemed staged. The sky too blue and clear. Not a natural sky, but like one of those you get in old technicolour films. She walked down the steps and along the pavement, pulling the hood of her jacket over her head. She didn't feel like going home, but she supposed that that was where she ought to go. She walked down the street to another street and then another. She saw that the missing cat poster was still there and walked up to it to get a good look at the picture, which was now fogged and water-blurred down one edge. Wanting to see something in the cat that would confirm it to have been the same Tiger that she had found. But it was hard to tell anything from the picture. Maybe she would get a cat one day. The thought cheered her up a bit, taking away some of the glumness that seemed to weigh in dragging at the lower half of her body. She thought about what the newspaper article had said about her. Wilful...defiant...devious. It seemed a bit extreme, and what mean things to say about the victim of a kidnap. People are supposed to say nice things about you, like when you're dead. She wondered who had described her like that. The more she thought about it the more upset she felt. But if you thought about it, wilful just meant that you could be determined and get things done. That wasn't so bad. Most people were pathetic, so anyone who was not pathetic was labelled as wilful. Defiant just meant you knew your own mind and thought different things to everyone else. That was no bad thing. Devious, well, they were just plain wrong about that. She supposed they had been referring to her telling stories and got their adjectives a bit skewed. She thought that they must have meant imaginative or creative. People round her neck of the woods, sometimes, they had trouble finding the right word for the right moment. People were always saying things like, *What's the word?* or *It'll come to me later,* and then say the first word that popped into their heads anyway, even if it wasn't quite right, like they were just glad to be done with the talking. She supposed that's how they had come up with the word devious. That's how it would have been. The reporters would have been asking a lot of questions and people wouldn't like all the questions. Or maybe the newspaper had come up with it to make the story more interesting, they'd throw anyone under a bus for a good angle. Even a child. Even a kidnap victim.

She had spent a lot of time on that ransom note. Making it look like the business. This was the first she had heard about it, though she'd checked on the TV news when Bob and Gina weren't around. She didn't want Bob finding out about it. She hadn't wanted him suspecting that it was anything to do with her. And that Gina! She knew she was going to be trouble. Even before she arrived, she had known it.

*

Sherrie-Lee was hungry. She didn't know how many hours she had been wandering the streets. She just put one foot in front of another, just taking any direction that occurred to her in the moment between steps. Sometimes her mind followed various thoughts, sometimes her mind was blank. She found herself walking through the lower part of town looking at the shop windows, the reflections in the glass, the displays inside. She couldn't say whether she had already walked this way as this was the first time she seemed conscious of where she was walking. The first time today that she had paid attention to her surroundings. At the TV shop that doubled as a pawn shop there were two rows of televisions. Someone who looked like her mother was multiplied across the screens in various sizes and shades and brightnesses. She stopped and watched, her insides shifting and shrinking on seeing that it really was her mother. The news ticker at the bottom of the screen read: The mother of Sherrie-Lee Connors appeals for her safe return. Her mam looked small and crumpled, with red shadows around her eyes. She stood beside a woman wearing a suit jacket and an I'm-all-the-business-perm. People who didn't know her mother would think she looked like a mother devastated by the disappearance of her child, Sherrie-Lee thought to herself. They would see it and feel a whole load of sympathy for her. The truth of it was that she always looked like that, even those shadows beneath her eyes. But somehow, on the screen, she looked even smaller and more hopeless and defence-less than she did in real life. The whole thing must be painful to her, she didn't even like to have her photo taken. Thinking of this fact made Sherrie-Lee feel sorry for her. She watched her as her mouth moved and imagined what she might be saying. *If you've got our Sherrie-Lee, send her back. We miss her now we know she's gone.* The pains in her legs started up again, and something shot through the back of her head, some internal spasm. She willed her mother not to open her mouth too much, not to smile. *Don't show the world your missing teeth, Mam.* Then, mercifully, the perm woman touched her by the elbow and they both moved away. The presenter took their place, back in the newsroom.

Sherrie-Lee looked behind her and then in the other direction as if deciding where to walk next. She pulled her hood tightly around her face. Near the centre of town, she circled back on herself and went to sit in the park. There was no one else around. Only Sherrie-Lee and a statue on a stone plinth of someone in long robes, wearing a crown. Small flowers of different colours had been planted round the edge of the grass that circled the statue. The forced cheeriness of them seemed to mock her. The bright colours jarred. In her head she couldn't have felt more dejected and despondent. The thought that she should perhaps not go home, that she should go somewhere else, kept surfacing in her mind. Home was the last place she wanted to be. All the sense of gloom and failure folded in on itself. She could keep up the ransom story until they coughed up the money, she could just go and pick up the money when they left it, but they wouldn't just hand it over like that. They'd keep an eye on it and pick her up when she came to get it, even if she came in disguise and ran fast like she'd originally planned. They'd still get her. She'd just been naive thinking she could get away with it. Perhaps it was for the best that Gina had put a stop to everything. She might have dragged other people with her too. She tried to think of a story to distract herself, to give herself a bit of space to think things through, but no story came.

26

Lester walked through the streets, taking turnings at random, just to keep moving, to keep his thoughts running at a pace through his mind. He had no other desire but to get to the end of this rush of thoughts and return to some clarity. What a fool he'd been. And Gina, what did she make of it all? She'd been suspicious from the moment she arrived. Had she seen through everything? And now? The situation he'd allowed himself and Gina to be put in. *Fool*. He said the word aloud as he passed through a gateway that led to the canal. As though speaking the word would somehow give it a weight he could measure himself against, allowing him to see himself from the outside. The situation crashed around him as his mind grew into an awareness of what had been going on. As though he himself had had nothing to do with any of it. He saw it from all different angles at once. Gina wouldn't have put up with any of that. She was too reasonable and wanted everything to make an ordered kind of sense that she could relate to, taking comfort from that order at the same time. He stopped walking when he reached the canal, the surface a patched blue reflection of the sky. Murky at the edges, under the shadow of the reeds. A black and white dog jumped in near to where he was standing and swam out enthusiastically in a straight line. The still blue of the reflected sky was broken by rippled furrows as the dog powered its way through the water. Then it seemed to tire or change its mind, turning in an exaggerated arc to swim back to the bank. A man walked past as the animal pulled itself onto the bank, shaking itself and following after him.

Lester and the man exchanged a nod of acknowledgement, but no comment seemed necessary. Lester was glad that conversation had not been attempted. He breathed in deeply, filling even the outermost part of his lungs. He held his breath and slowly exhaled so that he had to focus only on the distorted rhythm of his own breathing. Again, he inhaled with increased restraint. Holding it. Five seconds. Seven seconds. Ten seconds. Exhaling. Whole minutes passed with his sole focus being the increased effort of his breathing.

He took up the path again in the direction that led away from town. The look on Gina's face, when she had come through the door holding the newspaper, came back to him. The wide-open expression of her eyes, glaring, questioning. Her words. *Don't you think this Sherrie-Lee Connors looks like our Zadie?* Not a question. A statement. An accusation. Furious. Taunting. The final proof of everything she held against him. What a complete fool he'd been to even let Zadie follow him home. To let her into his flat. And then when he had been determined that she should go home, he had let her convince him that it was in his best interests if she stayed, cutting the trail that might have led back to him if they picked her up and questioned her. He laughed at it now, thinking against his present predicament. She'd been convincing. He'd give her that much. Had she played him from the beginning? The kidnap plan. The ransom. Had it been in her mind from the very start? He thought of the word from the newspaper. Devious. He shook his head, embarrassed at how easy he'd been to convince. How he'd just gone along with things. He closed his eyes and stopped walking. He felt an urgency to get back to the flat. Take control of everything. He took his phone out of the pocket of his jeans to check the time. To see how long he'd been out walking. There were no missed calls. No messages from Gina. He thought back to when he left. The walking into the sofa as he was leaving the room. Too furious to see where he was going. The slam of the door behind him. And then when it was just the two of them, after he had left. What Gina would have said to Zadie? What *Zadie* would have said? He picked up the pace of his walk. The thought that Gina would've left invaded his mind. Taking root there. It would've been the final straw for her. She wouldn't have even needed to question Zadie. She would have known it all by then. She would have heard the slam of the front door and responded by packing her bags and going back home to her mam's. You don't get no second chances with a woman like Gina. Once she'd made up her mind about something. He felt hollow at the thought of it. The hollow doubled back through him at the thought that he'd brought it all on himself.

27

Sherrie-Lee headed towards the road that led towards her estate at the outskirts of town. She pulled her hood back, letting her hair blow about in the draughts made by passing cars. What did it matter if anyone saw her now? All that was over. She watched the cars as they passed her, trying not to breathe in all the traffic fumes, and thought that she should've taken the back road out of town. The passing cars seemed to slow until she was walking faster than they were moving. Just ahead she could see there was some obstruction in the road, but couldn't make out what it was. She increased her pace as she walked towards it. A wheel of some kind of cart was wavering in the air, the cart it was attached to upended, and a man was standing beside it. A small horse was laid on the ground in front of it, breathing unevenly. The back of its head was facing the pavement and Sherrie-Lee could see its eye moving around wildly, as though it was straining to see her.

What's wrong with it? she asked the man.

I dunno. She's had some kind of seizure. She was fine before and then she fell to her knees and just keeled over. The man crouched down by the head of the horse, loosening the bridle. Standing just above him, Sherrie-Lee could see that he had thick, entangled, blonde hair and that his skin was brown and freckled at the same time.

She crouched down next to him and patted the neck of the horse. The horse had sweated so much it made her hand wet. She was a deep chestnut brown with a rough, scruffy black mane falling about her neck. Her dark eye looked out, wild and knowing. There was mucus collected around the corner and spreading beneath it.

I've called my brother to come with his truck. His knee was shaking and jolting the elbow that rested upon it, up and down in rapid movements. In his hand was a black leather blinder that he had removed from the bridle of the horse. He stood up and looked back at the traffic building up behind, shoving the blinder into the pocket of his jeans. The two-lane road had been reduced to a single line of traffic as cars manoeuvred around the collapsed creature. People craned their necks to look down at the horse as they passed, slowing when they should have been speeding up, to get a better view.

The man bent down over the body of the horse, unbuckled the breeching strap and began unwinding it from the shaft of the sulky. Sherrie-Lee stroked the horse's neck as the man reached underneath. The creature snorted weakly but made no attempt to move, her eye seeming to calm and dull. The fur on her neck was slick and gritty with sweat. White lines of crusted salt marked the contours of her muscles. Her breathing became small and shallow. Looking up along the pavement ahead, Sherrie-Lee vaguely recognised a man walking towards them. Even at a distance he was familiar looking because of his mass of blonde dreadlocks: the man from the IDAW meetings. He walked in an uneven line, sometimes close to the wall and sometimes towards the outer edge of the pavement, seemingly absent and without purpose. He bent his knees slightly as he approached close to where Sherrie-Lee was kneeling.

What's happened here? he asked, his head bowed towards the kneeling girl.

The man said he thinks she's had a seizure. Sherrie-Lee nodded toward the fallen horse and continued stroking her neck.

He looked up and nodded towards the man, who had moved towards the sulky and was busy removing the trace straps from the singletree bar at the front of the cart.

A white pickup pulled up in front of them and a man in a check shirt got out of the passenger side. Alright, Ned, he said to the first man as he let the tailgate down at the back of the truck. Another man climbed out of the driver's side and came to join them. As the three of them spoke Sherrie-Lee felt something change in the horse. When she looked down at her face she saw that the animal's eye had changed. An opaque film had covered it and she realised, with a shock, that the horse was dead. She wanted to cry out and tell Ned, but some sense that he already knew held her back.

She continued stroking the neck to ease it through to the other side. The way she had done when her nan had died, when she had kept holding her hand for a long time afterwards, because it had seemed then that death was not an instant thing, but a kind of journey. A journey for which every being might need a bit of support for. She thought of all the life draining from the horse: the heart stopping, the organs closing down, the brain slowly ceasing to read the creature's body, its thoughts and sensations. All of what made her alive coming to an end.

The two men who had arrived in the truck pulled the sulky away from the back of the horse, sliding the left shaft from beneath the weight of her, parallel with the visible shaft above. They pulled the whole contraption to rest on the pavement. Deftly, and without speaking, they moved their attention to the horse herself. Ned came to stand by the front, the man in the check shirt at the rear end and the third one at the hip.

Would you give us a hand here? Ned said to the IDAW man, whom Sherrie-Lee had forgotten about until that moment. Stepping back to allow him to join the others at the horse's shoulder, she tried to remember his name.

There was a count of three, and the four men picked up the horse, straining against the weight as they began to lift her towards the back of the truck. Ned crouched under the front part of her to support the weight as they slid her part-way onto the truck, before jumping into the bed of the pickup to ease the bulk in by pulling at the breast plate and harness straps, while the others pushed and held the rest of the body up. Come on there, girl, he encouraged, exhaling the words in the last reserves of his breath. The labour was paused when only part of the horse's rump was still to be pushed into the back of the pickup. The trailing reins and straps were folded up and thrown next to the horse.

She's a weight for a small horse, the truck's driver said.

Aye, she is that, said the other man. One more push and we'll be done.

They heaved against the horse until the tailgate could be brought up and fastened. The sulky was placed on top of the creature, which didn't seem right to Sherrie-Lee. They passed the reins between the spokes of the wheels to keep the trap in place, then the three of them got into the front cabin and Sherrie-Lee and the IDAW man watched as they indicated into the traffic and drove away.

A few moments of silence passed between them before the IDAW man said to Sherrie-Lee, Hey. You're that new recruit, aren't you?

She was surprised that he'd remembered her at all.

I thought I recognised you. You know, we couldn't save that horse, but there are other animals that need us.

Sherrie-Lee was still thinking about the horse and didn't respond. She noticed he had a Proud to be Vegan badge on his cargo shorts, next to a black and white one with an interlocking V and A, which reminded her of that car logo. He wore a couple of other badges too. Ones she didn't recognise.

Do you want to hear about the animals that still need saving? What you up to now?

I was just on my way home.

He looked away when she said that, so she started to step away, get on her way.

If you have ten minutes to spare, we just got a bit of a mission with IDAW. I was just gonna drive out to a laboratory and give the place a bit of a reccy, if you want to come along and help?

Well. She hesitated. What do you want me to do?

Just have a look at the place. See what you think about it, you know, for the next meeting. I'll fill you in when we drive over there. They're pouring acid on beagles and then testing creams on them.

Wow, Sherrie-Lee said. That is horrible.

I know. They literally pour acid on the dogs' backs. I mean, onto their skin. Can you imagine how that burns? Our skin's all we got, man! He looked at her. He had moved to stand in the shadow of the wall. Even though he had blonde hair his eyelashes were dark so that he seemed to have thin blackish outlines to the outer rims of his pale blue eyes. It looked like the remnants of eyeliner. Like when someone wears makeup and goes to bed in it. The next day it looks like that.

Well? What do you think? Wanna come along?

Sherrie-Lee looked back along the road that she had come from. The traffic had lulled and exhaust fumes shimmered in the heat on an open stretch of tarmac. She thought about how it would be when she got home and breathed in a long slow breath. She felt the IDAW man edge slightly towards her.

He raised his eyebrows and half-smiled as though it was already a done deal and said, It won't take long and it'll be good to have someone else to back it up.

Okay. She couldn't really say no to helping those poor beagles.

They walked together in the direction Sherrie-Lee had already been headed, to where there was a white van parked up on the curb, its hazard lights flashing.

Heat gushed from the cab when he released the van door. She inhaled the smell of old grease and metal as she climbed up onto the seat and waited as he went round to his side. There was a whoosh of traffic as he opened his door. A car beeped at him. Wazzock, he muttered under his breath as he got in beside her.

She put on her seat belt.

He looked at her and seemed to stall. Actually, Sherrie-Lee, this is a secret mission. Best not have those cameras catching us on film, eh. He nodded towards the road ahead and unclunked her seat belt for her. Crouch down there for a bit. Just through the rest of town. I'll tell you when you can come out. Just in case we get seen.

Sherrie-Lee did as she was told. She noticed that he'd called her Sherrie-Lee when she'd always signed in as Zadie at the group. And he'd done a reccy of where all the cameras were. Well. That didn't mean much. So had she. When you lived on the edge, you had to be aware of all kinds of stuff that normal people never needed to pay attention to. She tried to find all her impressions of the man from the meetings she'd been to.

It's Robert? Right?

Robyn, he said quickly, looking into the rear view mirror.

They didn't say much for a while.

Saw your story in the paper. They got some story running on you, Sherrie-Lee.

Yep. I've seen it too.

Even on the news, they got it running. They say you been kidnapped.

Yeah, she sighed. It was a misunderstanding. A bit of a game that went wrong.

She thought about his name. It was a strange name for a man. Being called after a bird. It was a girl's name at best. She remembered that Robyn seemed to stay on the sidelines at the meetings. He'd not spoken until that last one and she couldn't remember him being at the town hall protest, or the one at the woodland. Perhaps he was more part of their intelligence. Focussing on new missions, targeting the right people and stuff like that. She thought back to the meeting she'd seen him speak at and thought that he had seemed to be part of the organising side. She thought briefly about mentioning the woodland protest. Holding her crouching position by the base of the seat, she saw that he had a long scar down the side of his leg, starting above his knee and stretching down the front of his shin. It was red and at least a centimetre thick. A proper medical scar. Not anything from some fall or accident. From a quick glance she saw that he was chewing some kind of small stick, like part of a cocktail stick. He moved it around in his mouth, chewing quickly, pushing it out so it protruded from his lips, before pulling it back in again.

You can come out now, he told her. He took his eyes off the road to glance at her quickly as she pulled herself up from the floor.

Sherrie-Lee sat back in the seat and put her seat belt on. In the sunlight that came through the windscreen, she could see all the dirt and the dust in the corners, beyond the reach of the wipers. Blonde hairs on Robyn's arms showed up golden and exaggerated where the light touched them. There were a lot of small, white scars on his hands and a thick line of dirt under his thumb nails.

So is the lab far? she asked.

Lab?

With the beagles.

He smiled. Nah. We're nearly there.

The van turned into an industrial estate, and they drove round it, pulling up opposite a low building, built from grey corrugated metal, or clad in the stuff. There were no windows in the building, no signs on the exterior. Sherrie-Lee supposed that when laboratories did these kinds of experiments they had to keep a low profile, so no one would know what was going on. There was a lot of stuff going on that people didn't know about. A lot of stuff. Much more than people could imagine. Much more than people would believe.

That's where it's all happening, he said, looking back from the building towards Sherrie-Lee, raising his left eyebrow. They were quiet again as they contemplated the building.

A game you said. How so? he asked.

She looked at him. Oh that, she said. Well, I got kind of carried away. I was staying at a friend's for a while and I wrote a ransom note to say that I'd been kidnapped. I didn't really expect it to get so out of hand. For them to take it so seriously. I mean, I wanted them to I suppose, when I wrote it, but didn't really expect it to all pan out like that.

No kidding? A genuine look of disbelief crossed his face.

Sherrie-Lee nodded.

That's pretty cool. I never met nobody before that staged their own kidnapping. I mean that is fucking something, Sherrie-Lee. He breathed out a low laugh.

She shrugged. She remembered the excitement that she herself had felt when Gina had come in with the newspaper and then how quickly it had all fallen away. It all seemed a long time ago to her now, even though it had all happened not much more than a few hours ago. Almost like it wasn't even her that had done it all. It seemed that far away. Another Sherrie-Lee in another universe. A random act spinning out of control.

Respect, Sherrie-Lee. Robyn said. Ha! He seemed to be thinking over what she said. After a few moments he added, And they didn't suspect a thing? He laughed again.

Sherrie-Lee thought about the beagles inside the building. She thought about where they might be and how many of them were kept in there.

So, you had someone who would pay the ransom, then?

My dad would pay it. Fifty thousand is nothing to him. He works for NASA so I don't get to see him much, she said, throwing in a tone of nonchalance, as though she were used to her wealthy dad and all the work he did for NASA.

NASA?

Yep. He's their expert on dark matter. It's essential to the working of the universe and it holds everything in place. And we wouldn't exist if it weren't for dark matter. It made the Big Bang possible. Dark matter is the future of space exploration.

So what did your note say then?

Just, you know, the basics. If the fifty thousand were handed over then I could be returned safe and sound. You know, basic ransom note stuff. How much. When. Where. You know, all the details you would need.

Robyn looked at her, raising his head in the beginnings of an exaggerated nod. He exhaled sharply. That is pretty impressive, Sherrie-Lee. Not many people could pull something like that off. I mean to think of it and be in a position to set it all up and pull it off. Not many people, Sherrie-Lee.

Sherrie-Lee shrugged and thought of Bob. Gina must have given him the letter by now. She wondered if everything was okay with them. If she'd been forgiven.

So how come you were just on your way home, then?

Suppose I got tired of the whole thing.

Just like that? Without picking up the money? There was a brightness in Robyn's eye. When you looked closely at his face you could see he was a lot older than he seemed.

Yeah. I dunno. It seems daft to me now. Sherrie-Lee felt overwhelmed by a wave of exhaustion, which seemed to come over her all at once. The pickup was set up for next Friday, she added quietly.

After all that work. And you just had a week to go. Robyn had kept the part-cocktail stick in his mouth throughout and now he held it between his front teeth. He seemed to be deep in thought, staring out at the low building ahead of them.

Think what that kind of money could do for the cause, Sherrie-Lee. We could still do it you know. Pick it up on Friday. What do you think?

Sherrie-Lee thought it over for a minute. She wouldn't have to go home at least. Not yet, anyway. But the whole thing seemed childish and naive to her now. It would be her who'd be picked up at the pickup. Simple as that. There was no way she would get away with it. She would be sent to some institution for delinquents like Keeley Downes's little brother. Even if they did cough up the money, which Gina had said that they never do. No, she couldn't agree to that. And what would Bob think of it all?

So you were just going back home? Were they expecting you then?

Yep. I should be there now. They'll be wondering what happened.

He started up the van.

Are we not going to get out, go have a look around? she asked, looking out at the building as they started to move away.

Next time.

What about the beagles in there now?

He smiled a half-amused, self-satisfied kind of smile and shifted the van into reverse, not answering Sherrie-Lee's question. Beagles were being tortured ten metres away and he was smiling. A shadow of worry re-entered part of her mind. His left arm gripped the back of her seat as he looked back behind them. She noticed that he smelled of stale sweat. It was not overpowering, like it had been building up for days. She just noticed it now that his arm was raised. Sweat from today that had dried and then been sweated over again.

It's good that people dedicate their time to helping animals, she said, trying to push this new nervousness aside but feeling it instead rise and swell in her throat.

Just helping protect them from people. Us humans. Something went wrong in our heads. We think we're the boss of everything. That everything is there for us to take from, to hunt and kill and harm. We think that all the other creatures are there for our benefit, for our profits. But that's all fucked. It's not how it should be. We got to learn how to co-exist. He wiped his mouth with the back of his hand and tapped the top of the steering wheel, impatiently.

Well, it's good that people like you are there to do it.

He huffed slightly. Problem is, protesting don't do no good. You gotta be more radical than that. People ignore protesting. You got to do things they can't ignore.

He looked at her, as if to gauge her reaction, before continuing in a more animated voice. The IDAW is okay, but it don't go far enough. He articulated the letters individually this time when he referenced the group. There was a mocking lilt to his voice when he said those letters. You got to do something they can't ignore. You've got to be prepared to go full in. It's a war. You gotta do some real damage, where it matters, be prepared to damage stuff and cost them money. That's all they really care about in the end. Profit. When things stop making a profit, that's when things change. You gotta target things. Learn people that that's the way things have to be done.

Sherrie-Lee sat quietly, looking ahead.

Fuck. Sherrie-Lee, just think what that kinda money could do for the cause. Did you know, Sherrie-Lee, just a few companies are responsible for destroying the whole fucking planet?

Chevron, Exxon, BP, Shell, Gazprom, Aramco. A few others. Fucked up the planet for their own gain. They got to pay for it. All the damage they've done. It's only fair. But nobody gives a fuck. All the politicians are interested in is all the backhanders they get from these people. All the bribes. These companies. These elites. They're the ones really in charge. And if anyone calls them out on it, they're the ones made to look starkers. And the more you say, the more fucking starkers you're made to look. Until in the end, you just go with it and go fucking raving mad. He lifted his hand and wiped across his eyebrow. He seemed to be pulling at his eyebrow, though it was done outside her field of vision and she couldn't get a proper look.

That's true, Sherrie-Lee said. It's okay to drop me anywhere here. I can just walk from here.

Yeah, over there. Or a bit further down, she added when a minute had gone by without him responding.

Sherrie-Lee, we need to think about that money a bit more. We don't want to be letting no opportunity go without thinking it all through, do we? Let's be reasonable about it. It's our due. You can't set up something like that, draw everyone in and then just walk away before you get your hands on the money.

After a few minutes he added, I mean fuck. Fuck. Fuck. He put his foot down on the accelerator and laughed a strange hiss through his teeth.

Sherrie-Lee's will melted, it pooled on the seat, to the floor. Making it feel wet, as though she'd peed herself. The draught of air coming through the open windows made her feel cold suddenly. She looked at him out of the corner of her eye. He had pulled himself up closer to the steering wheel and was looking ahead, intently. His eyes were narrowed and his lips moved as though reacting to the contours of some internal conversation he was having with himself. All the while, through all the talking and the hissing, he still kept the little bit of cocktail stick in his mouth.

We got to think this all through, he repeated. He spat the stick out of the window.

They'll be waiting for me at home, she said quietly. Her hands gripped each other on her lap and she dug her nails into the fingers of her other hand as they curled into each other more tightly.

But you're still kind of missing?

Sherrie-Lee's head tried to go in one direction. She swallowed hard as her throat narrowed and a fog swirled inside her skull. *Stay cool.* I was going home, she said quietly.

He looked at her to get the measure of her. She returned his look, directly in the eye to show it was the whole truth, but could not bring herself to say any more.

Fuck, he said again, banging the steering wheel with both palms.

They drove on in silence.

After a while of driving through country lanes, the van pulled up outside a small croft-like house, surrounded, on three sides, by fields. There were no other buildings around. The van started up again and drove onto the grass, bumping over the rough ground to the back of the building, so it was hidden away, even from the dirt road at the front.

We're gonna hang out here for a few days, Sherrie-Lee. See how things lie. His eyes narrowed, wrinkling up, as he looked at her. The van's automatic windows closed. There was a slight twitch in his upper lip. That's what we're gonna do, Sherrie-Lee. Wait here a few days. He looked straight into her eyes, but she showed no response. He had a lot of grey hair in his hairline above his forehead. He stayed staring at her as though waiting for her to say something.

Why? she said, not taking her eyes off him.

Robyn half-smiled, but didn't say anything. Then, without warning, he laughed loud and quick. When he stopped, there was no trace of any amusement in his face. He looked worried and serious. His left eye flickered.

The van clicked. Locked. She watched his reflection in the passenger door mirror, as he walked round the side of the house. She tried the doors anyway, when he was out of view. She thought she knew what he was up to. He was going to be predictable in that sense. But then, and this is what worried her, there was also something a bit sinister about him. Something too loose cannon. Like he could flip over some trivial thing. Do something senseless. The way he hissed through his teeth. There was something animal about it. Something deranged. That weird smile. The cold, odd look in his eyes.

She turned round in the seat and lifted herself up so she could see the house through the back window of the van. She could make out a single window in the back of the house. A torn curtain hung across it. There was nothing else, just that window. The torn curtain. The low roof.

She sat back in the seat and looked out at the fields which dipped away dramatically ahead of her. She felt remote from herself, removed as though she were a character in a film. Sheep were dotted about. Frozen to stillness by the distance. How passive they were, out there munching grass, indifferent to their own futures. They could all be going to the slaughterhouse tomorrow. It would make no difference. They would just carry on as they always did.

She chastised herself for the second or third time. She had felt that something was not quite right, even before she got in the van. She should have followed her instincts and not got suckered in with all that stuff about beagles. Probably it wasn't even true. He didn't seem to know what she was talking about when she'd asked about the lab. She'd read in a science magazine in the library about the importance of following your instincts. It wasn't just superstition. It was an inbuilt defence mechanism meant to alert you to danger. Instinct was part of our evolution. It was in our DNA, designed to protect us from predators. She had read all this stuff and knew it, but why hadn't she acted on it? She thought of the welfare woman at school, how she would look at her with an expression of forced patience and say, *Sherrie-Lee, to know and not to do is not to know.* It sort of made sense, now. Now that she thought of it in this new context. She had never tried to make sense of it before because she always felt the woman was too patronising, like a lot of those types. She was sure they meant well, most of them, but somehow they just always seemed to pitch the whole thing in the wrong way. They never really listened to anything you said, even though that is what they were paid to do. There was something insincere about them too. That's what got up her nose about them. The fakery. At least people were sincere where she came from.

28

She was woken up by a tap on the window. She looked up. It was Robyn smiling in an exaggerated way, close to the window. So close you could see spittle stretching between his teeth. His insane, wide smile. He was like the man from the fucking *Shining*. He held up two bags of crisps, one at either side of his head. He looked in, like he was expecting some kind of reaction, like a response to the crisps or something. He kept smiling and then he nodded towards her, the bags of crisps like oversized ears. He walked round the front of the van, opened the driver's door and put the stuff on the seat. He pulled out a plastic flask from a side pocket of his trousers and put that on the seat with the crisps.

He kept looking at her, as though he wanted to say something, or he wanted *her* to say something, then he shook his head and whistled through his teeth. One long note.

Well, Sherrie-Lee, it looks like you're still missing. They still got you on the news. He stayed standing in the door frame of the van, looking in on her. His eyes were wide and bright, glinting in the dark. He smiled again and nodded at her, and when he turned his head slightly as he changed his position in the door frame, he kept his eyes fixed on her. His chin jutting out slightly in a kind of challenge or like he was toying with the thought of saying something else.

Sherrie-Lee looked at him, but didn't say anything. He looked odd in this half-light of the van's open door. There were pale puffy patches under his eyes and at the sides of his mouth too.

He sighed and seemed to puff his chest out as he breathed, like she'd seen gorillas do in wildlife documentaries. She half-expected him to bang his chest with his fists and roar. He looked off, down towards the valley. There was no moon out, only a few scattered stars in the black sky. The meagre light escaping from the van showed up tufts of coarse, sere grasses in the field next to them. The darkness beyond was complete and silent. Even the sheep had quietened down.

Well, Sherrie-Lee. Goodnight, then. He stayed looking at her, grinning for a few exaggerated moments. He had this way of holding himself, his body seemed to hover before committing to a movement or as though he'd changed his mind at the last moment. He pulled away and closed the door of the van, without locking it.

Sherrie-Lee stayed absolutely still. Her breathing deepened. Her heart thudded so much she could hear it pounding in her ears. In the mirror, she watched as he retreated. Just before he disappeared from view, he turned round, holding his hand forward. Her hand went to the handle. Too late. He'd clicked it locked in the same instant. The van flashed in response and fell silent. From the corner of her eye she saw him through the mirror, standing at the end of the house, and although she couldn't make out his face any more she imagined him looking at her, pleased with himself and smiling.

Wacko, she muttered under her breath.

After a minute or so, she picked up one of the bags of crisps. Chicken flavoured, she read the packet. Nice, she said aloud. Some wacko vegan he is. She opened the bag and inhaled the delicious smell.

All the worrying she did about stuff so that it wouldn't happen. She hadn't seen this coming. If you're worried about specific things it stops them from happening. Things don't usually happen when you're worrying about them. She did all the worrying for

Joshy because he couldn't do it for himself. It was her worrying that kept him safe. That kept all the dangers away. If there was no one to keep their eye on the ball, to look out for him, there was no telling what might happen.

She thought about the green glass in the deserts of New Mexico. When the first atomic bomb was dropped there, the sand liquified in the heat from the blast as it was thrown into the air and became glass as it cooled and fell back to the desert floor. She'd had a piece of green glass in her collection. She'd found it whilst walking in the cemetery. One of the graves was covered with the stuff. But after she'd read about the green glass of New Mexico, she'd taken it back to the cemetery where it couldn't do any harm, just in case it came from there and was full of radiation.

29

Lester looked up at the traffic of legs walking on the street outside. Heels tapping sharply against the pavement, black loafers slapping the surface. Boots pounding. The call centre where he worked was in the basement of an office block in the centre of town. Through the elongated, rectangular windows near the ceiling the lower reaches of the street outside was visible. It was five-thirty and the numbers of passers-by had thronged as people finished work and left offices and shops. His own shift finished at six. He looked along his row at the other people talking into their headsets, facing computer screens. His last five calls had run to answer machines. He had pressed the key to indicate a call back each time and waited for his next call to come up. The calls came up automatically. Somebody had been sacked the week before for responding to a *fuck off* on the line with his own *Fuck off to you too, Sir*. That was what Lester had heard. The guy must have been really fed up with the job, because everyone who worked there knew that that would get you fired on the spot.

Rarely did Lester take the bus back from work, preferring to walk and save money. Already a couple of the small bars he walked past were filled with the after-work crowd. He glanced in through the large glass windows. People sat at stools around high tables in their business clothes, talking and drinking from wine glasses. A desire to be a part of it flooded into him and he thought briefly about calling Gina to come and meet him. Imagined himself waiting for her at one of the tables, a vodka and coke already purchased for her and there at the table when she arrived.

He turned to walk through the main pedestrian area. A bunch of high school kids milled around Market Square, sitting on the steps of the museum, drinking from cans of energy drinks. A large group of homeless people congregated at the other side of the steps, their bags of possessions behind them, piled up in the corner under the covered part of the entrance. A sleeping bag was already laid out. Pigeons strutted on stunted feet, others cooed and gobbled from window ledges above. A waiter stacked chairs outside an outdoor cafe, then dragged a table through the doorway. A woman poured frothy water into a drain outside the pie shop; she held a long-handled sweeping brush against her shoulder while she tipped the bucket with both hands. It felt good to be walking through town. The busyness of the place infected him with a buzz of optimism.

As he turned into his own neighbourhood, he saw that the big man, who often looked out and watched people from the corner plot of his garden, was there. He moved his weight from foot to foot when he saw Lester approach but did not acknowledge him when Lester nodded and said hello, which Lester always did even though the man never responded to his greeting. Whenever Lester saw him, he was always standing in the same place, wringing at his hands which he held in front of his chest, his face expressionless and child-like despite the size of him. Sometimes another man, decades older and half the size of the big man, was in the yard too. His dad, Lester had thought on first seeing him. Poor bastards.

Gina's suitcase was by the front door when Lester entered. Gina herself was in the living room, sitting neatly on the sofa.

What's up, Gina? He stood in the doorway.

It's still all over the news, Lester. She's still missing is what they're saying.

Lester rubbed at the sides of his mouth with his thumb and index finger.

I don't know what to say, Gina. He came to sit next to her on the edge of the sofa.

So much for that letter she left you, Lester.

Why's your bag out there?

Gina shrugged, I don't want to be getting mixed up with all this business, Lester. Whatever it is that's going on. I don't want to be part of it.

C'mon, Gina. There's nothing going on here. You're okay. He put his arm around her shoulder and pulled her towards him.

She resisted. Clearly something's going on, Lester. She shuffled around so that she was facing him. How could you get mixed up in all this after all we've been through? It doesn't make any sense.

Everything's gonna be okay. None of it has anything to do with us.

How can you say that? She stood up and walked towards the window.

All that stuff she said. I don't know if any of it's true. It's all such a mess.

Lester rubbed his face with both hands. He stood up and went to stand behind Gina.

I can't stay here, Lester. I don't know what to believe anymore.

30

She woke to the throb of her ankle and the sound of sheep, which seemed to have moved closer in the night. They bleated from one direction and then another in a kind of mass ventriloquy. It had taken her a long time to get to sleep, and she was still tired. And stiff. And hungry. She turned round to check on the house. There was no sign of life there. She wondered what time it was. The clock on the van showed only zeros whenever the engine was turned on. It seemed early. Outside, a light rain fell soundlessly. Mist veiled the distant hills, like the grey of the sky had been pulled down onto them. She longed to step outside. To let the rain fall on her skin, wetting her hair and face and clothes.

She thought about what Robyn had said, about all the stuff still being on the news. Bob would see that and wonder what was going on. He would think that she'd been lying in her letter. That she was still up to something. It was the least of her problems now, but somehow it was the thought that made her the saddest as she sat in the van weighing it all up. She remembered how he had looked before he walked out that last time. That wounded look. The anger. She imagined, again, how he must have felt. That he had trusted her and she had gone and done that to him. Sending a ransom note and not even telling him about it. Some friend she had been. She tried to picture them at home, him and Gina. She imagined that Gina would have quite a few things to say about the whole thing. *What was ya thinking, Lester? Harbouring a bank robber's daughter? If she even was that and not just some weird kid. Why, Lester, do ya go and get yerself so mixed up with all the wrong things that are going on, all the helpless cases?* She wondered if she had nagged the whole truth out of Bob, or worked it out. If Bob had let something slip, with all the commotion around the letter she left and the news story, and then with her still being missing and making it drag on for so much longer. He wasn't good at telling lies. Then she thought about how down in the dumps he had been when he hadn't been able to visit Gina that Sunday, and how sad he would be if all the goings on had made Gina up and leave him. Thinking of all this pushed her to the verge of crying. That Robyn was a piece of work. ASSHOLE, she said aloud, looking in the side mirrors to make sure he hadn't made an appearance.

Robyn had said a lot of weird shit. She couldn't take it all in, he rambled so much. He didn't have any friends. He had said that people weren't to be trusted, that only a fool trusted people. They were a delinquent species, wired for destruction. They were only ever in it for themselves. The ones that seemed to be on your side of things, they were the worst. You had to keep an eye on them even more than any of the others. That's the way it worked. You had to work them for your own gain. It wasn't true that humans were a social species, that was a political trick. A myth. They were a solitary species, anti-social at best. He had said something about how you only had to read Mack Velly to know that.

The funny thing was that she agreed with Robyn on most of the animal stuff, even though he was unhinged. People didn't care, they were selfish, and more than that they were irrational, incapable of acting even in their own best interests... No bees, no people... They would never take notice. *Every extinction brings you closer to your own extinction.* She had read that somewhere and thought it pretty cool, that. She wished she'd thought of it. People didn't want to listen. It always astonished her how little tolerance people had for the truth. Some people got it though. Some people knew it. Even a nut job like Robyn got it. It was a real concrete thing for some people. Look at the lament for the lost species she had gone to. Then she thought about how there had only been twelve people there. People were blind. They didn't care. Or at least, enough people didn't care. She had ideas of her own on the subject. She had even given it a name. She called it the Stupid Gene Theory. Everybody had this gene, but it was dormant until people hit their teens. Then somehow it got switched on around those years. She even had a theory that maybe this gene gets activated because of all those teenage hormones. It gets switched on and it never gets switched off again. And when this gene is activated people start to see things differently. All the things that are really important get sidelined and this gene tells them that stuff like caring for the animals and the world is not important. That it's childish and trivial. Some people are resistant to it switching on, but these people are very rare. When the stupid gene does get activated, people stop caring and act as though the destruction of the entire planet wasn't relevant to them. As though they could go and live on Mars or something, like they're all Elon-fucking-Musk. The whole thing was fucked. She hoped it would never happen to her, that she'd be one of those people resistant to the switching on of the stupid gene.

But that Robyn, all his talk of blowing stuff up. That was the problem with him. He was all skewed in his mind. He belonged in the big house on the edge of town. The thought of him made her feel on edge inside her stomach. His unpredictability. The weird smile, like it was some kind of mask that just appeared on its own. Always fixed in exactly the same way. He smiled at odd things too. That was another sign. She thought he was younger when she had seen him at the meetings, hanging around with those other people, who all looked to be in their twenties, maybe younger than that. But when you saw him in the daylight you could see all the lines in his skin, hundreds of them bunched around his eyes and across his forehead. She saw in a revelatory moment when he was talking and twitching that it wasn't about his dedication. He was a fraud on that front. He was unhinged. He had nothing else. She saw it clear and true. As though it were written down on a signpost pointing to him. Like the one to the folly. Only this one said *Nut Job*.

She wished she'd saved one of the bags of crisps from last night. That would've been the really smart thing to do. She was starving. She wondered what Joshy was doing, whether he was awake, if he'd had anything to eat yet. At home, it wasn't always certain that there'd be food, though they always tried to keep boxes of cereal bars in for Joshy. He could get very upset when he was hungry. She hoped someone was looking out for him. She didn't know how long she'd be stuck here. And then there was the other possibility too, but she didn't want to even think of that.

She had slept fitfully. Her body was tired of sitting in the van. She tried pulling her legs up and altering her position, but it only seemed to work for a few minutes. Her body would jolt awake, and it was hard to get comfortable; although it was July it was really cold at night. She tried lying down on the hard cold surface of the back of the van. She had heard somewhere, or probably she had read it in some book, that if you stay too long in the sitting position, it leads to blood clots in the brain and you die.

She had woken, full of a dream she had been having and of the ache of leaning her shoulder and head against the door of the van. She had been dreaming that she was in an IDAW meeting, and the woman with the Tintin hair was speaking, and all the people in the room were sitting listening to her. But when, in her dream, Sherrie-Lee looked around at them, they were not the people who were usually there but people she knew from other places. There was a librarian, not Claire, but someone else from the library, sitting just behind her. In her dream she was aware of trying to be discreet when looking at people, ready to look away if they looked at her. Though they didn't ever look at her. Nobody was even aware of her. Her social worker was there. She had a huge handbag on her lap and big looped earrings. And Luke was sitting on a chair on the stage, facing the people in the audience. Well, not really facing, but looking down, and he had his hair kind of drawn over his face. In the meeting they were discussing killing his dog, Pearl, because she was a freak of nature. Inbred. Pearl was nowhere to be seen. Nothing more was being said as the dream shifted into a silent phase and just before she woke up, she panicked that maybe it had already been done. That Pearl had already been killed. The dream left her feeling anxious. About the dog, she thought and then about how it might mean something else. How it might mean that something was going to go wrong or that something bad had happened at home.

31

Let's go, Sherrie-Lee would say to Joshy. *Come on.* Doubling up the enthusiasm for both of them.

She'd move about the room picking up one of his shoes and looking for the other one. She'd have a pair of his trousers over her arm while she looked for the shoe. He'd have his pyjamas on. He could go out in those. It would take ages getting him ready. But then she didn't want him going out in just his pyjamas, it made him seem disabled or something.

This is what it was like every time they went out. All the motions they had to go through. She missed it now though, that one focus for all her energies. She wouldn't feel annoyed by it any more if she got the chance to do it again. She wouldn't feel cross at him for not helping. She wouldn't even tell him to stop picking his nose. She tried to remember all the details about him. The way his right ear stuck out a bit and was always a bit red. The way his hair was a bit flattened at the back, from the way he always slept on it. Even his head was flattened in the same place. The way his big brown eyes always seemed concentrated somewhere else, they never looked at Sherrie-Lee, even when she was talking to him.

She thought of the documentary of the Frenchman with locked-in syndrome that she had watched. About how he was unable to move or talk. He could only blink with one of his eyelids. He had had a stroke and his wife had devised this whole way of communicating around her saying the letters of the alphabet out loud and him blinking when she got to the right letter. So they communicated like that. Letter by letter. How long it must take just to say a sentence. Imagine being loved like that. That someone would try so hard to find the thoughts trapped inside you.

From the dwindling light outside, Sherrie-Lee thought it must be gone ten o'clock. She was hungry. She must have been stuck in this van for about fifty or sixty hours. Every millimetre of the visible front part of the van had become familiar. The nick in the rubber seal near the bottom left-hand corner of the windscreen. The greenish lumps of dirt about ten centimetres across from that, nestled into the rim of the rubber. The white specks of dust on the dashboard above the steering wheel. She kicked half-heartedly at the passenger door with her left foot. She knew it was no good because she'd frustrated herself almost to tears by kicking at the windows and the back doors the day before. She thought that she'd damaged her right ankle too, maybe broken a bone in there. It still hurt a lot when she moved it. She'd always had weak ankles and knees and knew that there were a lot of bones in the foot. It was probably one of those that was broken. She could make a lot of noise, but there was no one around even to hear. If there was something heavy like one of those little fire extinguishers some vans have, or even a rock, she was sure she could smash a window and make a run for it. But there was nothing in the van except a coil of blue rope, and so far she hadn't thought of anything she could do with that. And there was the bucket which she used only reluctantly, drinking only a tiny amount of water when the dryness in her mouth and throat became uncomfortable.

The coming darkness felt hopeless and forlorn as all the colours began to disappear. Somewhere, deep inside her most primal self, she felt sad to see them go, as though the night would last forever and the day would never come again. She coaxed herself into telling a story; she didn't have the energy or the heart for one of the longer ones, so she told herself the one about the frog and the scorpion. The scorpion wanted to get to the other side of the river, so it said to the frog, Hey frog, please will you take me to the other side of the river? No way, said the frog. You're a scorpion and if I do that, you'll sting me.

Why would I do that? said the scorpion. If I did that you would die and sink and I would drown. I would not do that. The frog thought about it and saw reason in it. So the frog let the scorpion climb on his back and both of them started to cross the river. Half-way across, the scorpion stung the frog. The frog, startled, turned to the scorpion and said, Why did you do that? Now we will both die. The scorpion said, Because I am a scorpion.

It was a fable by somebody called Aesop. She'd memorised a few of them. They were short and easy to remember and bumped up her repertoire of stories without much effort. And although they were short there was a lot in some of them too. When you thought about them, they seemed to mean one thing and then another. This one was her favourite. It startled her when she first read it. It was shocking the message in it. That natures could not change. That you were what you were and couldn't improve on it. It ran wildly against what the PR of the world seemed to say. That you could be better, that everyone could change. It was a terrible message if you thought about it and it grated against Sherrie-Lee's essential optimism. Her belief that everybody could be better if they tried, if they really wanted to be. But even though it led to his death, the scorpion could not help himself. It was about self-destruction too. Short-sightedness. And that was everywhere. Look what people were doing to the planet. Then she thought about Robyn. He was definitely all scorpion. She was sure he had been bad for pretty much all of his life and could never be better. Was he born bad? Was he a bad baby, crying all the time and biting other babies so that even his mother couldn't stand him? Or did the badness come out later?

She wanted to tell herself a story to see if she still could. If she still could start one from the beginning and tell it through to the end. She supposed that she still could, even though she'd chosen a shorter one, to trick herself into doing it, almost. Though she saw too that there was no point in it. No point in any of it any more. Even if she wasn't stuck here in Robyn's van, there still wouldn't be any point. All that planning and dreaming and making stuff up. All that working towards becoming a storyteller. She could see now that it was all pointless.

32

So, we know it's this Friday, Sherrie-Lee. What we need now is the time and place. Robyn looked at her through the open door of the van, trying to be casual. And you were staying with a friend all that time?

Not the whole time. Sometimes I slept in empty houses, sometimes I snuck back to my own house after dark, when everyone else was asleep. She spoke slowly, pausing for effect. She let it sink in to his tiny deranged mind.

Wicked. He half-laughed. He looked at her, as if to weigh her up. In the light she saw that his teeth were a kind of grey colour. They were sort of crushed in, with a couple of them edging over the ones next to them. She'd never seen teeth like that before, even though nearly everyone she knew had something wrong with their teeth. He touched his chin and walked away from the van. He had his back towards Sherrie-Lee, while he looked out across the valley.

When he turned back towards her, he was still rubbing at his chin. You know what, Sherrie-Lee, we could strike a deal. We ought to get that money, put it to good use. Seeing as it's all set in motion. Finish the deal.

What's in it for me? she said, looking at him full in the face.

He was standing so close that she could see the muscles tighten in his jaw. A forced kind of smile stretched itself over the tightened muscles of his thin face. He nodded.

I see you, Sherrie-Lee. I see you.

33

Lester was hiding in a small, dank basement. It was dark except for a slit of light that came through the bottom of the closed door. The line of light diffused as it spread into the basement and showed up a long-abandoned spider's web. The web seemed to stretch and cover half the basement, the long threads broken and half-floating in the air, furred with dust. Outside, he could hear shutters banging. He closed his eyes to decipher the rhythm of the banging. Was it the erratic push of the wind, or more determined, like the testing of hands wanting to get inside? They were coming for him. Any minute now, they would be in. He looked around him, into the darkened room, hoping to find, half-hidden in the shadows, another door, to a room he hadn't noticed before, leading away from this one.

He was woken by the tunnelling of his own dreams and looked about himself, as though he was somewhere unfamiliar, not in his own room. He looked across at Gina, still sleeping, with her back towards him. He moved in closer to her so that his face was level with the nape of her neck, inhaling the warm smell of her. He closed his eyes to shut out the memory of his dream and the assault of waking. Sometimes he woke in the night from the banging sound of his dreams. On those nights he had to get out of bed to check there was no one coming for him. That the front door of his own house was safe.

You okay? Gina murmured to him, only half-awake.

Yeah, he said, nuzzling closer to her, his eyes wide open soaking in the reality of his room.

*

She had questioned him about Zadie, about Zadie's dad. More than once he thought she would leave. It hadn't helped that Zadie was still missing, that she was still in the news. He also wondered about that. Gina had continued with her questioning until he was beginning to feel sucked under by the vortex of lies, circling and layering into each other. Then all at once, by some mercy, his answers had seemed to satisfy her. Or at least formed a kind of network of coherent answers. Answers she could live with if she stopped asking more questions. That's all anyone really wanted, he thought. Though there was still something. She had been quiet over the last few days and sometimes she seemed to look at him in a long, ponderous way. Measuring something or other about him. She didn't get mad, the way some of the women he'd known used to. She internalised things, thought things through in her own way. Asked only what she needed to. That made it worse somehow. He wanted to tell her the truth about everything, just how it had happened, but he knew he couldn't. For her own sake as much as his. If she had kept on at him with her questions it would have felt better to keep up the lie. Would've made his defence more necessary.

Gina was on the phone to her sister when he came out of the shower. She didn't look at him when he entered the room, drying his hair roughly with a towel.

She's not used to her, she told him when she came off the phone. She was sitting on the arm of the chair.

She gets worried when Mam gets confused and worked up about things. Thinks something is happening all the time. She said Mam had got dressed in the middle of the night and when she asked her, where are you going, she said I'm going home. You are home, Mam, she told her. Then Mam burst into tears and said that this wasn't her home. It was an hour before she got her back to bed. That's how it is, I told her. When it happens to me, I just say, let's go to bed, Mam, and we'll go in the morning. She makes everything into a drama.

Lester came up behind her and rubbed her shoulders.

What's to become of everything, Lester?

He moved his thumbs to rub the back of her neck and kissed the top of her head.

How about me coming to live with you?

She pulled away from him and turned round to look at him, as though he had said something truly astonishing.

No. She wouldn't like that. She doesn't like men in the house, you know that, Lester. She wouldn't like that at all.

Or nearby, then. There's nothing to keep me here.

I don't know, Lester. That doesn't feel right.

He was silent then. Though he wondered what she meant about it not feeling right. Whether it was just about her mam, or whether it was something bigger than that, something that couldn't be solved in Gina's mind.

34

Eleven in the morning, Friday 29th, behind the bin facing the waste ground by the Millennium Industrial Park, Sherrie-Lee said.

He walked slowly in her direction, back to the open door of the van. When he was nearer, he bent his knees so he was closer to her level. He smiled. It was a different kind of smile. This one twitched. A vein in his forehead stuck out. Then he laughed. He threw his head back. A loud, quick burst of laughter. High-pitched. He looked back at her, staring into her eyes. And then laughed again. He was so close she could smell the sourness of his breath.

There, that wasn't hard was it. Eleven in the morning, behind the bin facing the waste ground by the Millennium Industrial Park, Robyn repeated. So now, we can just get this done, Sherrie-Lee. Everything goes okay, you can just go home.

It sounded simple, Sherrie-Lee thought afterwards. And however it worked out, she had no option but to give him all the details. Let it play through to the end. That way there was at least a small chance. If she refused. Well, she didn't know what might happen. She didn't like to think.

*

She stayed in the same position for a long time, letting weird, random thoughts enter her head and then leave again as though she had no will to oversee what went on in there. Robyn didn't

217

really care about the animals. He was a fake. Like that social worker she had once. Lorraine, with the oversized head and dinner lady body, and the exaggerated soft voice that didn't fit. Like she had practised that voice on purpose because she thought that was how to speak to children like Sherrie-Lee. Defective children. Patronising and superficial, with her nodding dog brain inside that big head, nodding and banging against the insides of her skull. The fake pretending-to-be-encouraging-smile that came with the job. It was practically part of the uniform. She was her social worker for four years, and one day Sherrie-Lee had seen her walking in town with a girl about her own age. Her daughter, Sherrie-Lee had guessed afterwards. She had been about to say hello to her, just out of politeness, though she didn't really feel like it, but as she approached, she saw that Lorraine was pretending that she hadn't seen her. She was pretending to be looking somewhere else, in a direction where there was no Sherrie-Lee.

She had to get control of her mind, she thought now. She had to take possession of it. Her mind jumped as though it was just out of reach. She had to keep her wits about her. It wasn't how she imagined it would be. She wasn't how she'd imagined she'd be. In her fantasy, being kidnapped had been a good thing. The start of something good. A new life. The life she was meant to have. That's how it had always run in her mind. It had played itself out without any threat, without detail. And she'd never imagined it would be so boring, all the long hours sitting alone in this van. She'd imagined her kidnapper to be someone she could be sympathetic to. Somebody who was kind. Like Bob had been. Whom she could like or could help become a better person. Robyn was none of these things. She felt no sympathy for him. No will to make any connection. She didn't want to make herself real for him, or entertain him with the Sherrie-Lee show.

She looked out at the fields, the sheep and the stone walls, all stretching out and falling away in front of her. She felt tired, but beyond that only a kind of numbness. Even her hunger had seeped away.

Dusk seemed to come on all at once, when the white disc of the sun dropped behind the hill. She watched it all passively. A new wave of missing Joshy crashed around her. If she got out of this okay, she would be a better sister to him. She would never abandon him again and she would do more with him, she wouldn't just leave him in front of the TV like everyone else did. She would take him on more walks. They would take the bus and go to the moors like she had done with Bob. It wasn't that far. She would learn the names of all the trees and the flowers and the birds and keep telling them to Joshy until he learned them too. It was important, that was. Learning the names of things. It was the first step towards looking after things, making them part of your world. And when she grew up and got a place of her own, Joshy could come and live with her. They would have a TV and a kitchen with a breakfast bar. And a fruit bowl full of fruit on the breakfast bar. Like normal people did.

She thought how she had brought it all on herself, by sending that ransom note. It had brought it all on for real. It had given Robyn the idea. Maybe he remembered seeing her at the IDAW meeting when her photo was appearing on the news, and then seeing her on the street with the horse had given him the opportunity, too. She felt certain that it had been just chance connections like that. That was all. Without her actions none of it would've happened. It was she who had invited fate like that. She scratched hard at her legs, though they weren't even aching. She leaned her head against the cold glass of the window and inhaled the smell of the dirt that lacquered the surface. She wondered if the Sherrie-Lee on the Earth-like planet in that distant universe brought on the same kind of problems that she did.

She looked out at the diminishing light. The leaching of the colour from the earth. The draining away, until it was just silhouettes. Then later still, even some of the silhouettes could no longer be seen. The position she was in was uncomfortable. She'd been sitting in it for too long, but she made no attempt to move. One by one, a few stars appeared. They'd probably been there for millions of years, Sherrie-Lee thought. Some of them might not even be there anymore. They are still seen because it takes so long for the light to reach us. A year is nothing to them. A human lifespan. Even a thousand years. A blink of an eye. She tried to imagine herself flying into all that space up there. Flying through all that time. Drifting. To the birth of the first stars. Coming through all that dark matter holding everything in place. Pushing it into existence. And before that, when it would just be blackness. Vast nothingness. No stars. No colour. No star dust or debris or milky ways. And then she imagined falling back through it, back to earth. A human life is no more than a speck of dust.

35

Sherrie-Lee sat muted and small inside the van. The outside loomed alien and impenetrable like a thing she could never again be part of. It breathed an indifference that would forever resist her presence. And this locked barrier of the van that she could not will herself out of was a big fuck-off sign of this. She had been expecting it to be all over at some point – that an ending would show itself, and she would know it: deep down in the depths of her stomach, in the pains in her legs, in the white blobs that came and went through her vision. She would know it in the dull thud at the back of her brain. She knew too that until then it would all be a kind of nothing. She had lost track of the order of days somewhere. Of which day it was, so that she could not work out which one came next. She tried to work up some coherent feeling, but nothing came. That was probably just as well, there was no telling exactly how long it would take. And she needed to reserve all she could until that time. Feeling took it out of people, drained people. It pulled them unnecessarily in all kinds of directions, fuelled by some spark and twist of the imagination. Messing them up, needlessly. People got on better in life when they put all feelings to the side. And the more terrible and tragic their lives the more they needed to do this, until eventually, in extreme cases, they must exist in the absence of all feeling. It tired and confused her, just thinking about it. She frowned into the distance and wondered how many hours she had spent in this van. If it had been five days, then it would have been around 120 hours. If it had been six, then 144. She should have kept better count of the days. It was hard to calculate, not having any proper access to the time. If she came out of all this, she would buy herself a watch and never be without it. She would make sure it always told the right time and make a point of looking at it all the time, just so she would know what time it was. Now, she was a double hostage, both to raving Robyn and to time itself. You wouldn't think not being able to keep track of time would be such a problem, given that everything was out of her control anyway, but it bothered Sherrie-Lee. She was a girl who liked to keep track of things. Keep a sense of order, even to what seemed beyond any order. She was extra-vulnerable, not knowing, like a piece of seaweed adrift.

Sherrie-Lee slipped into a deep sleep. She dreamt she was standing in a doorway looking out on a piece of scrubland. The doorway was the side door of a pub, *The Golden Lion*, which she knew well because when she was younger she would sometimes be sent to see if her older brother was in there. In her dream, she was standing in the doorway with a drink in her hand. A tramp came up to her and asked her for a drink, so she offered him one from her own glass, but he told her that he better have it from a different glass. She went inside to get him a new glass and poured some of her drink into it. She passed it to him and he drank it down in one go, like he was really thirsty. He drank it by throwing his head back and just pouring the liquid in. He smacked his lips together and said, looking at the glass, that that was good. That he needed that. Sherrie-Lee reached towards him to take the glass back, but instead of giving it back he looked out towards the waste ground opposite and threw the glass long and hard towards a wall some distance away. It was dark so they couldn't see the glass hit the wall, but they heard it smash. He looked back at her and smiled and said that some habits were hard to give up. When she woke, she didn't remember the dream straight away. It came to her minutes after waking when she was looking out at the landscape ahead of her. It was so clear when it came to her that she might have been remembering something that really happened. The tramp's face was so vivid. The round, reddened face, the sore on his lip. Dark brown smiling eyes and dark, straight hair flattened to his head. His beard.

Where do dreams come from? she thought as she looked out at the growing day. She had never seen the man before and yet there he was in her dream, so clear and real-looking. It was amazing to her that people so real could just be invented in a dream. Small miracles, conjuring up people. Perhaps these people have been seen before on the TV or in real life and have just been forgotten about on the surface. But the brain has stored images of them, deep inside, so that they can come out in dreams. If you really thought about it, it was something amazing. It was more amazing even than making up stories, because there were pictures too, which made it even more real. And everybody does it, even though they are asleep and their brain isn't even trying. The mind just playing on like a reel of film. On and on, image after image. She wondered, then, about blind people, people who have been blind from birth, what their dreams look like, because their brains wouldn't have a stack of images for their dreams to use. She wondered whether they saw images at all. She thought about this for a long time.

It had been a very long time since she'd had to go find her older brother in *The Golden Lion*, though it had been better at home when he was around, even though he was hardly ever at home even then. Grace was less mean, she might even have been on the borderline of nice sometimes. She didn't know why it was better. It was as though his presence brought a kind of order to the house, just by his existence there. There was more of a sense that everybody had a place.

She didn't like looking towards the driver's side and tried to avoid it as much as she could. That was Robyn's domain and she didn't want to think about him. Didn't want to spoil the inside quiet she felt about things. She wished she could open a window and feel the coolness of the night air on her face. Feel the breeze come through the window.

She looked up at the stars and thought of all the energy they contained. She looked at them and wondered at their silence. All that energy, all that fire raging, they should have been ringing out with deafening noise, screaming with rage into that vast emptiness. Even our own star in our own solar system was silent, all that distance away. It was possible, Sherrie-Lee thought, that that silence was where the future was heading, that all the animals would one day be just as silent. All the birds. There'd be no birdsong. No whirring of any insect. Everything would just be silence. All the creatures would be silent as stones. As fossils.

36

She missed Claire. She missed the conversations they used to have. Sometimes whole weeks would go by and Claire would be the only person that she had had a real conversation with. Claire always spoke to Sherrie- Lee as though she was a proper person and not defective at all. Even when Sherrie-Lee had made pronunciation mistakes, she had not made her feel small for not knowing the proper way to say something. She smiled now at the memory. The expression on Claire's face when Sherrie-Lee had told her of all the dev-*eye*-ants in her neighbourhood. The look of incomprehension, followed by a warm, amused smile of realisation. Deviants, she had told her the proper way to pronounce it. Sherrie-Lee had laughed too and confessed that she often mispronounced things when she tried out words she found in books. They'd agreed that some words were difficult to say if you just saw them written down. Claire had said that it was because English had a lot of silent letters and a lot of different rules for saying the same letters. The blue of Claire's hair had made the brown of her eyes stand out.

Sherrie-Lee had thought a lot about these conversations about words. It seemed like some incredible thing that these words had an existence beyond the books she found them in, that they should have a particular sound other than that suggested by the word's arrangement of letters. An order of stresses all their own. That they had a three-dimensional existence in the real world. That they had a sound and a shape that was known and recognised by other people.

These thoughts carried her into sleep so that the dreams that held her were comforting and calm.

*

She was woken by the click of the van door as Robyn climbed in beside her.

They drove in silence. The night air came in through the open windows, like a beckoning from a distant place. Unknown and cooling. She tried to think of all the distant places she could be in right now. All the places she had imagined herself in in the past. But at each name she conjured, her imagination blacked out and no images of anywhere would come to her mind. There was only the inside of the van. The road ahead of them. Robyn beside her. The familiar sweated-over smell of him. The sound of his snorted breath at intervals when he changed gear. He pulled a can of beer from a shelf in the car door and held it with one hand at the top of the steering wheel, pulling the ring pull off with the other hand. Gas hissed from the can and bubbles rose to the top. He took a long swig from the beer.

She wondered where they were going. Whether it was Friday already or whether he had other ideas, some other plan he'd concocted by himself. It was very dark. She recognised the outskirts of the city. A pub by a canal bridge. A block of flats. He drove fast. It must have been the middle of the night because there was no one around. He steered through a number of small side streets. Only a dim light from an occasional street lamp lit up the wet road and narrow pavements. In a darkened street near some disused factory buildings, he parked the van. He drank from the beer can and switched off the headlights. It was a dark, lonely place. The sides of the buildings surrounding them rose up, austere and foreboding.

He drained the can and squashed it in his hand. Opening the window wider, he tossed the can out onto the road. Sherrie-Lee heard the can clatter and roll on the asphalt and then the night returned to silence. She thought of all the insects that would crawl inside the can and not be able to get out.

Someone is going to just drop the money off then? And leave it there? Robyn said as he pressed the button to close the window.

Sherrie-Lee nodded but did not look at him.

Fuck, he hissed. He took money out of his pocket and straightened out the notes, placing them on the dashboard. Chewing at his thumb tip, he sighed and seemed deep in thought.

He half-turned in his seat and watched her for a minute, and then laughed. A short burst of laughter, maniacal and magnified, like it was the last time he would ever laugh. The odd high-pitch hurt Sherrie-Lee's ears. Still she kept herself from looking at him. He rubbed at his face with both hands. From his pocket, his phone pinged.

One minute, he said. Don't get no ideas. He took the money from the dashboard and got out of the van.

He had asked a lot of questions about the pickup during the day. She had gone over her answers in her head afterwards each time, examining them for mistakes, inconsistencies. Giving as little information as possible each time he asked. The necessary basics. *Don't elaborate and trip yourself up, Sherrie-Lee,* she had told herself again and again.

When he returned he started up the van straight away. Reversing without saying a word. Turning them around. Retracing the streets at speed. She had taken it to be the middle of the night, but as they approached country lanes she could see from the gathering light across the hills that it was towards morning. She must have slept for longer than she thought. The days and nights had taken on a kind of dazed endlessness, merging into each other. Time contracted and expanded and knew no sense of order. It was impossible to mark the passing of the hours, except from the position of the sun and moon. She slept and woke, regardless of the rhythm of day and night. Her food, when it was given to her, seemed also at strange, random times, so there was nothing to structure the day around. This is what it was like for captives all over the world.

Nothing had been said for a long time.

Rounding a lane, two pheasants could be seen on the road, a short distance ahead of them. Robyn put his foot down on the accelerator and sped up. One of the pheasants got away but the male had been slower to take off and they clipped it. The van slammed to a halt, throwing Sherrie-Lee forward into the pulled limits of her seat belt. Robyn got out. Sherrie-Lee watched him as he stood to look at the bird and then as he bent down closer and picked it up by its feet. She heard him open the rear door and place the creature in the back.

From the corner of her eye, she could see the satisfied look on his face when he climbed back into the van.

If it's road kill, it doesn't count, he said, almost to himself. You can still be vegan.

It wouldn't have been roadkill if you hadn't sped up to kill it, she thought, keeping the insight to herself.

Better for my table than some toff's, he said as he started up the van again. As bad as the fox hunting fuckers. Think they're above the law. That they can just do anything they like. He seemed to be talking to himself. He was speaking in a low voice and repeating himself almost as though he was telling a story.

Did you know, Sherrie-Lee, that the toffs release fifty million game birds every year just so they can shoot them? He looked towards her, then pulled himself nearer the steering wheel in agitation. Fifty million. Can you imagine how much damage to native species they do, how many frogs and lizards and bugs they eat? Toffs can do anything. They always get away with it. The one

228

up the road gets half a million in subsidies every year to look after his grouse moor. Never mind that he never pays any tax. Two hundred years ago land was taxed, but now only the little people pay tax. Nobody cares. But let the family down the road get a council house too quick and people want to lynch them. That's why they sold them all off, to stir up competition for the few that were left, to create hatred and divisions. To control a people, all you have to do is control who they hate, who they watch.

Sherrie-Lee looked back at the bird. She had never seen one this close. Even in the half-light inside the van, she could see what a beautiful bird it was. The iridescent sheen on its feathers. The green of its neck. Even the small feathers were intricately patterned with a deep copper shimmering where the light touched them. The tail feathers were as long as the body itself. Even run over and dead, the thing had an elegance about it.

I was in the hunt sabs once, Sherrie-Lee. Not for long, though. The hunters always think themselves above the law and the sabs just let them get away with it. All the sabs people ... They're just too law-abiding. You can't fight people who are above the law, without putting yourself above it too. You have to be prepared for some real action. That's the problem. They wouldn't listen ... It was all nicey nicey and swapping recipes for vegan cakes and shit. Educate the people about what is going on, that was their mantra. But people don't want to be educated. They don't want to know. And if you try to tell them, they think you're nuts. Sherrie-Lee was watching him out of the corner of her eye as he talked. The rest of her vision took in the blush colours of the dawn breaking through the low mists of the fields.

If you want to stop fox hunting, Sherrie-Lee, he looked towards her and she was forced to look back at him. His eye glinted in the low light, and he smiled a forced kind of smile and shook his head as he looked again into the road ahead. Shifting up a gear as he sped up, he continued, If you want to put a stop to it and the law aren't interested, even though you show footage of the men digging them out of their dens and throwing them and their cubs to the dogs, and the dogs ripping the foxes apart, you have to take action yourself. They go to the hunt in their cars, their four-wheel drives, so you get their number plates. You get the picture, Sherrie-Lee?

He looked at her for extended moments. She wanted to crawl into herself and disappear, all the selves she'd ever projected, stack them all back inside herself like those Russian dolls.

You know, Sherrie-Lee, we might just make a warrior out of you yet. She could feel him looking across at her, before continuing, You get their number plates. And from this you can track down where they live. Easy as fuck. You just Google it. Then if you really want to stop it, this is what you do. If you really want to stop it, you go to their house, a little shove on the door with a crowbar. Then, because they always sleep soundly, these people. People with no conscience always do. They have no cares, see. Then you take your sharpened screwdriver or knife and you stab them through the neck, through the jugular vein, just here. He pointed to his neck and looked at her until she looked where he was pointing. Just there, Sherrie-Lee. With force he pressed his finger into the side of her neck. The van veered into the edge of the grass at the side of the road and he had to return both hands to the steering wheel to right it. Or through the temple with the screwdriver, he continued. It's as simple as that, Sherrie-Lee. One push through the skin. Through the flesh, Sherrie-Lee. That's all it takes. He relaxed his hold of the steering wheel, which he had been gripping tighter in all his excitement, and slapped the top of it in conclusion.

He had been speaking calmly, over the top of the gripped steering wheel, over the growing frustration of the way of things. It was a practised calm, measured and paced, a way of speaking that poured calm over the un-calm throb of things, and she felt strangely calm, too. She looked into the back at the pheasant again. Its death had come quickly. Not like the traveller's horse. A few minutes ago it had been in the full of life. Running around with its friend. And now. She wondered at the change inside it. At what had happened inside its body to move it in an instant from life to death. The irreversible switching off that had moved through it. The stopping of what gave it life. The closing down.

37

There were dots in the distance, not sheep this time. These ones were coloured. Coloured dots. Farmers maybe, or walkers who had wandered off the trail. Sherrie-Lee watched them and wondered what direction they were moving in. They were so far away that they looked still. If they were moving upwards, they would be getting further away. Downwards and they'd be getting closer. Across from where they were was a stunted tree. She watched to see the direction they were headed in relation to the tree. She watched, not taking her eyes off the dots. Sometimes they seemed to draw closer together, sometimes further apart. She thought that they were definitely moving closer, they seemed more in line with the position of the tree, now. They had definitely been above it before. They were definitely walkers, too. A farmer would have a quad bike or tractor to get around on. She waited for them to appear under the line of the tree. Then waited for the dots to take on more of a shape. There seemed to be a red jacket growing out of one dot and a brown one out of the other. She reached across and pressed down hard on the horn until her hand grew tired and slipped. She reached again and pressed down with both hands. Through the side mirror, she saw Robyn approach from behind the van. She slunk back to her own seat and watched him raise his hand and wave to the people across the valley.

What the fuck are you doing? He climbed in beside her. Tomorrow is the pick-up day. Why the fuck are you ruining things now? We pick up the money tomorrow and if everything's okay, if we pull it off, you can go. Do you get that? Fuck. We pull it off. You can go. Fuck it, Sherrie-Lee, you don't want to be putting yourself into danger now.

He started up the van and drove off slowly. This way, he said, turning to her, it looks like the beeping was just a kid impatient to go somewhere. Don't be a fool, Sherrie-Lee. Don't wanna be trying to get one over on me now, Sherrie-Lee. His voice was a kind of low whisper, slowed to an exaggerated show of patience. The kind of voice that had an unspoken threat hidden into it, which broke through here and there, when the rise of the pitch couldn't be controlled. The kind of voice that said, *Don't let my fake patience run out, you don't want to see what will come in its place.* His eyes moved around quickly as he worked the van. Darting to the mirrors, to the people in the distance, away from Sherrie-Lee, to the fields ahead. His fake patience hadn't reached his face. In the darting eyes and the twitch, his face told a different story.

Sherrie-Lee thought about what he said about danger, and how he hadn't specified what danger. She thought about what he said, too, about letting her go after the pickup and how unlikely that would be. She was a witness after all. She knew his whereabouts, knew people from IDAW who knew him. Unless he was going to disappear, it was she who was a danger to him. And that's where her danger lay.

I'm warning you, Sherrie-Lee, don't be pulling any fast ones. He looked across at her and hissed through his teeth, then sped the van up, driving so fast that she felt herself thrown about beneath the hold of the seat belt, so she would know he meant business. That he was not a person to be played.

233

38

Good morning, Sherrie-Lee. He opened the passenger door of the van and held up a plate of beans and mashed potato. He put the plate on the seat next to her.

The presence of the plate brought up a flood of hunger inside her. Sherrie-Lee hesitated. It was some trick, she thought. Some game he was playing. *Do not show any interest in the food*, she told herself. *Don't give him that power.*

He stayed at the open doorway, looking in at her.

She couldn't stop herself from glancing down at the food.

He crouched down to draw her attention. So, this is the big day, Sherrie-Lee. The day of reckoning.

He pulled himself forward, steadying himself by holding on to the upper edge of the doorframe with the grip of one hand. She felt his gaze poke at her for a reaction. When Sherrie-Lee looked at him she saw that a worried look had darkened his face. His mouth was stretched into a thin line. He rubbed at his unshaven chin.

His jaw clenched and he narrowed his eyes, though he wasn't looking at her. His gaze went directly over her, through the window next to her, like he was thinking of something else entirely.

She looked down at the fork resting on the plate. White bubbles of bright light pushed themselves into Sherrie-Lee's eyes. Colour drained from her vision, then came back in patches, like a failure and return of pixels. She imagined the feel of the fork in her fingers. The feel of the hard metal in her hand. She didn't want to look at him again.

Robyn sighed and glanced sideways. Fuck, he said. He stood up and started to walk away. He walked back and closed the door. Then, moving round to her side, he looked down at her through the closed window from his standing position, and opened her door.

He did not say anything at first. His presence coupled with the silence was menacing and Sherrie-Lee felt the need to say something. It's for the animals, the money?

He laughed again. How about this? You're doing this because you have no fucking choice. His voice was half shout, half angry hiss. He widened his eyes at her, peering in closer to her face.

She looked down at the plate. She didn't like to be shouted at. Her mother used to shout at her like that. Uncontrolled rage, before the medicine spaced her out. That shout reached into the same hollow space left by her mother's rages from all that time ago. That they were still there inside her, and that she was conscious of them now, with everything else that was going on, threw her back, leaving her off-kilter within herself. Another, forgotten Sherrie-Lee popping up to bother her when she could well do without it.

We set off in an hour, he said, closing and then locking the door.

When Sherrie-Lee saw that he had gone, she took the fork and began to eat. It was the first food she had eaten from a plate in a long time. After the first few forkfuls, she slowed down and looked out at the landscape. She felt exhausted. Too tired to eat. She had, from boredom, memorised every detail of this landscape. She had spent so many hours gazing out at it. There was the line of trees on a distant hill. Each morning she had watched the sun rise up from behind it, burning off the blurred outlines of mist. The smooth crest of the same hill running out to the right and dipping down to meet the rise of another hill.

The food was cold, but that didn't matter. It was important to eat. She only felt full because she hadn't eaten, she knew that. She knew it from past experience. It was food and she was grateful for the way it filled her empty stomach, pushing at the nervousness that had been welling there since she woke early that morning.

If they were going to put out the bag of money, they would be preparing for it now. How could they not put it out? She thought of her conversation with Gina. How Gina had thought she was naive and silly to ask for a ransom. Your mam has fifty thousand, then? she had asked her, her voice sarcastic and pitying in equal measure. Is that how it worked? she thought over it again. If your family has the money, then they cough it up. If not, well, then it's curtains for all the poor people. She put it out of her mind. No matter how much she thought of it she was no closer to understanding how it worked. There was nothing more to do. She would see soon enough when they got there.

Later, when Robyn came back to the van, he took the plate from the driver's seat and laid it on the ground outside. They drove off without saying anything. Her stuff was still in the carrier bag at her feet, untouched from the time she had left Bob's. They drove to a patch of waste ground skirting an industrial estate, and slowed down.

So, this is where it's going to be? Robyn said without looking at her. They slowed by the bin, So, it's going to be dropped behind that?

Sherrie-Lee looked out of the window as they rolled past it. She had written the instruction in the letter, but seeing the bin now, it all seemed unreal. When she had scouted the area to put the details in the letter she never really imagined how it would be. That it would really happen.

You pick it up and walk with it to where I am going to show you.

They drove right round the waste ground to the other side. There was no one in sight. Not even a bird.

This is where I am going to park, when we do it for real. They turned into a small road between two buildings on one side and a warehouse on the other. They slowed, but they didn't stop. *I'll be watching you the whole time. This is the only place where you can park up without being seen, so we'll know if anyone else is watching.*

They drove off again, back into the country lanes, then pulled into a layby and stopped there. It seemed very quiet and still with the engine off. Neither of them spoke. Sherrie-Lee thought that Robyn must be off with his own thoughts, like she was. She wondered what he was thinking. Whether he was going over all the things that could go wrong, or whether he was thinking about what he would do with her if it all went as planned. It didn't seem like the kind of day that anything bad would happen to Sherrie-Lee. It was too bright and calm and quiet.

They drove around for a long time through the countryside. They passed field after field. Nothing more was said about the pickup. Nothing more was said about anything.

I have to go to the toilet, Sherrie-Lee said.

Robyn looked at her, *Can't you wait half an hour?*

Sherrie-Lee shook her head.

Okay, come on.

They both got out. She followed him to a bush that stuck out from the stone wall.

You can go there.

She looked doubtfully at the bush.

He stepped forward to give her space, and looked at the road in both directions. He seemed agitated.

She didn't want to go, what with Robyn being so close, but all her nervousness made her feel like she was going to pee herself. And in the last week she had been doing it in a bucket in a van. She felt she'd already pushed herself beyond being embarrassed. She was above all that by now. She crouched behind the bush and pulled her pants down. Felt the relaxation of that moment before

237

the pee comes out. Then nothing. Nothing would come out. She closed her eyes and tried again, making a psst sound to encourage herself.

Robyn stepped further away. When she stopped making the sound, he asked, Have you gone?

No.

Hurry up. We have to go.

Sherrie-Lee pulled up her pants and followed him back into the van.

Robyn pulled the van into a small empty car park at the other side of the industrial park. He took out a roll of wide black duct tape from the glove compartment, and got out of the van. She saw him at the front of the van pulling at a length of the tape, biting at it to tear it with his grey teeth. Then she saw him bend towards the number plate. He went to the back of the van and pulled out another length of tape.

He looked serious without all the insane smiling. This is it now, he said as they drove off again.

He pulled up, further down from where he said he would park up, then turned and said, You just go, walk across, get the bag and bring it back here.

They looked out the windscreen in the direction it was all going to happen. An old man in a flat cap walked with a stick along the waste ground at some distance. An old dog, a black and white terrier, walked alongside him.

They watched for a short while.

Go, was all Robyn said.

Sherrie-Lee got out of the van and began to walk across the waste ground in the direction of the litter bin. She heard the van roll into place behind her, the sound of its tyres on the gravel road.

Her legs felt funny. Not the pains, but something else. She had begun to be so conscious of her walk, of the maintained slowness of it, that her legs felt impossibly heavy, as though if she stopped thinking about the motion of walking they would stop working altogether and she would just collapse. She kept on, one step at a time.

She could see the bin quite clearly, one of those wide concrete ones with *Litter* written in black capital letters above the centre, but she couldn't make out anything behind it.

The sun baked down on the top of her head. When she got there, she saw that behind the bin was a black holdall. It was quite heavy, she realised when she went to pick it up. She pulled at the weight of the bag and looked back at the van. She could make out Robyn leaning forward over the steering wheel, watching.

Then she saw the old man running towards her. Get behind the bin, Sherrie-Lee, the old man called out in a surprisingly high-pitched voice.

She crouched down behind it, half-sitting on the bag. She could hear tyres screeching on the ground. She looked up and saw, through the open slot of the bin, a dark van blocking the road behind Robyn's van, and a silver car coming from the other direction.

You're alright, Sherrie-Lee. It wasn't an old man; it was a woman. You're safe now. We'll get you home soon. The woman was crouching down beside her, looking back at what was happening across the waste ground. The flat cap had fallen off. The terrier came running round to sniff at her. Even the dog didn't seem like an old dog any more, like it too had been play-acting. Now, rushing to sniff at everything, it seemed full of life. No longer the old dog of an old man. It seemed no time at all before the woman stood up and held a hand to beckon for Sherrie-Lee to follow her. Sherrie-Lee stepped out beside the woman. She saw that Robyn was in handcuffs and police were taking him into the vehicle that had been blocking the rear of his van. Bringing in Sherrie-Lee Connors now, the woman said towards her shoulder. The silver car was pulling round to where they were standing.

Everything is going to be alright now, Sherrie-Lee. We're going to go to the hospital for a while and then, when we know everything's okay, we'll go to the police station for a quick chat and then you can go home, Sherrie-Lee. How does that sound? As they got into the silver car, she told her that her name was Marion. The dog jumped in between them, sitting on its hind quarters at the edge of the back seat so that it had the best view out of the front windscreen. Marion told her that the dog's name was Leopold. Sherrie-Lee looked at Leopold as he swayed to the movement of the car, rebalancing himself as though he were skateboarding. There was an almost joyous look about him as he sat there, riding the movement of the car as he smile-panted, an air of triumph in his face. He didn't look like a Leopold.

Sherrie-Lee nodded, in recognition of his name, however unlikely it was. She looked at the black holdall that the police-woman had put into the back next to her and wondered if all the money was inside. She thought briefly about asking, then decided against it. She didn't want to know if it was not full of money – if Gina had been right.

39

We've called your mum to come down to the police station. It was Marion again. She came to sit opposite Sherrie-Lee and pulled her hand through her bobbed hair. Sherrie-Lee could tell she had thick hair because her hand had left furrowed lines in it. That would never happen with thin hair like her own.

All the corridors and rooms at the police station were painted a pale grey colour. There were no windows and all the light came from long bulbs high in the ceilings. There was nothing on the walls except for a few information posters. There was one near to where Sherrie-Lee was sitting, the one with the lady with scars on her face, telling how she hadn't worn a seat belt because she didn't want creases in her shirt. Sherrie-Lee wondered if she was a real person, this lady in the poster. The scar looked real. She looked down at her own hands, the shortened, bitten nails and the nail beds red and swollen. She clenched her fists to hide them.

She had waited in a lot of different rooms. Side rooms. Waiting rooms. Rooms at the side of things. There had been three different ones in the last four or five hours. She had waited in them alone or with the calm voice of an adult, measured and reassuring her. Explaining everything that was going on. You'd think she'd be used to waiting by now. All the days she had waited in the van. But when she waited alone in those extended minutes, which inflated and billowed out like sails, her impatience rose, pushed to its limits. It felt to Sherrie-Lee that life was going on in all the other rooms. In all the rooms that she waited next to. It was just like existence always felt to her, like it was all going on elsewhere.

The questioning had gone by in a haze. She drank two cups of hot chocolate from paper cups and told the ladies everything she knew. Marion was really nice, not like a copper at all. Sherrie-Lee told how she'd been kidnapped by Robyn and how he belonged to an animal rights group that she went along to also, and how he wasn't really vegan because he ate meat and chicken-flavoured crisps and how he had kept her in his van all this time and said the money was for the animals, but it wasn't really. And then, towards the end of the interview, how she'd had to go to the toilet in a bucket and how he'd made her write the ransom note, and where he lived and probably lots of other things too. But as soon as they came out of the interview room, into the chipped white light of the corridor, all of the things she had said seemed to fade away.

Marion went over to the front desk and asked if the mother had arrived yet. She didn't catch what the other lady said, but it must have been how her mam wasn't coming to get her, because Marion turned round to her smiling, and said that there'd been a change of plan, that she was going to drive her home herself, in a police car. And then she asked her, How does that sound? Sherrie-Lee had said, Alright in response, or she thought she had. She thought about her heartbeat, about how many beats she had already used up and about the day when she will have used all of them up, the full quota, and whether her heart will just stop or if it will slow down for the last thousand or so beats, and whether she will feel it all happening. She slipped her right hand inside her jacket and felt for her heartbeat.

It was beginning to get dark as they pulled up outside her house, Marion turned to her and said, Looks like the press are here.

They both looked out for a few moments. The press didn't look like much to Sherrie-Lee. Just a man in a brown jacket, taking a photo of the police car with his phone. Don't worry, Marion said. I'll go talk to him. You go ahead and get yourself inside.

She opened the front door of her house. The light was on in the hallway and there was a pile of the free newspapers that were delivered every week by the front door. Grace was walking from the kitchen, into the hallway and towards the stairs.

Ooh, look what the cat dragged in, she said when she saw her. Thought you'd been kidnapped. She didn't smile, or look pleased to see her, Sherrie-Lee noticed. Instead, Grace stood on the third step and swung over the banister to get a good look at her. So, where've you been then?

Sherrie-Lee shrugged and asked, Where's Joshy?

Autismo's where he always is. She nodded her head towards the front room and then took off up the stairs, two at a time, calling out, Mam, Sherrie-Lee's back.

Sherrie-Lee went in and sat next to Joshy in front of the TV. He was watching some idiot talk show. A man in a bright blue suit and a red tie was talking to some woman with long blonde hair and lots of makeup on, about which were their favourite airports and which were the worst ones.

What yer watching this rubbish for, Joshy? Shall I find you something better?

She sat back on the sofa and flicked at the TV with the remote. She felt Joshy move in closer to her and she put her hand on his shoulder and patted it. There was a new stain on the sofa, near to where her legs were. It was a dark grey colour so it was hard to tell what had made it. It was the shape of Italy. Joshy sat the way he always sat on the sofa, with his legs folded to his left side and the thumb of his left hand wedged into the folded joint at the back of his knee so that only his four grubby fingers were visible. Black lines of dirt showed under each of his overlong fingernails. One or two flecks of white spotted each nail. She took in all the familiar details of him, taking comfort from each of them. She would have liked to hug him, a long, big hug, but Joshy didn't like that kind of thing. She would have liked to hold him close and breathe in that warm, slightly sweet smell he always had. Just to keep everything at bay, all the loneliness and heaviness. The whole empty drabness. She thought about how she had always sensed that she and Joshy had been born into the wrong life, that they were meant to be somewhere else. But maybe everyone felt like that. Maybe you just had to get on with it.

The blue plastic toy figure that had been pushed behind the bars of the gas fire and never retrieved was still there. Sherrie-Lee had forgotten all about it and only now recognised its familiar position. Head down, nose-diving into a fire that was never lit, its blue legs sticking up like some dead, forgotten creature.

It's good to see ya, Joshy, she said looking at him. A sad kind of smile on her face. The face she had on when she was determined to hold up both parts of the conversation.

Joshy kept looking at the TV. He didn't say anything. It was nothing personal. When the TV was on, it just absorbed all his attention. That was all.

On the floor by the sofa was the tin that held Joshy's fossils. She picked it up and put it on her lap. She moved the stones with her hand across the metal base of the tin. The metal had become dulled from all the years of stones grazing the surface, so that in the bottom of the tin you could no longer see your reflection. In the sides, which were less scratched, part of a chin could be caught. A mouth, the side of a nose. Fragments of a face. The stones made a scratching sound as she pushed them around inside the tin. She turned each of them over until she found the one genuine fossil. The one with the ammonite half-secreted away within it. She picked it up and turned it over in her hand, thinking about all the millions of years it had existed through. Feeling at its solid coldness.

Reading Group Guide

The author has provided these questions to inspire discussion at reading groups, based on some of the characters, themes and issues in the novel.

1. Why did the author choose to focus much of the narrative on the voice of a twelve-year-old?

2. What is the significance of the title, *Fossils*? How does it work as a metaphor for alienation?

3. Why is the scene in the art gallery significant?

4. To what extent is Sherrie-Lee suffering from climate/extinction grief? Do you think this will become more common among young people as the climate crisis worsens?

5. In what ways do we see Bob/Lester becoming increasingly sceptical of Sherrie-Lee? How does he think of her by the end of the novel? Will the future bring them another meeting?

6. What does the future hold for Lester and Gina? Will they stay together?

7. How does storytelling function for Sherrie-Lee? Did you think this function halts at a certain point in the novel? Do you think she'll continue telling stories in her future?

8. How important is the local library for Sherrie-Lee?

9. More than 4.3 million children live in poverty in the UK. How is Sherrie-Lee's life affected by poverty?

10. What factors in Sherrie-Lee's life contribute to her feeling 'less than normal'?

11. Sherrie-Lee's mum is present only twice in the novel – first as a voice from another room and secondly on TV screens behind a shop window. Why has the author presented her like this?

12. Why is the section with Robyn included in the book? What does it bring to the structure of the story?

13. How does the relationship between Gina and Sherrie-Lee develop?

14. How does Sherrie-Lee relate to the different members of her family?

15. How is truth presented within the novel? How does Sherrie-Lee perceive it?

16. Why is so much space given to dreams in the novel?

17. How does Sherrie-Lee regard her community? How does she regard wider society?

18. In what ways does the novel engage with political issues?

Interview with the Author

Q: Sherrie-Lee is compelling: she makes me think of the young generation fighting for climate justice, when adults have so far failed. Where did the inspiration for this character come from?

A: When I first started to work on this novel, I wanted to construct it partially as a frame story – but one that grounds storytelling in the contemporary mundane world rather than a quasi-mystical one. I wanted to fix it in the messy, incoherent experience of real life, and I tried out various scenarios before Sherrie-Lee came to me. The names Sherrie-Lee and Zadie refer to Scheherazade in the original frame story *One Thousand and One Nights*. Once Sherrie-Lee arrived (and she arrived fully-fledged), she took over the narrative. I thought she was entirely fictional, though I began to realise as I wrote that she reminded me of a girl I knew growing up, and another I once taught. Both had difficult home lives and were spirited characters, so, on a subconscious level at least, they are part of the inspiration. Sherrie-Lee's sense of humour is characteristic of the community I grew up in. That came naturally and is an important part of her resilience. Her extinction grief is a kind of existential sorrow that is impossible to solve.

Q: Libraries are important in this story and crucial for Sherrie-Lee's wealth of knowledge. She gets a great deal of security from them and from Claire, the librarian she meets. What role did libraries play in your childhood and growth as an author?

A: I can't remember libraries in much detail from my childhood, and I was quite late to begin reading, though I remember the comfort of the reading corner in childhood classrooms. Libraries were important to me as a young adult as somewhere calming to go, somewhere warm, dry and comforting, and I still love them. They are among the few places you can simply pass time quietly alongside other people. You don't bother anyone, nobody bothers you, you don't have to spend any money – they are special places for these reasons alone. And, of course, the books. The selection on offer has been assembled over time, for the people who use the library. There is no need for libraries to promote the latest celebrity titles that bookshops feel they need to stock to survive. Claire is entirely made up, but a couple of months ago I heard on the radio someone recalling a fabulous librarian with blue hair, so I like to think that she exists somewhere, handing out books and conversation to Sherrie-Lees wherever she may be.

Q: Many different stories are threaded through this novel: Sherrie-Lee's own stories, her deceptions, and the lies she has told other people. What role does storytelling play in Sherrie-Lee's universe, and what role do stories play in our own?

A: Storytelling is essential in Sherrie-Lee's universe. It's how she makes sense of the world, how she tries to control chaos in her life, and how she tries to control others. Channelling thoughts and feelings through stories is her defence mechanism. She reaches for stories when things are going wrong, and she tries to reorder her world by ordering narratives. She sees many of the problems around her as consequences of the lack of 'proper' stories. Perhaps she is recognising something in the human condition itself: that human beings are storytelling creatures who live by meanings. The tradition of storytelling is a manifestation of this. There is a political function in the way that stories accumulate through connection. People share stories to communicate meanings, but also to unpack myths (such as origin myths) that generally support the status quo. For instance, fairy stories often operate to deliver self-reliance. This is where we encounter and overcome our fears and demons, where we reach a state of self-possession, ready to take on the world. All cultures have these traditions.

For Sherrie-Lee, telling stories is one of the fundamental ways she overcomes her sense of alienation. For example, when she learns the stories (habits, particularities) of different birds, she recognises it as 'finding a way in' to connect to the natural world, the first step toward caring about wild things. This represents a general alienation that is part of modern life, and in many ways *Fossils* is an allegory of alienation and a yearning to connect.

Q: The characters Sherrie-Lee meets at the environmental group are often hypocritical and behave in the exploitative ways they claim to fight against. Is this a comment about real-world leaders?

A: Only Robyn is such a character. He is a bad person. It just happens that he is also an activist. He does not represent anything, but is just a character in his own right. This is not to deny the hypocrisy and corruption of those in power in real life – never has it seemed so acute as now, in the current state of affairs in the UK, but Robyn is simply an opportunist, a miscreant, seeking to make money out of the situation. He is a bad character who behaves erratically and says extreme things, but at times he says true things, too. There are other references in the book that ridicule and critique these hypocrisies – political, institutional, cultural. They are there to be picked up by readers, though the story itself is always the main thing.

Q: There's a clear juxtaposition between Sherrie-Lee's ability to be cynical about the adults in her life and the sincerity and drive she has in her desire for creating a better world. Was this something you felt you could only capture with a young protagonist?

A: I felt that a young protagonist could get across things that would sound naive for an older character, because this is the way much of the dominant political discourse frames it. Concern for the environment is sidelined – a strategy to silence ideas that don't support what I like to call the *charlatanismo* of current politics. Absurd profits continue to be funnelled to the 'right people' while vulnerable groups are demonised. Most politicans have no will to protect the environment. Sherrie-Lee notices this and sees how powerless people are treated, and is frustrated and outraged by this. She sees it because she lives among vulnerable people herself.

All children and young people I have known want to create a better world. It is irrational *not* to want this, especially for children, before they become jaded. There is too much lip service paid to environmental concerns, functioning as a kind of balm. We are in denial, we refuse to engage with these problems effectively, and there is no political will in most parts of the world. When we hear of a green policy being implemented, however minor, I think we are comforted and allow ourselves to switch off. Sherrie-Lee sees this. Thank goodness for movements like Extinction Rebellion and Wild Justice, because they will make change possible.

I found while writing that a young protagonist could connect with the powerlessness and silencing of the natural world, because children are also powerless. So, although it was limiting in some ways to tell the story through twelve-year-old eyes, it also allowed an exploration of connections to those aspects of the world that lie at the margins of our experience. I am interested in what goes on in those spaces, at the margins – and what perspective is not limited in some way?

I know or have known people similar to characters in the novel and I wanted to give space to these voices, which I don't often see depicted in literature.

Alison Armstrong is a writer. She won a Northern Writers' Award for short fiction in 2017 and a Literature Matters Award from the Royal Society of Literature in 2020. She lives in Lancashire. Fossils *is her first book.*